THE Concordances
OF THE
RED
SERPENT

WILLIAM MEIKLE

GRYPHONWOOD

The Concordances of the Red Serpent

Copyright © 2011, 2016 by William Meikle

ISBN: 978-1-940095-51-6

Cover design and interior formatting by J. Kent Holloway

Gryphonwood Press
PO Box 28910, Santa Fe, NM 87592

www.gryphonwoodpress.com

Printed in the United States of America

For wee Scotsmen everywhere.

Gryphonwood Books by William Meikle

The Concordances of the Red Serpent

Island Life

The Invasion

Berserker

The Valley

The Midnight Eye Files

The Amulet

The Sirens
The Skin Game

The Watchers Trilogy

The Coming of the King

The Battle for the Throne

Culloden

Patty Doyle's blog consisted of twenty lines of rubbish and two lines of truth.

The rubbish got her fired.

The truth got her into real trouble.

Not that she knew it as she stepped into Doug Richards' office the next morning.

He waylaid her as soon as she walked in the front door, not even giving her a chance to take her coat off.

"Come into my office," he said.

"Why don't you come to mine? George will have hot donuts," Patty said, smiling.

Richards was having none of it. He strode away across the hallway, and Patty had to break into a stuttering run to catch up. Her heels beat a martial rhythm on the marble floor.

The redness at Richards' cheeks and the brusque way he waved her into the room told her there was something up. The fact that Patty caught her satchel on the door handle, and took three attempts to free it, didn't improve his mood any.

"When you're ready," he said sarcastically.

Patty disentangled the satchel and turned.

Richards was already standing behind his desk, using it as a bulwark between them. He motioned to the seat opposite him.

"Sit."

"I'm not a dog," she said. She smiled, expecting some repartee, but once more Richards said nothing, just pointed at the chair.

"Not had your coffee yet Doug?" she said.

"No. And you won't be having yours either," he said. "I want you out of here inside the hour."

At first she wasn't even sure she'd heard him properly. She'd been busy noticing the yellow splotch of mustard on the man's red tie, and hadn't yet caught up with the importance of the conversation.

"What? You're sending me to another office? But…"

He stopped her.

"No. Not another office. Out of the door, as in fired, dismissed, sacked, booted up the ass and gone."

"What? We've run out of funding again?"

"No," Doug said. "I've run out of patience."

He lifted a sheet of paper and read.

"*Doug Richards doesn't know his ass from his elbow. Why anyone would put him in charge of the department is beyond me.*"

He stopped.

"Any of this sounding familiar to you?"

He went back to reading.

"*He's a petty, small minded accountant with a cash register where his heart should be.*"

"It was only a bit of fun on my blog," Patty said. "I didn't mean anything by it."

"And I don't mean anything by this," he replied.

He handed Patsy an envelope.

"There's three months wages. Bye-bye. Clear your desk. And don't let the door bang you on the backside on the way out."

Patty stood outside the door, still trying to figure out exactly what had happened.

Fired, dismissed, sacked, booted up the ass and gone.

That kind of thing didn't happen here. The most excitement they had each day was when George brought in the donuts and they had to decide which flavor they wanted.

Well they'll have something else to talk about now.

She looked at the envelope in her hand, solid proof that it hadn't just been a dream. She'd never taken to Richards as a boss. John Tanner had been much better, an old school intellectual who'd understood the sheer joy to be had of handling books produced centuries before. When Tanner had to retire and Richards was brought in they had given him the benefit of the doubt... for all of two weeks, until the first project meeting. Richards talked of little else but budget, restrictions, and penny-pinching.

Patty had realized, even more than a year ago, that she'd never like the man. But she'd never have thought it would lead to her dismissal.

She barely remembered writing the blog. Yesterday had been a long day. She'd spent it working on a manuscript written in such a tiny, crabbed hand that she needed a magnifier to read it. By lunchtime she'd had a raging headache that aspirin only barely shifted. Four more hours after that and she'd felt like there was a small man with a big hammer working just behind her eyes.

She'd got home and soaked in a hot bath, then she'd had a few glasses of wine. On retrospect that had probably been a bad idea.

An even worse one had been signing on to the *Lonely Singles* chat-room. She'd had to fight off three creeps in the first half-hour and the headache started to come back. So she'd had some more wine.

Things got a bit blurred after that. She barely remembered being egged on by some of her on-line confidants to post her thoughts about *her tight-assed boss*. After yet another glass of wine she'd posted her blog, then immediately fell into bed.

She hadn't even remembered the blog this morning, let alone considered that Richards would have been following it.

She should have known better. Richards was just the kind to want to know everything about his employees.

But it can't have been that bad? Could it?

She considered walking straight back into his office and having it out with him. But, in the same way she knew he was a tight-ass, she also knew that he never changed his mind after a decision was made. He considered it a sign of weakness.

Patty walked around the hallway, three times, trying to loosen the knot that had tied itself in her stomach. She only stopped when she caught sight of Richards watching her. The man had a tight little smile on his face that Patty wanted to punch out of him.

To keep that urge at bay, she headed to the one place she knew she'd get sympathy. By the time she got back to her office she was angry, both with herself, and with Doug Richards… but mostly with Richards.

"Who does that asshole think he is?" she said loudly as she pushed the door open.

Nobody answered.

There was a smell in the air she didn't recognize. It burned, in her sinuses and in her throat.

"Whose cat died?" she said.

That was Jill Stanley's cue for a fart joke, but she didn't take it. Patty discovered why seconds later. She walked through the door to find the secretary sprawled face down across the photocopier. Her rear was in the air.

"You're *not* photocopying your face again are," Patty said. "You couldn't see for an hour the last time."

Jill Stanley didn't move.

"Come on Jill, stop playing *silly buggers*."

Jill was a long way from playing.

"Come on Jill," Patty said, a note of hysteria starting in her voice. "Blink, fart, do something. This *isn't* funny."

She had walked far enough to get a view of the secretary's face. Jill's dead eyes started blankly back at her.

Patty backed away, but she couldn't take her eyes off the trail of blood and saliva that ran down the side of the copier from Jill's mouth.

"*Jill?*" she whispered.

She hit a chair with her heel, stumbled, almost fell. She put out a hand to steady herself.

And felt something soft and wet. She looked down, and immediately backed away again into the corner of the room. She packed herself against the walls until she could go no further. Her hands shook, and she'd developed a twitch in the corner of her mouth that was threatening to turn into full-blown sobbing.

George Brookes had been her friend from the very first. He was the one who showed her the ropes, the one who told her which of the managers could be trusted, and which was a "*weasley little shit who'll screw you over to get ahead.*" George was the man who would open a window and shoo a fly out rather than kill it, the man who had pictures done by his kids on the wall above his desk. Patty looked at the big bright cards painted by the boys, and hot tears sprang at the corners of her eyes.

A cup of coffee sat on the desk in front of him, and a box with sugar and flour dust on the top sat next to that. But George wouldn't be eating any more coffee and donuts.

He sat at his desk, upright in his chair. His eyes were closed and it might have been mistaken for sleep. But his head hung back at an unusual angle, starting at the point that Patty had touched... a gaping wet hole in his neck. Patty knew that George would have a white shirt on, after all, it was Tuesday. But everything was red.

More tears came, and Patty lifted her hand to brush them away. Something red came into view, and she had to struggle to focus. Her hand looked like she'd put on a crimson glove.

A scream was about to start inside her, but she couldn't let it out.

Not when the place is so quiet.

She stood in the corner for a long time, shaking, trying to will her legs to move.

"*Don't be such a mouse Patty,*" George said in her head from years past. "*We won't bite.*"

"Oh George," Patty whispered. "I'm so sorry."

She looked round to the main door of the office.

"*Run,*" a voice said inside her. "*Nobody will blame you if you run.*"

She looked across the work area. Her desk was in another office at the end of a narrow hall lined with bookcases. There was only one other office off the corridor, and she couldn't do anything else until she'd looked into it.

Mary would be there, sucking a fake cigarette and fanning her face in mock indignation at the heat. Patty would sit opposite her, and they'd chat, about men, about the television, about just how dull life was. It would be just like any other day.

And after the chat, I'll just go back to work, and everything will be fine and dandy.

"Mary?" she called out, but it was barely more than a whisper. "Are you there?"

Finally her legs obeyed an order to move.

She sidled past George, trying not to look too closely, but unable to take her eyes off the red stain that ran all the way from neck to crotch.

Oh George. Sarah is going to be so upset with you.

She could still see Jill lying over the photocopier, so she walked faster. Once she was in the book lined corridor she could almost believe that things might turn out fine after all.

The door to the admin office lay slightly ajar, but that wasn't unusual, Mary was in and out all the time, fetching and carrying reports and mail and generally making her presence felt as the *driver* of the unit.

"Mary?" Patty whispered, and pushed the door open.

Mary Collins was there. But she wasn't talking.

The administrator also sat at her desk, baby blue eyes staring straight at Patty. There was a new third eye in the center of her forehead, the barest trickle of blood running from a black hole. It was neat, almost tidy. Which was more than could be said for the wall behind her. It looked like a Jackson Pollock starter kit. Red spots and dark blotches ran in a long fan across the white of the wall.

Once more Patty backed off. New tears bunched up in her eyes, and she wiped them away. Her breath came hot and hitching. But still she couldn't scream. She retreated to the corridor, pulling the admin office door closed behind her.

I'll come back later Mary, when you're less busy.

Once more she looked back at the main door out of the office, but she had one more room she needed to look in. She stood at the door of her office for long seconds. The door was closed, and she couldn't bring herself to turn the handle.

What if I'm in there? What if I'm dead?

She knew the thought was irrational, but the way the day was going so far, anything was possible. She listened with an ear to the door but there was no sound. The brass handle felt cold to the touch at first, but she stood there long enough for it to warm.

Finally she opened the door. She didn't go in, just let the door swing open.

There *was* someone in the room, but like everyone else in the unit, he was keeping quiet. He lay on the floor, blood pooling on the carpet from a wound just above his ear.

Patty didn't know him. He wore a sharp, expensive suit, and his leather shoes still had a price tag stuck on the sole. That, and he fact he looked to be dead, was all she knew about him.

She stepped forward.

Someone moved to her right and grabbed her arm. This time she was able to scream, but it was cut off by a hand put quickly across her mouth.

"Shush," a soft voice said in her ear. "They're still here."

She tried to squirm clear, but she was held tight.

"Didn't you hear me? They're after *you*. They're still here."

She let herself go limp in the man's arms.

"Better," he said quietly. "Now come with me. We have to get you out of here."

She felt him relax. Only slightly, but enough for her to push free and away from him. She almost fell over the body on the floor but managed to tip-toe around it and turn to face the one who'd held her.

A slight, thin man stood in front of her. Patty herself was quite small, and used to looking up at men, but the man's face was at her eye-level. He had an open, friendly smile, and only his eyes betrayed some tension.

"I hope you're not going to do anything stupid like scream?" he said in a lilting accent that she couldn't quite place.

Patty looked at the open door, but that was where the *other* things she was trying not to think about had happened.

"I'm sorry about your friends," the man said softly. "But we can't help them now. We've got to get you out of here."

He held out a hand. Patty ignored it.

"Did you kill them?" she said.

"The ones outside? No," he replied. He kicked at the body at his feet. "This one, yes. If I hadn't you would be as dead as the others."

He moved to the door and held out the hand again.

"Now please. Come with me. I can help."

Help. That sounds good.

Patty took a last look at the body on the floor then took the offered hand.

2

By the time Mike Turner arrived on the scene the place was full of forensics techs and patrolmen. He almost turned on his heel at the door.

I really don't want to do this anymore.

The sight of cops taking statements, technicians carrying equipment back and forth, the relentless busy nature of a new crime scene had excited him, once upon a time. Not anymore. Now he dreaded what lay inside, a dread that pulled at his gut and made him nauseous.

Or maybe that's just last night's whisky.

The press had already got wind that something was going on, and three different television crews jostled for position behind a barrier. They all shouted at Mike as he left his car but Mike had learned many years ago never to talk to them -- at least not before clearing it with his Captain first. He ignored their increasingly shrill demands and walked, slowly, towards the scene.

He took a minute to stand out on the road and survey the building. It didn't look like a slaughterhouse, but then, they rarely did. Mike drove past this one most days of the week, and had never registered what went on inside. The name above the door didn't give much away. *Morrisons. The Bibliophiles*, it read. Even now he wasn't quite sure what that meant. Was it a bookstore? If so, it had no frontage on the street, just a security door leading into a hallway that could just be seen through tinted glass.

Whatever they did, it smelled of money -- that was apparent as soon as he opened the door.

He showed his badge to the officer stationed there.

"It's a bad one Lieutenant," the young officer said.

"Aren't they all, son?"

The officer looked at Turner as if he might be slightly mad. The Lieutenant was getting used to that look. He'd been seeing it a lot recently… from his Sergeant mostly, but also from the guy at the newspaper stand, the bartender at the Two Hounds and the kid at the checkout in the supermarket. He knew what it meant. He just wasn't sure he was prepared to do anything about it.

"Where's the party?" he asked, and was directed through a series of oak-lined corridors.

There's money here all right. And lots of it.

More forensics men dusting for prints created a trail that he could easily follow until he came to where the cops were gathered.

Like wasps to a honey pot.

The door was marked *Cataloging*, but that didn't help him much either.

He got the look again from Mendoza when he walked into the office.

"Lieutenant," she said, cagily, as if he might bite.

"Sergeant," he replied. "What delights have we got to-day?"

As quickly as it had come, the look was gone, and she was all business.

"It's a multiple. Three office workers."

"Take me through it," Turner said.

Mendoza led him into the office. Mike winced at the color scheme, lime green did not go well with mahogany.

"I'd go mad if I had to work in this," he muttered.

It was only after the initial shock of the green passed that he started to pay attention to the office itself. It was a small room, barely fifteen feet across, containing three desks, four cabinets, and two bodies.

They walked over to where a young woman was sprawled across the photocopier. A forensics tech was on the floor at her feet, looking for fibers.

Mike felt close to tears.

"Jill Stanley, 22," Mendoza began. "Nothing on her record but a couple of traffic violations. She got banged up a bit, and her neck is broken. Best guess is she was thrown against the wall, and not gently either."

Mike walked round the forensics tech to see the body more clearly. The girl's eyes stared accusingly at Mike.

You should have done something, they said. He looked away from her face, but that didn't help. The secretary's skirt, short already, had hitched up so that the top of her thighs showed, and there was a glimpse of red panties.

"Get her off there and covered up as soon as you can," he said.

"Forensics will be a while yet and…"

"And that poor dead girl is flashing her ass for all the world to see. Let's give her back some dignity, shall we?"

This time it was the technician who gave Mike that look, but Mike was long past caring.

"Are you OK boss?" Mendoza said, but Mike had already turned away. Seeing George Brookes didn't improve his mood any. He tried to concentrate on the desk instead of the body, but that only made him acutely aware of the crude drawings on the wall above, the primary colors and stick figures that told of happy kids, waiting for daddy to come home. The sick feeling hung heavy in his gut again.

At least Brookes' eyes were closed. But the gaping hole in his neck looked like a large extra mouth.

You should have done something, it said before Mike had to look away.

"Garrotte," Mendoza said. "Probably piano wire. George here was 45, married, three kids and seems to have been tied to this desk since he was twenty. A steady, straight, office worker who never did anything wrong to anyone in his life."

"Any connection to the secretary?"

"Nothing apart from the job," she replied. "And there's more."

She lifted Brookes' hand. When Mike bent he saw that three of the fingernails had been torn off forcibly."

"He was tortured first," Mendoza said.

"Of course he was," Mike replied sadly.

There were more forensics men dusting for prints in the small corridor that led to offices at the back. The walls here were lined in more of the dark wood, and the low ceiling, painted dark brown, gave the effect of a long dark tunnel. Suddenly Mike felt claustrophobic. He stopped. His breath came in hot hitches.

Mendoza stood at his side, but Mike wouldn't look at her, and when she put out a hand he brushed her away.

"Just show me the rest," he said brusquely. "That's what I'm here for isn't it?"

He got the *look* again.

"After you," she said, and motioned him along the corridor.

He stood at the office door and looked in at the woman with an extra hole in her head sitting at the desk.

"Mary Collins," Mendoza said. "Gunshot wound, single shot, point blank range. I doubt if she was even given time to speak."

She spoke now, but only Mike heard her.

You should have done something.

He gave Mary Collins' body no more than a cursory glance before looking into the office opposite.

The first thing he noticed was a large pool of blood on the floor.

"So who does this belong to?" he asked Mendoza.

"We don't know yet boss. The room belongs to a Patty Doyle, but there's no sign of her."

"So this could be hers?"

"Or someone else's."

Mike ran a hand through his thinning hair.

I'm getting too old for this shit.

"Any weapons found?"

"No," Mendoza replied. "We're missing a gun, a garrotte and probably a set of pliers."

"Well I suppose we should start with Doyle. What have we got on her?"

"Not a lot. She's an indexer and cataloguer. She lost her job this morning."

"Well, at least we have a motive," Mike said. "What goes on here? What's the line of business?"

"Indexing, digitizing and cataloguing of rare books."

Mike looked around, taking in the mahogany woodwork.

"Looks like there's plenty of money in it."

"We're checking their financial records now," Mendoza said. "We've also sent a patrol car to the woman's apartment, and we have her boss waiting for you in his office."

"The boss isn't a suspect?"

"No. He found the bodies. He's a wreck."

I know how he feels.

As he followed Mendoza he tried to muster up some enthusiasm. It got harder every day. All he could see in his mind were the dead, crying for a vengeance that never came.

You should have done something.

That was the trouble. Lately he felt impotent in the face of a world that didn't care, where human life was a commodity to be traded, with less value given to it than pork-belly futures. Every day he saw promising lives cut short early, every day he wondered if there was any point in even trying to stem the flow.

Looking forward wasn't any better. Every morning when he looked in the mirror he saw an older man. Just in the past year what little hair he had left had started to gray, first at the temples, and now scattered all through. He felt tired almost all the time, and most of his muscle had started to run to fat. It seemed like yesterday that he was pounding the track for an hour without getting out of breath. Now he'd be lucky to manage a minute. He was falling apart, slow inch by slow inch, with only the enthusiasm for the job keeping him going.

Now even that had failed him. Here he was, one year away from his pension. Normally it should be something to look forward to, but for Mike it was a black hole waiting for him to fall in; a pit he wouldn't escape. Today he'd managed to pull himself out of the armchair, get dressed, and look presentable enough to pass for an NYPD Lieutenant.

How long will it be before I can't even do that?

"Mike?" Mendoza said softly.

They were alone in a hallway, and the Sergeant had touched his arm lightly, bringing him back to what passed for reality.

"Are you OK Mike?" she asked.

"Well enough," he replied, brusquely, until he saw the concern in her face. He put his hand over hers and forced a smile that he didn't believe in.

"It's OK Sam," he said. "Just the black dog again. You know how it gets me?"

She nodded.

"It's been biting your ass for a while now though Mike. Isn't it about time you had it muzzled?"

He patted her hand and tried to muster up something that would satisfy her.

"I've just been feeling a bit under the weather. It's nothing a few beers won't cure."

She smiled up at him, and something inside him softened. Not a lot, but enough to get him through a few more minutes.

"I'll take you up on that later boss," she said.

Doug Richards' office door opened, and both detectives dropped their hands to their sides, fast.

By the time they walked into the office they had their game faces on.

Sam was right. He is a wreck.

Richards sat behind a large desk, but he didn't look like he belonged there. His hair was awry, as if he'd been tugging at it. At some point that morning he'd spilled mustard on his tie, then tried to clean it. An off-yellow blob sat on the red tie, and he was worrying at it as Mike and Sam came in. He looked up, and his eyes were red-rimmed and bleary with tears.

"They're all dead. Aren't they," he said, and immediately started to sob. He scratched at the yellow blob on his tie with a thumbnail, and was starting to wear the material so much that the threads of the tie were unraveling.

The young officer who'd opened the door whispered at Mike's side.

"He's been like that for an hour now Lieutenant. Shall I call for a psych eval?"

Mike ignored him, moved forward and sat opposite Richards.

"Mr. Richards?"

The man kept sobbing.

"Mr. Richards, you're right. They're all dead."

The man kept rubbing at the tie, concentrating hard on it as if it was the important thing in the world.

And to him, right now, it is, Mike thought. *It's the only thing between him and oblivion.*

"I need your help," Mike said.

Richards looked up.

"*My* help?"

He had a hitch in his voice, but Mike's hunch had been right. Asking for help had got his attention.

"Yes," Mike replied being careful to keep his voice soft and unthreatening. "We need someone who knows this office."

"That would be me," Richards said. He let the tie fall against his shirt and looked into Mike's eyes. "I'm sorry. It's all been such a shock."

"Just take your time sir. Tell me what happened," Mike said. That was all he needed to say.

It all came out of Richards in a flood.

"I went down to the vaults to check on a manuscript. When I got there I found the door was lying wide open. Now that thing has to be hermetically sealed. We're fully controlled for moisture and temperature, and even slight variations can rot the books faster than spit. Well, when I saw that door open I just flipped. It just had to have been Doyle. I was still angry with her anyway, and this just sent me over the top. She'd been so rude, even after I sacked her. I marched across to her office. I knew she'd still be there, spreading sedition among her little troop of performing monkeys. I was determined to nip it in the bud. Forcibly if I had to.

"I pushed the office door open and strode in and…"

He stopped, the blood draining from his face, eyes starting to roll up in their sockets.

Mike banged his fist on the desk, hard.

The noise brought Richards back. He picked up his tie and started rubbing the yellow spot again.

"They're all dead," he whispered.

"We know what you saw," Mike said softly. "Back up a bit. You terminated Ms. Doyle's employment. Can you tell us why?"

At first Mike thought the man wasn't going to reply. He was still playing with his tie. Mike was about to bang the desk again when Richards reached into his desk and brought out a sheet of paper.

He passed it to Mike.

"I wouldn't normally bother about our staff's personal lives, but Doyle never liked me. And I didn't know why. So I started reading her blog… just to try to get a picture of what was going on in her head and…"

He shut up, and Mike saw the lonely little man behind the facade.

He loves her. He loves her, but can't show it.

It was a print out of a blog posting, by Patty Doyle, dated the night before. The print had been done of the whole page, and also showed a small picture of Ms. Doyle in the top corner. She looked to be a petit blonde, with a happy smile.

A cataloguer of failures was the heading. It continued:

> *"Doug Richards doesn't know his ass from his elbow. Why anyone would put him in charge of the department is beyond me. He's a petty, small-minded accountant with a cash register where his heart should be.*
>
> *"He has no feel for the history, the tradition. All he thinks about are dollar signs and bookkeeping. He's probably got a small dick as well… all petty tyrants like him are obviously over compensating for something.*
>
> *"Take this morning. I was working on "The Twelve Concordances of the Red Serpent" when he came in and told me to stop, as I'd used up the budget.*
>
> *"How can you use up a budget on a piece of history? The small-minded fool has no soul, no poetry, no heart.*
>
> *"The sooner we get rid of him, the better the department will be, and we can get back to doing what we do best."*

Mike read it twice.

"You can see why I had to talk to her," Richards said.

"And you fired her?"

Richards sobbed again.

"Damned right. She's a flake. She should have gone years ago."

I think you're protesting too much, Mike thought.

"Flaky enough to take it out on the staff in the office?" Mendoza asked.

Richards jerked in his chair as if he'd been shot.

"You don't think… no, she wouldn't… she couldn't…"

Then he stopped.

"But... that would make it my fault," he whispered. "All my fault."

He started to shake, and went back to rubbing at the tie, furiously this time.

"Mr. Richards," Mendoza began.

"No Sergeant," Mike said sadly. "Leave him be. Just leave him be."

Mike rose and left.

Mendoza followed straight behind him. She pulled at his arm when they were out in the corridor.

"What was that all about boss? He might know something..."

Mike shook her off.

"All that poor bastard knows is pain. What's our motto? Protect and Serve? We'd be doing neither for him if we kept at him in the state he's in."

"But we've got nothing else," Mendoza began.

"Then maybe you should be doing something about it rather than standing here?"

He got that look again, but she was a good soldier, she left him alone.

He'd told Mendoza it was "*Nothing a few beers won't cure*," but he'd lied. Whisky was the only thing that was going to fix this, and even that would only be a temporary reprieve. While he'd been looking at the bodies earlier, he hadn't been thinking about the job, hadn't been careful to look for clues; he'd been thinking about booze, and how much he just wanted to lose himself in it.

It had started last year. Juliet Wozniak had been a society figure, rich, well liked, good looking, and as evil a bitch as ever walked the planet. Mike's team was called when the kids disappeared. The case dragged on for weeks, and Mike knew that the woman was bad.

But I never pushed it.

They found her three children dead in a cellar, having been starved, beaten and tortured over a period of months. The sight of those three small bodies had broken something in him, and Mike saw them every time he closed his eyes at night. And every night they accused him.

You should have done something Mikey.

Every new case brought them back again, and more and more the bottle called, with its promise of oblivion, for a while.

He had no idea how long he stood there in the corridor, and he didn't really care.

He was brought back to the present by Mendoza's return.

"Are you holding up boss?"

Mike nodded.

"That beer is looking awfully good about now though. You do know that this has all the makings of a circus?"

Now it was her turn to nod.

"The Captain's going to be all over us on this one. We need to be on the ball."

"I know," Mike said wearily. "Go on then. What have we got?"

"We might have a break boss. This place has cameras everywhere. They've got full security footage from this morning, and there's some stuff on it you need to see."

Backstage at *Morrisons* wasn't as salubrious as the front office. They walked through a *Staff Only* door into a maze of corridors. The walls weren't painted, mahogany was conspicuous by its absence, and the doors to all the rooms were little more than rectangles of plywood with locks in them.

"Could be worse," Mendoza said. "They could have had more of that green paint."

She led Mike to a small back room. A security guard sat in front of a 3x3 rack of monitors showing views of the building, inside and out. He was watching the barrier where the television crews had been joined by gawkers from the public.

"Say, is that her?" he said to Mike, pointing at the screen. A famous newscaster stood there, haranguing a bored looking cop.

"Yes. That's her," Mike said. "Just be thankful you can't hear her. She can strip paint at ten yards."

"Nice tits though," the guard said, then realized that Mendoza was there. He went a deep shade of red and started mumbling apologies.

Mike laughed for the first time since entering the building.

"Suddenly *my* day doesn't seem quite so bad after all," he said to Mendoza. "So what have we got?"

"Run the tapes," she said. "And stop where we did earlier."

The guard fumbled with some buttons and dials on his desk, but finally got things to work.

Mendoza tapped at one of the screens.

"We have two unknown males arriving, two minutes apart. Here's the first."

The picture stopped, showing a tall male in a sharp suit entering the main door.

"There's no security on that door?" Mike asked.

"Yes, there is," the guard said. "But he had the codes. And so did this one."

He ran the tape forward.

A much smaller, much thinner man walked up to the door, tapped in the codes, and entered.

"Have we got enough for FROG?" Mike asked Mendoza.

"For the first one, yes, we got a pretty good full on shot of his face. The second... not so sure."

"Get it over to the lab boys ASAP anyway," he said. "Is there any more footage of them inside the building?"

The security guard answered.

"Afraid not. One of them had some kind of jammer on him. All we've got is snow."

"And shouldn't somebody have noticed?"

The guard wouldn't meet Mike in the eye.

"I was out the back having a smoke. I get a five minute break every hour."

"And who knows this?" Mendoza said.

"Just about everybody that ever comes to the office regularly," he replied.

Mike tapped at the monitor.

"And a couple of extra guests it would seem."

He looked at the screens for long seconds.

"Do we have the Doyle woman coming in?"

"Yes," Mendoza replied. "Five minutes before either man."

"How about the parking lot or the surrounding streets... any eyes on them?"

"The lot has only worker's cars in it. Nothing yet from the street but we're canvassing for more footage from wherever we can get it."

"Good," Mike said. "Looks like you've got it covered. I'll see you back at the precinct."

He got the look again as he turned and left. He knew Mendoza was only concerned for him. In fact, she was one of the few things that took the edge off the depths of the blackness.

But not today.

He went out into the city, heading for a bar. Any bar.

3

Patty stared out of the car window and wondered how she'd got to this point. She felt nauseous. Her world had narrowed to a long dark tunnel. Down at the far end she saw the city passing by, but it didn't look like anything she recognized as real.

Her mind had become a kaleidoscope of ever shifting figures that were fractured and distorted just enough that she could not quite make out what they signified. She saw Jill Stanley, who looked like she'd applied her make up badly… there was just too much red, and her skin was too pale. And George looked like he'd cut himself shaving and forgot to stem the flow. Then there was Mary, with one big eye, staring, always staring.

Closing her eyes didn't help, for then things started to become clearer, and if she allowed that, then she'd also have to allow the scream that was waiting to let go.

She knew there was a man in the driver's seat beside her. She remembered him leading her by the hand out of her office. There had been something back there that she should be thinking about, but every time her mind got close the tunnel contracted further and left her in darkness.

And her hand itched. She'd looked down at it, just once, but looked away quickly. Too much red again, a deep red that wouldn't go away, even after rubbing her hand forcibly against the material of the car seat.

She watched the tunnel, and the city beyond. She was vaguely aware that they had already circled the Park twice, but as she didn't know where she was going, she refused to let it worry her. Not yet anyway.

The man beside her kept up a constant stream of chatter, but that's all it was to her… background noise, like you hear in a restaurant, other people's lives. She kept it at bay by thinking of her childhood.

Her mother's voice came to her.

Our Patty's a worrier.

Patty was sitting in the garden, playing with Tom from next door. Rather, Tom was playing, running behind bushes and firing off a toy gun from behind them. Patty sat in the dead center of the lawn and watched everything that was happening. But she didn't move. She was wearing her clean dress, and if she moved, it might get dirty, then she'd have to wash it. And choose something else to wear. And there might not be anything suitable in the wardrobe. So she contented herself with sitting.

What's she got to worry about?

Her Aunt Sarah's voice this time. Aunt Sarah laughed too much, and too loudly. Patty thought it might be the gin that did it. But she wouldn't ask about it, couldn't ask, just in case she was wrong and made a fool of herself.

Aunt Sarah spoke again.

She's got her whole life ahead of her.

Her mom had laughed.

That's what she's worried about.

Hot summer days by cool ponds, with ice cream and lemonade.

She'd been happy then, and she could be again, just sitting, watching the world pass her by.

If only the annoying little man would stop chattering.

He hadn't shut up since they got in the car. Patty was only vaguely aware of some of the topics he'd covered so far, but she was pretty sure they'd already run the gamut of religion, politics and sport. Now he was onto some conspiracy theory involving Knights Templar and the search for the Holy Grail. It was like being with a bunch of frat boys at a drinking session that had gone on far too long into the night.

But at least the frat boys had the good grace to go to sleep.

And it wasn't just the chattering. He almost buzzed with nervous energy. He slapped the steering wheel with his hands in time to a martial rhythm; he drove like a maniac, taking corners too fast and cutting in on people just for the hell of it and, in between the chattering he whistled off-key jigs and reels. Every ten seconds his gaze made a round trip, from out of the windshield, to Patty, to the rear view mirror, then back to the view outside the car.

This time he spotted that Patty was looking at him.

"We're clear," he said. "There's no one following us."

Why would someone be following us?

His hand touched her arm, and she brushed it off brusquely.

"You haven't heard a single word I've said, have you?" he asked. Again she noticed the lilt in his voice, the hint of an accent. He was also dressed strangely.

You don't see many three-piece tweed suits these days.

The suit looked rough, almost hairy. Beneath the jacket and vest he had a bright yellow shirt, open at the neck where unruly tufts of graying hair seemed to be trying to escape.

She put out a hand to touch the cloth of the jacket.

"Three generations of wee women on Harris labored long and hard to make this," he said, and laughed. There was that accent again, although she still couldn't place it.

But it was enough to get her interest, to pull her out of the tunnel.

Reality came at her like an express train and the darkness beckoned, but the man touched her arm again.

"Look, I'm sorry about your friends. But there are things we need to do if we're to be safe."

"Safe?" she whispered. And suddenly it hit her. She started to cry. At first it was no more than a quiet sob, but it quickly became shoulder hunching, wracking wails as tears ran down her cheeks.

The man beside her let it run its course.

"Better?" he asked when she finally quieted.

And, in truth, she did feel better. She wouldn't be healed. Not for a while, maybe not ever. But she could function. She was ready for answers.

"Who the hell are you?" she asked.

"Seton," he said. "Alex Seton."

"I don't want to know your name," Patty said vehemently. "I want to know *who* you are, and what the hell is going on."

He laughed loudly.

"What's so funny?" she said.

"Everything," he said. "And nothing."

He smiled. It looked like something he did a lot.

"I'll tell you what I know," he said. "But first, I need to know where it is."

"Where what is?"

"The document you were working on."

Patty felt like she'd fallen into the *Twilight Zone*. She couldn't quite get a grasp of the conversation, and the small man looked and sounded more like a demented pixie from a bad dream.

"What document?" she said, exasperated.

"I read your blog," Seton said. "You said you were working on *The Twelve Concordances of the Red Serpent*."

Patty felt anger growing in her, and fought it down.

"You want to know about a fourteenth century journal? My friends are dead. They're lying back there in the office and they're *dead*."

"I know," Seton said softly. "I was there, remember. I was there because of the journal. And so was the suit who killed them."

Patty still couldn't put the facts together in any way that made sense to her.

"It just an old journal," she said finally. "Why would anyone kill for it?"

"I think I know," Seton said. "And I'll tell you. But, please, tell me where it is. We need to get to it before they do."

Patty's brain was finally starting to click into gear. Slowly, but she was getting there.

And Mama Doyle didn't raise any idiots.

"Stop the car," she said. "Stop right now. I'm going to the police."

Much to her surprise he pulled over to the curb. She reached for the door.

"I can't stop you," he said. "But just listen to me. Just for a minute?"

She took her hand off the door handle.

"I'm not a prisoner?"

He laughed again.

"I don't see what's so funny," Patty said.

"No, you wouldn't," he replied, and that set him off laughing again.

She reached for the door handle again.

"No, please?" he said, and this time he looked serious, although there was a twinkle in his eye that Patty suspected was always there. "This is important."

She sat back in the seat.

"OK. I'm listening."

He took out a cigarette case, opened it and offered her one. She shook her head.

"It's been a bad enough day already," she said.

He tapped a cigarette ostentatiously against the case, flourished a Zippo lighter, and finally lit up before talking.

"I'm a journalist," he said. "And I specialize in – well, let's just say, the *obscure*. A couple of months ago I discovered someone was looking for the *Concordances*…and they were prepared to step on as many toes as required to get it."

"Why…" Patty started.

He raised a hand.

"We don't have time. This is the short version. You'll get the long one later, if we're given the chance."

That sounds ominous.

He took a long draw on the cigarette.

"I've been following their tracks for weeks now. Yesterday, the one I've been tracking accessed your blog. He called out the heavies to get the journal. And I got there just in time to save you."

That didn't tell Patty a great deal more than she knew already, apart from the fact that her drunken blog had been a *really* bad idea.

"That's it?"

"That's it," he said.

"You're right. That is the short version. I've got a lot of questions."

He nodded.

"But they'll have to wait. By now they'll already know what happened back at your office. We need to find that journal before they do."

"Why?" Patty said. "What makes that particular manuscript so important?"

He suddenly looked serious.

"Because more people will be killed if we don't find it. Possibly many more."

"And I'm just supposed to trust you?"

He stared straight at her.

"You've got to start somewhere," he said, and looked at his watch. "And the clock is ticking."

Her hand moved towards the door again.

"Ms. Doyle," he said softly. "If you leave now, you'll never know why."

Once more she put her hand back in her lap. She wanted answers. More than that, she needed answers. And she owed the dead staring eyes of her friends more than just running to the cops.

"Please Ms. Doyle. Just tell me. Where is the journal?"

She sighed loudly, just to let him know who was in charge here.

"It came in last week. There wasn't much to it. Abstracting and indexing only took a couple of hours. I finished working on it yesterday afternoon," she said. "Jill had it couriered back to the owner. She's very efficient. I don't know what we'd do without her…"

She stopped, suddenly remembering. Tears came again.

Seton put a hand on her arm.

"Who's the owner?"

Normally she wouldn't know that information, but Doug Richards had made a point of mentioning this one, a man so rich that *everyone* knew who he was.

"Carslyle, the newspaper man. He lives…"

"I know where he lives," Seton said, and suddenly his eyes lost their twinkle, replaced by a hard stare.

"Hold on," he said as he started the engine. "I think we're in for a bumpy ride."

4

It was guilt that eventually drove Mike out of the bar.

It took him a while to notice it though.

Mike had always liked bars. Quiet ones, loud ones, small intimate ones, large empty barns that echoed like cathedrals; they all talked to him, reminded him of better days and happier times. The one he'd chosen today was an old friend, from back when he'd been a young detective who still found working the Homicide squad a rewarding experience.

This one qualified as *small, intimate*. Any more than ten people inside and it started to feel crowded. But it was a place for drinkers. There were no television sets, no juke-boxes. There was just some gentle jazz in the background and the clink of ice against glass. Sometimes there would be a low murmur of conversation, but voices were rarely ever raised in more than a whisper. Jack, the bartender, had been here as long as Mike had been coming, and Mike's patronage extended back nearly twenty years now.

He used to come here after his shift, to sip beer and watch people, to shoot the breeze with Jack about the latest ball game, or just to disengage his brain and drift. The place had undergone several slight changes of decor over the years since then, but the barstools were still comfortable, and the booze still got you drunk. The fact that he got drunk faster and more often than he used to wasn't the fault of the bar.

Nobody's fault but mine.

It was only when he realized he hadn't thought about the case since entering the bar that the guilt started. He looked up and saw that he was the only person in the room, sitting alone and nursing his fourth whisky. Even Jack was giving him a wide berth.

He drained the last finger of whisky in one gulp and put the glass down, too heavily, on the bar.

The thud sounded like the last nail going in to Mike's coffin.

Suddenly he was disgusted with himself. The Force deserved better from him. Mendoza deserved *much* better from him.

"Another, Lieutenant?" Jack asked as he took the glass away.

Mike shook his head, but part of him was sorely tempted. He pushed it away into a dark place where it could fester until later.

"I've had too much already," he said.

"See you later then," Jack said.

Mike didn't answer. He didn't need to. Both of them knew that it wouldn't be long until he was back in the same seat.

It wouldn't be long at all.

He left the bar and squinted against the lancing sunlight that threatened to spear his brain. It brought on an immediate headache, a pounding just behind his left eye. He almost turned straight round and headed back into the comforting dark of the bar. It was only the thought of Mendoza carrying the caseload for him that kept him moving.

She'd been carrying him a lot recently, running static for his increasingly long absences from his desk, keeping up with his paperwork, and doing most of his job for him. He hadn't asked her to do it, hadn't thanked her for it, but he was grateful that she was there.

But for how long? How long can you treat her like a doormat and expect her to stay there?

As he walked back towards the precinct he could already feel the call of the bottle. He was vaguely aware that his daily intake of booze was rising, and rising fast… he had a collection of empty bottles in his apartment that accused him every time he walked passed them. He was drinking for breakfast, lunch and supper, with a little extra during the night at times to get him back to sleep. So far he'd fought off the urge to buy a quart for the bottom drawer of his desk, but he knew that day wasn't too far off.

Mendoza raised an eyebrow as he entered the office, but that was all. The rest of the team kept their heads down until Mike was in his room. A murmur of conversation followed him inside. He knew they were talking about him, knew that only Mendoza was holding things together. It didn't help his mood any.

He sat down in his chair, hard, and sighed deeply as the Sergeant knocked on the open door and entered. Not for the first time he realized just what an attractive woman she was.

Mediterranean genes. That was the considered opinion in the locker room. They showed in the black hair and dark complexion, but it was her blue eyes that pulled him in and trapped him, every time.

Well, almost every time.

The look she gave him as she entered told him that he wasn't number one on the popularity charts.

She carried a sheaf of papers, and Mike tried to divert her attention by getting the first word in.

"Give me some good news Sam, please?"

He could tell it hadn't worked as she closed the door behind her.

"We need to talk, Mike," she said.

When women say that, it's usually time for men to shut up and listen.

"No," he replied. "You need to talk. I don't need it at all."

She sat in the chair opposite and stared at him.

"You don't look good boss."

"Too much healthy living," Mike replied, trying to keep the tone light. She wasn't having any of it.

"The Captain was looking for you. Nearly an hour ago," she said.

"Did he find me?"

He didn't get a laugh.

"It's not funny Mike. You're screwing up. And it's not just me who notices. What the hell is wrong with you?"

"Nothing a…"

"…few beers can't fix?" she finished for him. "Yes. I've heard that already today. And I didn't believe it the first time. Come on Mike, it's me, Sam, that's asking."

Mike didn't like what he saw in her eyes now. He started rearranging the papers on his desk, just to avoid it. It looked too much like pity.

"Mike?" she said softly. "*Talk* to me."

He put the papers down and looked at her. Something inside him lurched, and suddenly he realized he *was* going to talk after all.

"Do you want the truth or the B.S.?" he said quietly.

This time he did get a laugh, but there wasn't much humor in it, and it didn't reach her eyes.

"I think I've had enough of the B.S. You owe me the truth."

Mike sat back in his chair and stared at the ceiling.

"I suppose I do."

He took a long pause before he spoke. When he did it was to articulate something he'd been thinking all day.

"I'm getting too old for this shit," he said.

"Aren't we all?"

"No Sam, I mean it. I'm frazzled, on the edge. And I can't see a way out. It started with the Wozniak kids, and it's all been downhill from there."

"Then take some leave. God knows you've got enough built up."

"In the middle of a triple homicide case? That wouldn't look good."

"News-flash boss. It already looks as bad as it's gonna get."

Mike fell quiet. He kept his gaze on the ceiling, frightened that, if he looked at her, there would be more of that *pity* there.

I don't think I can take too much of that.

"I can't do it any more Sam. I'm old and I'm tired. But the job's the only thing keeping me from the bottle," he said.

He looked down from the ceiling. She was still staring intently at him. He managed to raise a smile.

"Even if it isn't doing a very good job of it."

"I knew the Wozniak case hit you hard," she said. "But I didn't realize how hard."

"Neither did I," Mike said. "Not at first. But I started to dream, then I started to drink to stop the dreams. Then I just seemed to keep on drinking."

"There was a time you would have come to me first," Sam said quietly. "Remember?"

And he did remember.

A week after the Wozniak case Mike had the first of the dreams; the three pairs of sad, dead eyes of the tortured children, staring up at him.

You should have done something.

He'd still been shaken when he got to work, and a dark depression hung over him all day. Sam went to the bar with him after the shift, and listened as he rambled, and drank, and rambled some more. She'd helped him to bed, and stayed on his couch. The next morning they made breakfast together like it was the most natural thing in the world.

It had lasted three months. He'd almost been contented. But work romances don't last, cop romances don't last, and boss/underling romances don't last. They'd been thrice doomed.

And yet they'd nearly made it, until the night he'd turned up at her place drunk and looking for a fight. He'd got one. She'd kicked his ass around the room then thrown him out into the street.

"I remember the bruises," he said, coming back to the present.

She looked him in the eye.

"I'm ready to try again," she said.

"I'm not," he replied without thinking, then realized, too late, that he'd said the wrong thing.

It wasn't pity in her eyes now, it was hurt, and that was worse.

Sam sat back in the chair and started shuffling the papers she'd brought in with her. Now it was her turn not to look him in the eye.

"Just try to stay off the booze for a day or two Lieutenant," she said, all business. "We've got a killer to catch."

"Sam, I'm sorry," he said.

And he was. But he'd learned a long time ago that you can't turn the clock back. The only way to deal with mistakes was to learn from them and try to do better.

"So am I," she replied. "Now can we get to business or are you going to be a pitiful bastard again?"

Mike forced himself upright in the chair.

"If that's the way you want it, Sam?"

She nodded. This time she did look him in the eye, and gave him a flinty stare that cut like a knife.

"That's the way I want it," she said.

She put a sheet of paper on the desk in front of him.

"Forensics got a match on the suit. FROG found him easily enough and the DNA from the blood on the carpet confirm it. His name is Dave Ross."

Mike lifted the sheet and read the docket. It gave name, age, and current address. He had one arrest, nearly ten years before, for aggravated assault. It also gave a current job description.

"Security guard? Do we know who for?"

"We're chasing him down now. Should have it in the next five minutes or so."

"Anything else?"

"Still no news on the other man on the tapes, and no sign of Doyle at her apartment. Their pictures are in circulation."

"And what about forensics? Anything else there?"

"They're still trying to figure out who did who and when. But we have another mystery. Forensics say that given the amount of blood they found, Ross must have bled out. There's no way he walked away."

"They could be wrong," Mike said. "It wouldn't exactly be the first time they made a mistake."

Sam shook her head.

"You saw the blood Mike. It did look like a big pool to me."

"So what are they saying? Whoever killed him took the body with them?"

He tapped at the docket in his hand.

"He's down here as six-two and nearly two hundred pounds. That's a helluva lump to be carrying around, never mind getting it out of the building unseen."

"Yet the fact is, he's gone," Sam said.

"So we have a conspiracy? The other man, Doyle and Ross all in it together?"

"I don't think so. If that was the case, who did Ross?" Mike though about it.

"But if it's not the case, where did Ross's body go?" Sam nodded.

"That's what's got forensics thinking. And there's something else. We haven't any footage of what went on inside the building. But we got these from afterwards."

She passed him two pictures. One showed Doyle and the small man leaving in a blue saloon. The other showed a black van with tinted windows. The windows were so dark the driver could not be made out. Time stamps on the pictures showed they were taken about ten minutes apart.

"Plates?" Mike asked, then put up a hand. "No. Let me guess. Forensics are working on it?"

He got a small smile.

Not much. But something to be going on with.

"We don't have much to go on. Not till we get a fix on Ross," Sam said.

"OK then," Mike said, standing. "Let's get me some coffee. It's time that I was sober."

That got him a longer, slower, smile, and suddenly he found he liked it. He liked it a lot.

"I'll go chase up on Ross," Sam said. "Meet you at the Java."

The smile kept the darkness at bay all the way to the small area that served as the coffee stop. The coffee had been stewing for so long that it was almost chewy. Mike poured a tall cup of it. It gave his heart a kick-start and chased the whisky around in his stomach. For the first time that day, Mike started feeling like a cop again.

All I need is a donut and I'm set.

He was about to pour another coffee when Sam arrived.

"We've got a lead," she said. "But I'm not sure I like it."

"Tell me anyway," Mike said, and tried a smile of his own. It didn't feel right. He was badly out of practice.

Sam was too preoccupied to notice.

"Somebody's missing a security guard named Ross. And they say they've got info we need to hear."

"That's a bit of a coincidence, that they ring us just as we're looking for their man."

"Yes," Sam said. "That's what I thought as well. But it got someone's attention. The call came from Adams Pharmaceuticals, and they want us to go over there."

"Who wants us to go over there?"

"The Brass. The Captain got a call from high up. And we've to tread carefully."

"Ah. One of those calls."

"Yep. One of *those* calls. I hate the political shit."

"Comes with the territory Sergeant," Mike said, putting down the coffee. "Let's go and see how a multi-national pharmaceuticals company is involved in our very local triple homicide. If nothing else, the lies should be creative."

5

"Why?" Patty asked again.

They'd left the city behind a quarter of an hour ago, and neither of them had spoken much in that time. Now they drove along a wooded road, and hadn't passed any traffic since they'd turned off the highway.

Patty's thoughts were beginning to calm. There was still no quiet point for her to settle on, but she no longer felt like screaming, and that was a start.

"There's that question again," Seton said. "I told you. They're after the journal."

"But..."

"Why?" Seton said, in a fair approximation of her voice. He smiled and laughed again. "Curiosity killed the cat you know?"

Patty stared straight ahead. *Killed* wasn't a word she was going to be thinking about any time soon. Panic kept fluttering around her, and if she let it, it would fill her; quite possibly consume her. She was used to an anchored life. Calm, uncluttered regularity was her aim for each day. This particular day wasn't quite going to plan. Her mind kept going back to her blog.

"Doug Richards doesn't know his ass from his elbow."

Why couldn't they just have killed Richards.

She immediately felt bad just for thinking it, but it wouldn't go away. Her blog had got her friends killed. It was going to take a long time for her to come to terms with that.

If I ever can.

It was something George once told her that got her thinking clearer.

"When the wind starts to blow, it's best not to fight it. Go with it, and you'll move much faster."

Of course, George had been talking about a particularly difficult transcription, but it had stuck with Patty.

Go with it.

She pushed herself upright in her seat and spoke directly to Seton.

"Where are we going?"

"To Carslyle's country house, remember?"

Remembering was something she was trying hard not to do.

"What makes you think Carslyle will see us?" she said.

Seton laughed out loud and beat a rhythm on the steering wheel.

"What makes you think he won't?"

"Well, for a start, he's just about the richest man on the planet."

"And rich men never see people?"

Surprising herself, Patty managed a laugh.

"You know what I mean," she said. "He's a recluse."

"A recluse with a thing for rare manuscripts," Seton said. He looked at Patty and grinned. "Say, you don't know anybody who's a specialist in those do you?"

Once more Patty laughed before she remembered exactly why she was here.

Seton must have seen something in her face. He slowed down slightly and put a hand on her shoulder.

"It's OK to laugh you know?"

But that just made her think of George, and the new red grin under his chin.

"No," she said. "It isn't. I feel *so* guilty."

He pulled the car over onto a grass verge and turned off the engine.

"It wasn't your fault."

"It was *my* bloody blog that started this."

Seton lit himself another cigarette and opened his driver side window to let the smoke out.

"No," he said softly. "If it's anyone's fault, it's mine. I should have done something before now. "

"Tell me," Patty said.

He shook his head.

"Not yet. Carslyle first. Now are you *sure* you're OK?"

She nodded. He ground out the cigarette and started back onto the road.

Patty pulled down the sun visor and looked at herself in the vanity mirror.

"You're taking me to see one of the richest men in the world looking like *this*?"

Her make-up was streaked in pale brown and white stripes across her face. She'd have looked cat-like if her eyes weren't so red and puffy and her hair wasn't standing at acute angles to her scalp.

"You look just fine to me," Seton said. Patty checked his face to see if she was being mocked, but he *looked* serious enough.

"But if you think you can improve on perfection, you might find what you need on the back seat," Seton said, not taking his eyes from the road. "I brought your satchel from the office."

Just holding the satchel grounded her back in *her* life for a few seconds. She clung tightly to it, holding it against her chest for a second before opening it. Just as she did so, her cell phone started to ring.

"Give that here," Seton said as she picked it out of the satchel.

Patty ignored him and flipped the phone open. Her finger was just about to take the call when Seton took his right hand from the wheel and picked the phone from her hand.

He tossed it, still ringing, out of the open window onto the roadside.

"That might have been important," Patty said indignantly.

"And it might have been the police," Seton replied. "What would you have told them?"

"I don't know."

I don't know.

That just about summed up her day so far.

Patty spent the next five minutes fixing her face and hair. The mundane routine of it grounded her, brought her back to a semblance of reality. She found a bottle of water in her bag and, with a handkerchief, started to remove the blood from her hands. She managed to get them looking mostly clean, but no matter how hard she rubbed the blood away, she suspected she'd always remember it having been there.

It might never feel completely clean again.

"I need to know why," she said softly.

"We *all* need to know," Seton replied, suddenly serious. "And that's what this is all about, in part."

He lit another cigarette.

"You smoke too much," she said.

"And you think too much. In my book that makes us even."

Try as she might, she didn't have a good answer for that one. Seton didn't give her time to worry about it.

"What do you remember of the journal?" he asked.

The *Concordances* manuscript had come in last week, and Doug Richards had passed it straight to her.

"This belongs to John Carslyle, you know… the newspaper man?" he said. "He's one of our patrons, and donated over a hundred grand last year. There's a rumor he might put money into a new climate controlled vault. Put it on the top of your pile."

That was it. No *please*, no *thank you*. Not that she'd expected anything else from the man. Her blog had just been an outward manifestation of something she'd thought since he was put in charge. He had no feel for the history. He was a bean counter.

All those thoughts had gone when she lifted the journal. It was old and delicate, and she took great care with it as she prepared the initial description.

> *Author:* {*Unknown.*}
> *Title: The Twelve Concordances of the Red Serpent*
> *Language: Old Scots.*
> *Origin: Edinburgh, Scotland, 1329*
> *Binding: Bound in dark brown calf over wooden boards. Heavily ornamented, gold tooled.*
> *Frontispiece inscription: Ye Twelve Concordances of ye Red Serpent. In wch is succinctly and methodically handled, the stone of ye philosophers, his excellent effectes and admirable vertues; and, the better to attaine to the originall and true meanes of perfection, inriched with Figures representing the proper colors to lyfe as they successively appere in the practice of this blessed worke.*
> *Description: Illuminated manuscript on parchment. 28 leaves. 21 x 13 cm. Single column of 19 lines. Textblock: 14 x 8.5 cm.*
> *Decoration: Text has illuminated Gothic initials "M" and "T" and bar borders ending in knotwork corners decorated in gold, red, blue, and purple paint on folio 2r.*

*Some paint has offset onto facing blank. Headings and
initials in red and blue throughout. Four full-color minia-
ture paintings with gold within full-page floral borders;
numerous vine-leaf and gold initials with floral pen work
extensions.*

Those were just words, and they failed to describe the
beauty of the book itself. Patty's job was to preserve that
beauty by digitizing the work, and cataloguing and indexing
its contents so that they could be added to databases and
allow researchers access to works that might previously
have lain forgotten in libraries.

It isn't something that people usually get killed for.

She didn't realize that she'd spoken aloud until Seton
replied.

"This time it is," he said.

"I don't understand," Patty said. The tears were close
again.

Seton sucked smoke and looked like he was trying to
make up his mind about something.

"Let me tell you a wee story," he finally said. "You'll
have heard some of it before, but not it all. You might not
think it pertinent at first, but listen anyway. It'll make more
sense later.

"It starts in Scotland, in 1328, while *The Bruce* was still
on the throne," he said, before pausing. "Actually, it started
a while before that. On the 24th of June 1314 the armies of
The Bruce, heavily outnumbered by their English rivals, but
using tactics that prevented the English army from deploy-
ing its strength, won victory at Bannockburn. Scotland was
taken back from English control. The Declaration of
Independence signed at Arbroath in 1320 was the culmina-
tion of *The Bruce*'s career and sealed his position. Scotland

had become the first nation state in Europe and the first to have territorial unity under a single King. This became widely recognized in May 1328. A peace treaty with the auld enemy was signed at Northampton. Tired and disillusioned from decades of fighting, the English King finally recognized Scotland as an independent kingdom and Robert Bruce as King.

"Unfortunately *The Bruce* wasn't going to live long enough to savor the moment. He was gravely ill, and had been for a long time. His enemies started to spread rumors that the King was a leper; a great stigma at that time."

Patty interrupted him.

"Wasn't his father a leper? Didn't I see it in that movie?"

Seton laughed, louder than anything before.

"You saw *that*? Historical accuracy has never been Hollywood's strongpoint, but they really pushed the boat out on that one. Did you know that *The Bruce*'s nickname was Braveheart?"

Seton smiled, as if at a private joke, and sucked some more smoke. Outside the car the trees on either side of the road had got more closely packed…so much so that Patty once more felt she was travelling down a dark tunnel. Seton's story had pushed her own aside for a short time, but it was still there, waiting to rush in and engulf her if she gave it an opening.

"How much further?" she asked.

"As far as it needs to be," Seton said, and smiled. "Now, do you want the story or not?"

Patty waved her hand at him to continue.

"The father wasn't a leper," Seton said. "And neither was *The Bruce*. He had none of the disfigurement or lesions associated with the disease.

"But something afflicted him. These days we'd call it cancer, and treat it accordingly. But if it was cancer, it was one that had been with him for a long time, back as far as 1307. Doctors were called from all over Europe, and they diagnosed a variety of cures, from leeches and bloodletting to tincture of mercury and mandrake.

"Nothing worked, and the great man was getting weaker by the day. Until a stranger appeared, an old man. Some say he was a Templar, with lore learned in the Holy Land. Whatever his story, the old man showed the Royal Court that he knew arcane secrets. He offered to help the King, in return for protection from Rome and the Pope.

"So began the experiment, the treatment of the King and the attempt to renew his vigor. It was all written down and collated, every detail recorded in a code known only to the writer himself. There were twelve steps in all; twelve *Concordances*."

"That's all well and good," Patty said. "And I can see how it could be a fascinating historical document. But it's still not enough to kill people for."

"It is if the experiment was successful," Seton said.

6

Adams Pharmaceuticals was a recent addition to the city skyline. They'd moved into one of the old docks in the late nineties and spent years putting up an office block that was a huge glittering monument to their success.

Driving down towards the dock felt like taking a journey back in time. Mike spent his first five years on the force here, walking these streets. He knew them intimately. There was the liquor store where he'd made his first arrest, there was the bar where he'd had to use his gun for the first time, and there on the corner just outside the old dock gates were the hookers waiting for the boats to come in. They hadn't changed much over the years; different girls, same old job.

The far end of the docklands was a different matter entirely. It had changed out of all recognition. Sanitized, cleaned up and buffed to a shine, the Adams office block gleamed in the sun.

"What do you know about this outfit?" Mike asked as Sam drove them into the vast car park.

"Adams inherited it," Sam replied. "It's a family business, going back at least a hundred years. According to legend great grand-pappy Adams was a snake oil salesman out West who discovered an old Apache remedy for headaches that actually worked. The company has been growing ever since. Apart from the fact that they're richer than Croesus, I only know what we've all seen on the ads. *Building Better Bodies…* quite a neat slogan."

"And it obviously pays well," Mike said.

The building they pulled up beside was a colossal sculpture of tinted glass and metal in angles and surfaces that caught the sun like a well-cut diamond. It towered above them, six stories high and over a hundred yards long.

"Good thing we're not intimidated by a lot of money, isn't it boss?" Sam said, and Mike found himself smiling.

It even felt natural.

The impression of wealth was only reinforced further when they walked into the lobby.

Lobby is too small a word for it.

Chrome pillars arched a hundred feet overhead, like the bones of a giant reptile. Beyond the bones, seamlessly integrated, a holographic projection showed a sky that was always blue, a sun that always shone. They had to walk across thirty yards of marble flooring just to reach the receptionist. All the way Mike felt like shouting, just to see if there would be an echo.

"You must be the police," the girl behind the counter said.

"And you must be the receptionist," Sam replied. "Hopefully we've finished stating the obvious. We have an appointment."

The girl directed them to an elevator cab that was bigger than Mike's bedroom.

"Mr. Adams is waiting for you in the Penthouse," she said.

"Does he have any pets?" Mike asked, but that only got him a blank stare that lasted until the doors shut on them and they started going up.

"The top man himself eh?" Mike said.

"Looks like it boss. This must be bigger than we thought."

"The bigger it gets, the more shit will be coming down from on high. Time to get the gum-boots and umbrella out again."

Sam wasn't paying attention. She was reading a plaque that was fixed on the elevator cab's wall.

"Adams Pharmaceuticals is a global service provider at the forefront of the pharmaceutical industry with operations in the USA, Africa, Asia and Europe.

"The organization comprises seven well-established, integrated companies and can provide an all-inclusive, seamless 'one-stop-shop' facility with services ranging from diagnostics, research and development, API manufacture, formulation development through clinical trials to delivery of finished product. Alternatively, depending on requirements, clients may create a partnership with a single division.

"Each customer is guaranteed a dedicated hands-on project management service to meet individual needs ensuring clients will experience continued success in all their ventures."

"What the hell does that even mean?" Mike asked as the doors began to open with a ping.

"It means we do research," a voice said. The doors opened fully and a white haired man stood there, a hand outstretched. "And we do it well."

Mike took the proffered hand and shook it.

"Mike Turner," he said.

"Alan Adams," the other man replied. It was hard to guess his age. His hair was white, but his face was smooth and unlined and he didn't have the turkey neck that you often saw in men getting on a bit in years. Mike couldn't see any signs of plastic surgery, but that didn't mean it hadn't been done... not when the man was as rich as Adam's appeared to be. His suit was silk, tailored and sleek. His tie-pin was a diamond Liz Taylor wouldn't have turned down, and his shoes looked like twenty cobblers had toiled over each stitch.

Sam shook the man's hand as well. Mike spotted that she had taken an instant dislike to him. It wasn't anything that anyone else would notice, just a subtle distancing of herself from closer contact. It was enough to put Mike on guard though... he'd learned to trust Sam's instincts.

"Research into what, if I may ask?" Mike said.

The man didn't reply. To Mike and Sam's amazement he dropped to the floor and started performing push-ups, thirty of them in rapid succession before springing to his feet.

"If I tried that I'd be puking for a week," Mike said.

Adams smiled.

"You're a detective. Let's see some of your reasoning skills. What age am I?" he said.

Mike took a closer look at him. On a second look he looked older than he'd first appeared. Small, almost invisible, crow's feet were long established at the corners of his eyes. The area around his Adam's apple showed some signs of sagging... not a lot, but enough to notice. His hands looked older than the rest of him, the skin tightly stretched across the knuckles, slightly gray and translucent.

"Come on detective, what's your best guess?"

"Sixty," Mike said, taking five years off his estimate for kindness sake.

Almost at the same moment, Sam said, "Eighty-two."

Adams had started to smile at Mike's estimate, but it quickly changed. Mike saw it in his eyes. This man was a charmer, but there was a shark underneath, and they'd just caught a glimpse of it.

"Someone's been doing their homework," he said.

"Well, if you're going to walk into the lion's den, it pays to know when it's dinner time."

"Luckily for you I've eaten already," Adams said.

Mike saw Sam's eyes show her anger, but Adams wasn't looking at her.

"Yes," he said, turning back to Mike. "She's right. I'm eighty-two years old. You see before you the product of clean living... and the proper application of pharmaceuticals. And that's what my company does... we find ways of improving the human condition, for longer."

"I've seen the ad... *Building better bodies*?" Mike said.

Adams smiled again, and the charmer was back.

"Precisely. To use an old cinema metaphor, I'm at the front of the house, the most visible exemplar of the company ethos."

He waved them towards a desk in front of a picture window.

"Come and sit," he said. "There's something you need to hear."

Adams sat with his back to the view, and Mike and Sam sat down opposite him. Adams started talking and at first Mike missed what he'd said, entranced by the view out over the city.

The window ran the full length of the wall. It had a slight tint to it that gave the skyline a slightly yellow tinge, almost sepia. It only served to accentuate the jagged peaks and valleys of the cityscape. The river shone like a lake of gold beneath and Mike was hypnotized by the activity of the tugs and pilot boats.

It was Sam's voice that brought him back to the conversation.

"So this man Ross... he was one of yours?" she said to Adams.

"Yes," Adams said.

"And you have no idea where he is?"

Adams smiled, and the shark was there again.

"No. That's why we called you."

Sam took a picture from her inside pocket. When she laid it on the desk Mike saw it was the one taken outside the scene of the murders.

"Is this him?" she asked.

Adams lifted the picture and looked at it.

"It could be," he said. "I'm not sure."

"How about this man?"

Sam put the picture of the second, smaller man on the desk.

"Ah yes. Him I *do* recognize. He's the reason I called you here. His name's Alex Seton. I think he's the reason that Ross has disappeared."

Sam and Mike looked at each other. Sam raised an eyebrow. Mike had played across the poker table from her enough times to know it was deliberate.

"How do you know him... this man Seton?" Mike asked.

Adams sat back in his chair.

"Firstly, I must ask that this conversation remains strictly confidential. It involves trade secrets worth billions of dollars in the right hands. It cannot leave this room."

"Drop the clichés Mr. Adams," Mike said. "We're homicide detectives, investigating a triple murder. If you don't tell us what you know, we'll just find a different way of getting the information. And our different way might not be subtle."

Adams sighed, and smiled. Suddenly Mike realized that the man had them where he wanted them. He was always going to tell them, but now it looked like he'd been forced into doing it.

"We run many experiments in this building," Adams began. "Not all of them are always, shall we say, *entirely* ethical. Seton was a volunteer for one of our new drug trials, something we've tried on rats and Rhesus monkeys, but never before on humans."

"Do you get a *lot* of volunteers for that kind of thing?" Sam said. "Isn't it a bit like Russian Roulette?"

Adams smiled across the desk at her.

"You'd be surprised what people will do for money," he said.

"I doubt that very much Mr. Adams."

Sam was on the verge of letting her dislike show. Mike had only seen her this antagonistic once before, and that was with the Wozniak woman *after* they'd caught her. She really hadn't taken to Adams. Mike decided to move the conversation on... if they stayed on this line Sam was likely to have the old man by the throat in the next few minutes.

"What was the trial trying to prove?"

"Can we leave that for the moment?" Adams said. "It's actually not important. What's important is that there were... unexpected side effects. Seton became increasingly paranoid, borderline psychotic. He started to believe we were holding him prisoner. It was all tied up in his mind with a conspiracy theory about the Knights Templar.

"And yesterday it all came to a head. He escaped, badly injuring one of our orderlies in the process. I sent Ross after him.

"Why didn't you call us immediately?" Sam said.

Adams looked at her. This time he didn't smile, and the shark was most definitely at home.

"Trade secrets," he said. "We don't need the publicity."

"Hold on to your hat Mr. Adams, publicity will be coming with the territory on this one," Mike said. "We have a triple homicide. And your company is right in the middle of it."

Adams didn't seem particularly worried.

"I'd *prefer* to keep things between ourselves, but we can handle the press if we need to," he said. "And I'm sure you'll find that Seton was the one responsible."

"Why are you so sure?" Sam asked.

"Seton was a mistake. We vet all of our volunteers for suitability long before any testing begins. Seton found a way to hide his history from us, and we've since discovered that he was flaky even before the trial. A regrettable lapse in our screening procedure I'm afraid."

You don't look afraid of anything.

Mike had finally figured out why Sam didn't like this man. He was too cocky, too self-assured, and he'd shown them all the respect he'd accord to the man who cleaned the executive toilet. To Adams they were just a means to an end, an end that he meant to have work in his favor, whatever it took.

"What if it was Ross who did the killings?" Sam said. "Will you be *handling* the press then?"

Adams started at her blankly.

"That's not a possibility. Mr. Ross has been in our employ for years and has an exemplary record."

"That's funny," Mike said. "We have an aggravated assault charge on his record ourselves."

Adams waived a hand at Mike.

"Old news. I know all about that. A youthful indiscretion. I'm sure if we looked into your record we'd find some closets with skeletons in the back Lieutenant?"

He knows about the drinking. The bastard has been checking up on me.

Sam had noticed as well.

"But if it was Ross? What happens then?" Sam persisted.

"Then Adams Pharmaceuticals will see he has the best lawyers in the country on his side," the old man said. "Just like the police, we look after our own."

"Those lawyers of yours might have some trouble representing him," Mike said. "We found an awful lot of his blood at the crime scene."

Adams didn't even flinch.

"All the more reason for you to find him quickly then, don't you think?"

He knew already. Mike thought. But Adams wasn't the only one who could keep a poker face.

Adams stood up. Mike and Sam did likewise.

"Just catch Seton," Adams said to Mike. "I'm sure I can persuade the Commissioner to give you a medal or something."

He smiled, and the charmer was back, but Mike could still see the shark. From now on, with this man, he'd always see the shark.

"We may need to come back with more questions?"

Adams started to shepherd them towards the elevator.

"My secretary will meet you in reception," he said. "She has full details on Seton."

"And Ross?" Sam asked as they entered the elevator.

Adams turned to her, pushing the button to close the door as he spoke.

"And Ross," he said. "But please, Sergeant. Don't mistake me for an idiot. You don't like me. I can see that. Whether it's because I'm richer, smarter or fitter than you I don't know, and I don't care. Your dislike for me doesn't matter. Seton is dangerously deluded. And if you don't stop him, more people will die."

7

"We're there," Seton said. They'd been travelling alongside a high brick wall for several minutes, looking for an entrance. Finally they found a gap that led to a semi-circular turning area and a set of large iron gates. He stopped the car and turned to Patty.

"Did you ever meet Carslyle in person, or talk to him?"

"No. There was no need and…"

Seton interrupted.

"What about your boss, Richards? Did he meet Carslyle? Or did they know each other before?"

"No," Patty said. "Richards would have mentioned it if they had. He would have been so full of himself. No. It was all done online as far as I know."

"The wonders of the electronic age," Seton said, and laughed again. "Good. Just follow my lead and we should be OK."

He started the car again and drove slowly towards the gates.

They didn't open.

"OK," Seton said. "Time for Plan B."

He wound down the window and shouted into a security box that was fixed to the wall at the side.

"Hello?"

The box squawked at them.

"What's your business here?"

Seton put on an atrocious American accent. He sounded like a heavy from a Forties gangster movie, and Patty had to struggle to contain a giggle.

"My name's Doug Richards. My associate and I need to see Mr. Carslyle."

"Do you have an appointment?"

"No. But tell him my name. And tell him it's about the Concordances. We have a possible problem with authenticity."

The squawk box went quiet.

"There's no problem with the manuscript," Patty whispered.

"But Carslyle doesn't know that, does he?" Seton replied.

"He'll never let us in," Patty said.

"Wanna bet doll?" Seton replied in the bad accent.

"No. And do me a favor. Drop the stage act. It won't work."

Seton smiled.

"But it got your attention to focus on the job in hand, so it did its job."

Patty was about to reply when the box squeaked again.

"Come on through. Just stay in your car and follow the driveway. You'll be met up at the house."

The gates opened soundlessly and Seton drove through onto the gravel driveway.

"He'll never let us in," Seton said sotto voce.

"Lap it up," Patty replied. "We'll see if you're so cocky when we get to the house."

"Oh ye of little faith," he said. "Trust me. I have a plan."

"And it's been going so well so far, hasn't it?" Patty said.

Seton merely smiled.

"You're alive, I'm alive, the company doesn't have the Concordances and I've got us a foot in the door of the richest man in the State. Give me some credit."

He drummed on the steering wheel and started to sing. *Hi Ho, Hi Ho, it's off to work we go.*

Patty had to contain herself to stop singing along, but she had a smile on her face as they continued along the gravel driveway.

It seemed to go on forever through a long channel of poplars and cedars. On either side of them sat acres of perfectly manicured lawns, studded with large broad-leaved trees. After a few minutes they passed a long crescent shaped lake that had a fountain throwing water almost as high as the trees. Finally they caught their first glimpse of the house, but it took another minute to reach it. It was a huge rambling edifice of gray stone, complete with gothic turrets and a slate roof. Ivy grew wild up all the walls, party obscuring high leaded windows. A flagpole on the highest turret flew both a Stars and Stripes and a Union Jack.

"That's not a house," Patty said. "That's a castle."

"Actually it's an English Gothic revival Manor house," Seton said. "It was originally set in an estate in Worcester-shire and was built in the mid-Nineteenth Century. Sometime between the wars it fell into ruin, and Carslyle's grandfather bought it and had it shipped over, brick by brick. It cost him a fortune."

"How do you know this stuff?"

Seton just smiled again.

"It's my job. It's what I do."

He pulled the car to a stop outside a sweeping set of stone steps that led to an imposing doorway. They parked beside an antique car.

Seton pointed at the sleek maroon convertible.

"That's a 1941 Lincoln Continental cabriolet. It was originally designed as a custom-bodied special for Edsel Ford. The engine is a long-stroke V-12 derived from Ford's flat-head V-8. The 1940 model had a history of inadequate water passages and poor oil flow, though these problems were mostly corrected by the time this model came out. It's a beautiful thing to drive."

Patty just looked at him in amazement.

"It's my job. It's what I do," Seton said again.

He got out of the car, walked round the side and opened Patty's door to let her get out. As she was negotiating her way out of the car the main door of the Manor opened and a tall thin man came down the steps towards them. Patty had seen his face in the papers.

But he never looked like he'd lost his temper before now.

His face was red, flushed, and he'd clearly worked himself up into a lather while waiting for them to arrive.

"Mr. Richards," he shouted. "I'll have you know there is absolutely no question as to the authenticity of the Concordances. I…"

Seton ran up and met him halfway down the steps. He thrust out a hand that Carslyle couldn't refuse to shake and started to talk, all in one breath, not pausing enough to give Carslyle time to think, let alone reply.

"Mr. Carslyle. It's a pleasure to finally meet you. I find all this modern fad of doing business electronically to be terribly depersonalizing. I was saying the very same thing to my assistant Ms. Doyle on the way here. Wasn't I Ms. Doyle?"

Patty recognized her cue. She walked up the steps and took Carslyle's hand.

"That you were Mr. Richards. And may I say Mr. Carslyle you have a very fine Manor here. Gothic revival unless I'm very much mistaken?"

Between the pair of them they got Carslyle turned and headed back up the steps. Seton winked at Patty behind the man's back as they got to the large oak doors of the house.

Patty was surprised to find herself winking back.

As soon as they entered the hallway beyond the door Patty felt distinctly underdressed. It was as if they had walked onto the set of a BBC costume drama. There was even a suit of armor next to the door and a tall grandfather clock in a corner. Staircases led up from four different spots to dark, echoing hallways above. The wood-paneled walls were further lined with huge portraits of stern faced men, and the carpet was so deep and lush that it felt like walking through a meadow,

Not that Carslyle noticed. They may have managed to get him inside, but he was still full of bluster and concern. He was naturally pale, with high cheekbones and thin lips, but his color was high, red at the cheeks, eyes wide and staring. His hands grabbed and released at the air in front of him, as if he was practicing strangling a small pet... or a small person.

"Now see here Richards," he said, nearly shouting. "You can't come here casting aspersions at the provenance of the Concordances. I paid good money for that manuscript and..."

"And that's the problem," Seton said softly. "We have concerns that you may have been swindled."

Carslyle looked like he might explode.

"Swindled? How the blazes do you come to that conclusion?"

"I'm very sorry Mr. Carslyle. We have to follow these things up," Seton continued. "We had a call from the CID in Scotland. They have caught a man who claims to be selling copies of the manuscript. Mr. McGuire from Linlithgow? I believe you've had dealings with him?"

Carslyle went very quiet. The redness drained from his face, leaving him pale and wan.

"How in the hell do you know that?"

I was just wondering the same thing, Patty thought.

"The same way I know that only the real Concordances came with a sheaf of papers inside. A folio of twenty sheets, hand written in the Seventeenth Century and claiming to be a re-enactment of the original experiment," Seton said.

Carslyle stood very still for long seconds. At first Patty thought he was going to ignore Seton completely.

"Mr. Richards," Carslyle finally said. "How in God's name do you now about them? There is no way that anyone knew about the papers inside. I only discovered them when I was examining the manuscript. They were sewn into the back cover."

"So you have them then?" Seton said. "That's very good. If they're the originals then we have proof that you have the real Concordances after all."

"Indeed I do. Let's finish this charade once and for all. Come this way."

Carslyle strode away from them into a room beyond. Seton made to follow, but Patty pulled him back.

"What are you doing?" she whispered.

"What we came for," Seton whispered back, and winked again. "Trust me. I'm good at this stuff."

Before she could reply Seton followed Carslyle into the room.

Patty looked at the main door to the outside.

I can go. Just go now, get in the car and go.

But, God forgive her, she was intrigued. Shaking her head, Patty followed Seton and Carslyle.

She walked into the grandest library she'd ever seen. She'd always been impressed when she visited the vaults at the office; at the stacks of ancient books and scrolls nearly packed and catalogued. But that was just a concrete box. Here the books had been showcased in a wondrous confection of dark wooden bookcases, high stained glass windows and cast iron staircases that spiraled up through row after row of splendors reaching to a high vaulted ceiling of oak beams above them.

Given the time, Patty would have been happy wandering among the shelves for weeks. She wanted to walk over and pick books at random, just to see what treasures lay there.

She heard a laugh from further across the room. It echoed, sounding out of place and somehow irreverent in such a setting.

"Close your mouth Ms. Doyle," Seton said. "You never know what could get in."

She looked across to where Seton and Carslyle stood over a small table near the largest window. She had only just dragged her eyes away from the stacks, but the window caught her attention before she'd gone three more steps.

It was at least fifteen feet tall, and the glass glowed where sunlight hit it, like gold melted in a furnace. It showed a figure standing on a border. On the left hand side of the window was a winter scene, a snow covered landscape that twinkled with frost and reflected harsh moonlight in dark shadows that seemed to creep across the view.

On the right hand side it was summer. Children played in a field of green with lambs and foals. A glorious sun lit everything in deep gold that seemed warm against Patty's face.

The watcher had two faces. An old wrinkled visage watched the summer scene, while a fresh faced youth watched the snowfall in winter.

Patty couldn't take her eyes off it.

Seton spoke.

"Here's another fact for you. Did you know that in the Eighth Century, the Arab chemist Jabir ibn Hayyan described forty-six original recipes for producing colored glass in The Book of the Hidden Pearl?" he asked her. "It's directly from him that that whole history of stained glass windows, from then to now, descends.

"And I have a copy of that book right here," Carslyle said. "Second tier, case 4, third row down. I got it from a chap in Istanbul. Paid a pretty penny for it as well, I can tell you. And there's an interesting story about the making of the window itself. It seems…"

"I don't care how it was made," Patty said quietly, interrupting him. "It's beautiful."

Seton came over and took her by the arm.

"That it is Ms. Doyle. But come. It seems we've found the proof that Mr. Carslyle's copy of the Concordances is indeed the original."

He led her to the table.

Carslyle already had the manuscript open in front of him. Beside it he laid out sheets of thin, almost translucent paper, showing row after row of text written in a very small, but very neat print. Patty leaned over and read the start of the first page:

> *Extractio Animae Solis: or a Triall upon Sol, for the Extraction of Philosophical earth. The Author has putt doon the consequences of his Experiments therein, from the beginning to the end, by way of Journal; in the sure and sertin hope of the resurrection and the life, in this year of oor lord sixteen hunner an forty. Putt doon here in the keep by the wee port by the shore.*

Begin a fast of forty days starting during the full moon of May, drinking only May dew collected with a cloth of pure white linen and eating only a biscuit or crust of dried bread.

Seton took the pages away from her, lifted them and counted them all.

"But there are only sixteen," he said.

"Yes," Carslyle replied. "And that's all that was inside. And I can assure you, the binding had never been tampered with before last week. I have the stitching saved. Look."

Carslyle bent to open a desk drawer.

At the same moment, Seton lifted a heavy glass ashtray from the desk and clubbed Carslyle, hard, across the back of the head.

Carslyle fell to the carpet. The only sound was a dull thud as he hit the floor.

Patty felt a new scream rising. Once more the day had taken a lurch, and she was no more ready for it now than she had been earlier.

"What?" she said, then, more urgently. "Why?"

"Did you think he was just going to give us these?" Seton asked, collecting up the papers and the manuscript. "Here. Put them in your bag."

She ignored him and bent to the ground.

"You've killed him," she said.

"No," Seton replied, taking the satchel from her. "I didn't hit him that hard. I didn't even break the skin. Look for yourself. There's no blood. And he's breathing."

Patty checked, placing her fingers at the side of the man's neck.

There was a fast but steady pulse, and Carslyle was breathing, but he was out cold.

"See," Seton said. "Now come on. We've got to get out of here."

The sight of Carslyle on the floor overlaid in Patty's mind with another man, who was also lying on the floor.

"Did you hit the man in my office like this?" Patty said as she rose. Suddenly Seton's smile didn't look very friendly to her.

"Look, I had to do it," he said, stepping towards her.

Patty took another step back. She was trying to remember how far away the door was behind her, calculating whether she could reach it and close it before he caught her.

He waved the manuscript and papers at her.

"This is what's important. If these fell into the wrong hands…"

"What? People will die? People are dying already. And you're the one killing them."

She backed away further.

He placed the papers and the manuscript carefully in the satchel before replying.

"Ms. Doyle," Seton said. "Please listen to me. You're in terrible danger."

"Oh? I hadn't noticed," Patty replied.

"I mean it," Seton said. "As I told you…"

"You've told me nothing," Patty shouted. "Nothing but obfuscation and lies."

"I haven't told you any lies," Seton said quietly.

"And you haven't told me any truths."

She was almost at the door. She steeled herself to make a run for it.

"And he won't," a voice said behind her from the doorway.

She turned.

It was a tall man in a suit that had once been expensive but was now crumpled, and stained down the left-hand side with dried blood. The last time she'd seen him he'd been lying on the floor of her office. He still looked pale, and a new bandage wrapped around his head concealed the earlier wound.

"Patty," Seton said quietly. "Come over here beside me."

"Don't listen to him Ms. Doyle," the suited man said. "Mr. Seton isn't himself."

"Patty, please." Seton said. "Come away from him. He's the one."

Patty looked from one man to the other.

"To hell with you both," she said, and made a run for the door.

8

Mike and Sam sat in the car going over the material that Adams' secretary had handed them.

"What do you think boss?" Sam said.

"About Adams? Like you, I don't like him. Then again, that's no reason not to believe him."

"All the reason I need. I'm pretty sure he was lying to us," Sam said. "And not just that, but he was laughing at us all the time we were up there."

Mike nodded.

"I got that too. But was it a big honking lie to cover up involvement in the murders, or just a small one to protect his business? We've got too many unanswered questions. We need to focus on eliminating some of them. Let's begin with Seton."

Sam held up a file.

"I've got a home address for him."

"Good. We'll start there."

While Sam drove, Mike read Seton's file. The picture on the front didn't tell him much. It showed a small thin-faced man with a broad smile. Even in the picture his eyes looked like they danced with glee. There was a single page of personal details. Born in Scotland, moved to the States in the Eighties, occupation described as Researcher.

Well that covers a multitude of sins.

The rest of the file was a bald record of the man's time at the hospital. There wasn't much to read. After two minutes he put it down.

"OK. We've got a forty-five year old Scotsman who volunteers for a drug trial."

He waved the file in the air.

"Adams hasn't given us much to go on. Every detail of the trial itself is missing. All we have is an admission date, on Monday last week, and some dates and times of a series of procedures."

"As for Seton, there's very little background. We've got age, address, and phone number. Next of kin is down as unknown, and previous illnesses is marked as none. There's no other medical records attached. It looks like the trial starts as soon as he admits himself, on Monday last week.

"Something goes wrong, he absconds, and starts killing people because, according to Adams, he's now got paranoia concerning a centuries old conspiracy that means to do something bad. The notes don't say what the bad thing is, but it has got Seton so worked up that he kills at least three people this morning. With me so far?"

Sam nodded.

"So, the company, worried that the failure of their trial will get out and damage their rep, sends a security guard after Seton. We find that person's blood... a lot of it. But no body. Ross has disappeared. And so has one of the workers in the office, Ms. Doyle. It's pretty obvious there was something in the office that Seton was after, but we don't know whether he found it. Does that sum up the situation?"

"Pretty concisely boss. That, and the fact that Adams seems awfully keen for us to find Seton. He showed little or no concern for the man Ross."

"I spotted that too," Mike said. "I can't see how all the pieces fit yet. But obviously our priorities currently coincide with Adams'. Find Seton, and at least some things will be clearer."

"We'll be at his house in five minutes," Sam said.

"Good. Just do me a favor and stop at the next bar. I'm parched."

She gave him a little sideways look.

He burst out laughing.

"Got ya," he said, and laughed again.

She hit him, hard, in the shoulder, then had to concentrate on the road.

"Now there's the Mike Turner I know," she said. "It's nice to see him back."

"Make the most of it honey," Mike said, not sure whether he was joking or not. "The beast could be back at any time."

In truth, Mike hadn't thought about a drink since before they'd entered Adams Pharmaceuticals. Whether it was the mystery element, or whether it was just that he was getting out of the office, he realized that the case had him hooked. He was going to be with it now till the end, wherever that might be and however long it might take to get there.

Judging by what we've got so far, that could be quite a while.

He picked up Ross's file. It told him even less then Seton's.

"Did we send a squad car to Ross's place?" he asked.

"Already done before we left the precinct," Sam said. "Nobody's home. We've got two guys on stake-out in case that changes."

There was a mug shot that showed a thin pale, pock-marked face and hard eyes that seemed too close together, staring, unsmiling, straight at the camera.

Stapled to that was the barest details of his employment; five years service, no reprimands, but no promotions either, a steady but small pay rise each August.

It was while Mike was running his fingers idly over the paper that he noticed the small raised tear in the top left-hand corner. He examined it more closely.

"There was another sheet of paper stapled in here," he said.

"Do you want to bet Adams had it removed before handing it to us?"

"No thanks. Those odds are too high for me. But I wonder what it was?"

"Just something else to keep us awake at night," Sam replied. "Another mystery."

"We've got too many of them already."

They pulled up in the street outside the address they'd been given for Seton. It sat in a row of red-brick houses in the Old Quarter. The road was wide, cobbled, and stank of money, from the mock-Victorian street lighting to the wrought iron fencing, to the tall square elegance of the buildings themselves. Seton's house was a mid-terraced townhouse, with a large oak door, high fluted windows and a balcony near the top that Mike guessed would give a grandstand view out over the city.

He whistled quietly.

"I'd give my left testicle to be able to afford a place like this."

"And I'd give your right one to join you. What do these places go for, a mill?"

"And then some," Mike said as they left the car. "We're moving in rarefied circles today."

As they approached the imposing front door Mike saw that it was slightly ajar. Without speaking he motioned Sam off to one side and took out his service pistol.

He poked the door lightly and it swung open.

"Mr. Seton? NYPD. If you're in there, come on out. We need to ask you a few questions."

There was no answer.

"Cover me," he whispered to Sam, and stepped inside.

A long dark hallway led away into the main part of the house. A staircase led up into darkness. Mike stood still for several heartbeats but there was no sound in the house.

The hallway had four doors, all but one of them closed.

"Mr. Seton?" he called out, but he was already ninety percent sure the house was empty. He headed for the open door, motioning for Sam to follow.

At least we're inside, and we won't need the hassle of getting a warrant.

Somebody had got there before them.

Seton was obviously a book lover, but whoever had gone through the house didn't share his passion. Books were torn and scattered over the floor, covering every inch of the carpet alongside overturned bookshelves and a badly busted laptop computer. Two leather armchairs sat in front of an open fireplace. They looked expensive. They'd also cost a lot to repair, as someone had taken a knife to them, searching the upholstery, and none too carefully at that.

"Somebody was looking for something in a hurry," Sam said as she stepped in beside him from the hallway.

"Sure looks that way," Mike said. Sam headed further into the house while Mike looked around the main room.

Besides a huge book collection, Seton had little else that told of his history. There were no family pictures, no possessions that would speak of a family history, in short, none of the usual things cops looked for when trying to make connections in a case.

Sam came back.

"Nobody home boss."

"And precious little here that looks like a home either." Sam looked around.

"It's the same upstairs. I don't think Seton spends much time here. There's hardly any clothes in the closets, and only one bed made up."

Mike ran a hand through his hair.

"OK. Let's get forensics over here and see what they can dig up."

A large map on the wall caught Mike's eye. As he moved closer he saw it was a road map of Scotland dotted with a large number of brightly colored pins. If there was a pattern to their distribution, he couldn't see it.

Meanwhile Sam sifted among the torn books at her feet.

"Didn't Adams say that the drug trial brought on Seton's paranoia?"

Mike nodded, still staring at the map.

"That's what the man said."

"Well it looks like it was pretty highly developed before then… unless he bought an awful lot of books in the past couple of days.

She read out some titles; The Holy Blood and The Holy Grail, Servants of the Cross, Our Templar Heritage, The Concordance Mysteries, The Coming of the King, The Sword and The Grail.

"And that's just for starters," she said. "Although most of it seems like nonsense. Listen to this."

Without the Sun and its shadow, the Moon, we can have no tinging quicksilver, and he is foolish who attempts to accomplish our Magistery in their absence. On the other hand he who knows how to tinge quicksilver with the Sun and Moon is in possession of our arcanum which may be-

come red sulphur, but at first is called white sulphur. Gold is the father, and silver the mother of the proximate substance of our Stone, for out of these bodies, prepared with their sulphur or arsenic, is our medicine elicited.

"What in the name of the wee man does that mean?" Sam laughed.

"I have no idea," she replied. "But it sounds like the sort of stuff any self-respecting conspiracy theorist might lap right up."

"No tin foil hats?"

"No," Sam said, looking at the spines of more of the books. "It's not the government this one's obsessed with. It's historical. And mainly based on the Templars."

Mike sighed.

"So Adams told us at least one truth?"

"Maybe more than one," Sam said. "Look at these."

She pointed to something at her feet.

Her shuffling had uncovered a series of black and white photographs, all showing the exterior of the crime scene, taken from somewhere across the street from Morrisons. Someone had used a high magnification lens, taking pictures of staff members heading in to work.

In close up, people could be seen punching entry codes into the security pad. There were four pictures for each staff member, each showing a number being entered. The numbers were ringed in black felt pen, but it was the people that drew Mike's attention. Even in tight close ups he recognized three of them.

He'd seen them all dead earlier that morning.

9

Patty almost made it to the door.

At first she thought the newcomer was going to stand aside and let her through. Instead he stepped in front of her, blocking her path. She moved to her left, but he mirrored her and again stood in her way. He put out a hand and grabbed her by the shoulder.

"I'm sorry Miss. My orders include both of you."

Patty tried to push him to one side, but he wouldn't budge.

"Let me past," she said.

His hand tightened on her shoulder and squeezed. Not too hard. Not yet.

"Now calm down Miss," he said. "I don't want to hurt you."

"Touch her, and this time I won't make the mistake I did earlier," Seton said behind her.

The thin man laughed, and Patty noticed for the first time that his skin was stretched, tight and smooth across his cheeks, as if he'd had plastic surgery. When he smiled he looked like an over-ripe plum about to burst.

"The mistake earlier was all mine."

Once more Patty tried to push past. He took his hand from her shoulder and grabbed her lower arm. He pulled her towards him, bringing a flare of pain.

"I said, calm down."

Seton moved two steps forward.

"I wouldn't," the thin man said. With his free hand he took a pistol from inside his jacket.

"Now we're all going to take a ride," he said. "And we're all going to be calm. Understood?"

Patty nodded. Seton didn't reply.

"I'm going nowhere," Seton said.

The thin man pointed the gun at him.

"I was told to bring you back alive, if possible. Looks like it might not be possible."

Carslyle chose that moment to wake up. He moved, and groaned. The thin man's gun arm moved to point at him.

Things happened fast.

Seton dove forward, coming in low under the gun. Patty squirmed away to one side, almost overbalancing as Seton's weight hit and the two men fell in a bundle of arms and legs.

They rolled, wrestling on the floor, Seton trying to get to the gun, the other man trying to get an angle to shoot. Patty danced around them, looking for a way to help Seton.

Finally she got an opening. She kicked out hard, and the gun arm went limp. Seizing his chance, Seton swung the satchel around and hit the thin man on the side of the head... right on the spot of the previous wound.

He let out a single low grunt, then his eyes rolled up in their sockets. He lay in a heap, the bandage already soaking red.

Seton kicked the gun away and it rattled into a corner.

He took Patty's hand.

"Time to go again," he said.

She looked at him, then down at the two men on the ground. It was the memory of the flare of pain when the thin man grabbed her that got her moving.

"The lesser of two evils is it?" she asked.

"If it means you'll come with me, yes."

Carslyle was on his knees now, trying to get to his feet. He looked unsteady and pale, but his voice was almost a bellow.

"Richards, you bastard. I'll see you in jail for this," he shouted.

Seton pulled Patty away.

"It's *really* time to go," he said. He put out a hand. "What's it to be doll?" he said in the ridiculous American accent.

I've come this far.

She took Seton's hand. Together they ran out into the hall and out of the front door.

A black SUV was parked beside their car, its driver side door open.

Seton almost pulled her to the car then shoved the satchel into her arms.

"Get in," he said. "Quick."

A shot ran out and the stained glass window shattered, colored glass tinkling to the ground around them as the two-faced figure collapsed in on himself, and summer and winter merged into a small pile of fragments. There was another shot, then silence.

"What was that?"

Seton was already on the driver's side and getting into the car.

"Carslyle killing Ross, or the other way around. Either way, we're still in trouble. Now will you come on."

Patty got into the car and before she had time to get her seatbelt hooked in Seton gunned the accelerator. Gravel flew and spattered as they spun, only just in control, out onto the driveway.

They narrowly avoided hitting a pair of stone lions, and the rear wheels spun again as they swerved onto the grass, gouging a brown stain in the otherwise perfect lawn, but finally Seton got them on a straight line and heading down the drive.

Do you always drive like this?" Patty asked.

"No," Seton replied, laughing. "Sometimes I'm in a hurry."

Something hit the back of the car with a thud that reverberated through the whole bodywork. A second later the back window fell in with a tinkling crash.

"Get your head down," Seton shouted, and pushed the car even harder. He turned the wheel hard, spinning them off the drive and onto the grass where they bounced and skidded, zigzagging from side to side as fast as he could turn the wheel. Another bullet pinged off the bodywork.

"Somebody is shooting at us," Patty said.

Seton laughed again, and reverted to the American accent.

"So many guns, so few brains," he said, and threw the car to the left just in time to avoid going into the lake. As they spun round Patty caught sight of the black SUV coming down the drive behind them.

"He's coming."

"I know."

Seton somehow got them back onto the drive and they approached the entrance gate doing over seventy miles an hour. The gate started to close as they approached it.

"Hold on," Seton said, and pointed the car at the closing gap.

Patty closed her eyes.

"Look out boys," Seton shouted. "Coming through."

They made it... just. A wing mirror ripped free and pinged off the gate, and Patty would never forget the tearing metallic rasp as they scratched the whole side of the car, but a second later they screeched onto the road.

She looked back.

The black SUV was behind them, on the far side of the now closed gate. The car rammed into the ironwork, hard, and the whole structure shook, but didn't give.

The thin man got out of the black car and started firing after them. Patty lost sight of him as they turned and headed away along the side of the tall brick wall.

Seton laughed aloud and banged the steering wheel.

"Woo hoo!" he shouted.

Patty sat back in the seat and tried to breathe deeply. Her heart pounded in her ears, and her fingers trembled.

Seton was still smiling. He started to drum on the steering wheel again.

"Well, *that* was fun," he said.

"Depends how you define *fun*," Patty replied.

He looked over at her.

"Come on. You can't tell me you didn't enjoy it? Not even a little bit?"

"It's the most excitement I've had since the last time somebody shot at me," she said. She meant it to be sarcastic, but, deep down, she realized there was some truth in it.

I did enjoy it. I enjoyed it a lot.

"Are all your days like this?" she asked.

Seton smiled.

"Every day is special, if you let it be."

"Where did you get that? On a greeting card?" Patty replied sarcastically.

Suddenly he looked solemn.

"Look, I know this is difficult for you."

"Oh, you think?"

"And I promise, I'll tell you the whole story. But first, we need to find somewhere to lie low for the night. They'll be looking for us."

"Who will?" she said, getting exasperated.

"Cops, Ross, more company men, reporters. Just about everybody I'd imagine. We've just burgled the richest man in the State."

"And tell me again why it's a bad idea to let them find us?"

He took a cigarette out and lit it.

"That's part of the long story. But I can give you another small bit of it, if that'll help?"

It was her turn to sigh again.

"Give me one of those cigarettes then," she said. "I picked the wrong day to quit smoking."

She took a cigarette from him and lit up using the car's lighter. The first draw left her almost dizzy, but she stuck with it. Patty and cigarettes were old friends. It was just going to take a little while to get reacquainted.

"So where were we earlier?" Seton said, absently.

"Robert the Bruce?" Patty said. "And some kind of an experiment?"

"Ah yes," Seton said, and settled into a sing-song story telling voice that was strangely soothing.

"It's 1328, in Stirling. The King hasn't been seen for thirty days, and rumors have spread that he is already dead. Factions are jockeying for the throne, and south of the border the English army is sharpening its swords, hoping for an easy kill. The people are frightened, unsure what awaits them if they lose their brave-heart, their talisman. Everywhere there are whispers and plotters.

"Deep in the castle, the Concordances experiment is reaching its climax. The Bruce lies abed, his breathing shallow, his face as white as alabaster. His courtiers stand in corners, muttering among themselves, and at the foot of

the bed an axe-man waits, ready to take the life of the alchemist should the King die.

"But, wonder of wonders, he does not die. Instead he takes in one long, stuttering breath. The courtiers move in, fearing it will be his last, but by the time the breath is exhaled, the color has started to rise in his cheeks, and by the time he takes a second his eyes are clear and bright as of old.

"Of course, it is greeted as a great miracle among the populace when the Bruce walks among them, looking as young as the man who won the victory at Bannockburn nigh on fifteen years before.

"The courtiers are not so pleased. Many are envious of the King's renewed vigor, and some of those who wished the King dead, look to the alchemist as the man who had laid waste to their plotting.

"The alchemist is taken in the depths of night, spirited away to a dark place where he can be questioned and his secrets unlocked. But the plotters never find his Journal. The Twelve Concordances of the Red Serpent stays hidden.

"And the alchemist never betrays his secret, even under the most undue tortures imaginable. They keep him alive for full on forty days, until he is little more than a running sore of weeping wounds and burns. And still he does not speak, merely silently gives up his life rather than betray his creation."

Seton had a far away look in his eye. The car started to drift alarmingly to the left.

"Watch the road," Patty said.

And it was then that she noticed that they were on a coastal highway, with the sea to her right hand side.

"This isn't the way back to the city. Where the hell are we?"

"Don't worry," Seton said. "We're safe. I've got a house out along the coast here that no one knows about."

"That's not what I asked."

Seton ignored her and finished his story.

"In the end of course, and only a year later, the plotters got their way. Without the alchemist, the secret was lost, and after only a few months the Bruce relapsed into illness. It had however given him enough time to organize the country and his successor. Strenuous attempts were made to keep the King alive, but no other alchemists could recreate the experiment. The King died, and the *Journal of the Concordances* was never found."

"Until now?" Patty said.

"Well, that's not entirely true. It surfaced once, in the Seventeenth Century but…"

"Let me guess," Patty said. "That's when the papers we found at Carslyle's were written?"

"Smart *and* beautiful," Seton said.

"Flattery will get you exactly nowhere," Patty replied. "So what do the papers detail?"

"Later," Seton said. "That's part of…"

"The big story?" Patty finished for him. "This big story better be worth waiting for."

"We'll get to it soon," Seton said. "I promise. But first, some food and rest."

At the mention of food Patty's stomach grumbled. She hadn't eaten since breakfast, hadn't even thought of eating. But now that it had been mentioned, she could think of little else.

"Food sounds good. How far is it to this place of yours?"

"Another forty miles or so."

"Wake me when we get there," Patty said, and closed her eyes.

She tried to let her mind drift, to find a calm place.

That was a big mistake.

The day had passed in a blur for her, not giving her much time to think, or remember. But as soon as she closed her eyes it all came rushing back.

One image dominated all the others, that of Mary, sitting at her desk, her new eye staring accusingly.

If Seton was right, Patty had started it, in that stupid blog. Too much wine and not enough brains. It was a lethal combination. And so it had proved. There she had been, angry with Doug Richards, ready to vent.

And because of that stupidity, her friends had been killed.

It's all my fault.

Hot tears ran down her cheeks.

She let then come.

It was obvious that Seton knew far more than he was telling. He *could* be the one responsible for killing her friends, but somehow she doubted it. There was something gentle, almost child-like about his manner. And he'd shown genuine concern for her, back at Carslyle's house.

Equally obviously the thin man was involved somehow. She suspected he was the murderer. But that raised a whole new bunch of questions, about who he worked for, how Seton knew he'd be at their office, and what they wanted with a fourteenth century Scots journal, wanted so bad that it was worth killing for.

Her brain just wasn't fit for processing that much information after the day she'd had. It finally shut itself down and left her, thankful, in the deep blackness of sleep.

10

Mike and Sam stood over Carslyle's dead body and Mike swore under his breath. The newspaper man stared back up at him, a neat red hole just above his eyes, and a messy red mass of gore on the carpet beneath him.

A breeze blew through the gap where a stained glass window had been, dislodging some more pieces of glass that fell, tinkling, to the carpet.

"The shit's *really* going to hit the fan when this gets out boss," Sam said.

Mike nodded.

"I suppose I still can't get you to drop me off at the nearest bar?"

Sam smiled sadly.

"And I suppose there's no mistake that it was Seton?" Mike continued.

"We've got his voice recording as he came in the gate," Sam said. "He said he was Doug Richards, but they were also caught on camera. Just a single shot, but it's definitely him, and the Doyle woman."

"And also the damned black car again?"

"And also the damned black car again," Sam confirmed.

I'm really getting too old for this shit.

"So whose is the blood over there?" Mike asked, pointing toward the door.

"No idea yet. It's gone to forensics. But if you want a guess, I'd say it's our missing man Ross."

"Any reason why you think that?"

"The black car for one," Sam said. "And it looks like Ross is going to show wherever Seton has been."

Mike nodded.

"Find one, we'll find the other. But why Carslyle?"

He looked around at the library.

"More bloody books. Could that be the motive?"

"Maybe. The books are expensive enough," Sam said. "The insurance covers them for over twenty million dollars."

Mike whistled.

"When they entered, they said to the machine at the gate they were here about The Concordances," Sam said, "Whatever that is."

Mike suddenly remembered Doyle's blog.

"*Take this morning. I was working on* 'The Twelve Concordances of the Red Serpent' *when he came in and told me to stop, as I'd used up the budget.*"

"Find me a phone."

Sam pointed out to the hallway.

"We passed one on the way in."

Five minutes later Mike got put through to Doug Richards.

"Mr. Richards? Detective Turner. Can you tell me if your Ms. Doyle was working on anything belonging to Mr. John Carslyle?"

Richards still sounded shaky.

"I'm afraid that's confidential information," he said. "Mr. Carslyle is a very private man and…"

"And he's busy being privately dead," Mike said. "I don't have time to be polite Mr. Richards. Nor do I have time to go through official channels. Something links your office and Mr. Carslyle… something that has now got at least four people killed. I need to know what."

He put the phone down seconds later.

"We're looking for a book; *The Twelve Concordances of the Red Serpent*. Richards says it's worth at least three million, so it also seems we have a motive."

He walked towards the door with a new spring in his step.

"Come on Sam. The game's afoot."

11

Patty came awake with a start.

Night was falling. They were driving along a narrow country road, the car's headlights illuminating trees stretched in an arch overhead.

"How long was I asleep?"

"Just about an hour," Seton said.

Patty's mouth felt like something small and furry had slept in it.

"Do you have any water?"

"Not in the car. But we're only a minute away."

He was true to his word. They emerged from the tree-lined road into a bay dotted with half a dozen houses, barely visible in the growing gloom.

"Home is the sailor, home from the sea," Seton whispered.

He pulled the car up beside a long low house set on the shore just off the road. Once more he got out of the car and came round to open her door.

Her back creaked and complained as she pushed herself out of the seat, and she felt tired, as if she'd done a long session in the gym.

"I need a hot bath," she said.

"And hopefully you'll get one," Seton replied. "But it's been a while since I've been here, so don't set your hopes too high."

When he put a key in the main door and pushed it open a dusty odor met them at the entrance.

"It just needs a bit of airing," Seton said. He flicked a light switch, and seemed surprised when it worked.

"Looks like you'll get that bath," he said. "I'll check the boiler. Make yourself at home."

He left Patty standing in a room that looked it had been parachuted in from the nineteen seventies. Thick pile rugs covered the floor… what could be seen of it between the olive-green leatherette sofas. There was a lava lamp on a Formica-topped coffee table, and a fiber-optic lamp on a similar table near the large, mock-stone fireplace. The stereo system in the corner was large, brown and mostly wooden, as was the television.

She heard Seton clattering around in a room to the rear. Suddenly the whole house started to rumble.

"It's OK," Seton shouted. "That's just the boiler kicking in. It'll settle down eventually."

He came back into the room and ran a finger over the arm of a sofa. It came away dusty.

"Sorry," he said. "It's the cleaner's day off."

Patty was still standing near the door, unsure as to her next move.

"I just realized," she said quietly. "I don't have anything. No clothes, no overnight stuff. No…"

"That's OK," Seton said. "You'll find all manner of things in the washroom, and your room is directly opposite that. There's a wardrobe full of clothes to choose from."

She laughed.

"You're not my size."

He laughed along with her.

"No. But my ex-wife was. And she left plenty of clothes here. Her style might seem a bit old fashioned for your tastes, but I can tell you, it's good quality stuff. God knows I paid enough for it. Now, off you go. Do what women do. I'll see what's in the larder."

Patty took her time in the bathroom. It too was dated, but charmingly so, with porcelain fixtures and brass fittings. The old bath had claw and ball feet that looked like they'd been hacked from an eagle. The water was only lukewarm, but she soaked anyway, until she started to feel chilled. When she climbed out to dry herself off she realized she felt better.

Much better.

She laughed out loud when she looked in the closet in her room. Seton's wife must have been around some time ago. There were cheesecloth shirts and skirts galore in wild batik patterns, short leather hot-pants, large floppy hats, and more denim than a rock concert audience. It took her a while to find something she'd feel comfortable wearing, but she had fun trying things on.

A shout from the other room caught her attention.

"Supper's ready."

She settled for a plain white cotton shirt and a pair of faded denims, finishing off with Cuban-heeled cowboy boots. They were in fake snakeskin, and totally tasteless, but in a strange way she liked them. She checked herself out in the mirror before she left. She looked like a refugee from a Barbara Streisand convention.

But when she reached the kitchen Seton whistled as he turned and looked at her.

"If I was twenty years younger," he said. "You'd be in trouble."

He checked her up and down.

"Good choice," he said.

The smell of cooking meat reached her and her stomach rumbled.

"Something smells good," she replied.

"Hopefully better than it looks," Seton replied. "It's mostly out of tins I'm afraid."

He showed her through the kitchen to a small dining area with a picture window out over the bay. It was full dark now, but, with the subdued lighting in the room, Patty could see the moon glimmering on the water and, off to the left, the steadily blinking rays of a lighthouse.

"I could sit and look at this forever," Patty said.

"I know what you mean," Seton replied. "There's something about the sea, something both immensely permanent, yet also at the same time transitory and fleeting. It's never the same, yet it's always the same."

Patty laughed.

"You're not making any sense."

"Good," Seton replied. "Sensible is not a word with which I wish to be associated. Now excuse me, I've got a silly supper prepared."

He left her looking out at the view. She let the calm fill her.

Seton brought in the food and Patty devoured it, scarcely looking at what she was eating. It appeared to be a mixture of Spam, corn and beans but it tasted as delicious as any restaurant meal she'd ever had.

Seton laughed.

"Rarely has anyone enjoyed my cooking quite so much."

Patty looked down and realized she was wiping the last of the sauce from her plate with her fingers.

"Sorry," she said.

"No need to be," Seton replied. After the day you've had you're excused table manners."

Patty sat back in her chair.

"Speaking of the day I've had… you owe me a story. Give me one good reason why I can't go to the police."

"Oh, I can give you many of those," Seton said. "And you're right. I owe you an explanation. But it will take a while. Come through to the main room. There's coffee ready, and I found some single malt Scotch in the cupboard."

"I'll say one thing for you Seton. You sure know how to show a lady a good time."

Five minutes later they were settled in front of a log fire. The coffee was dark and bitter, and the whisky light and smooth. Patty drifted, almost dreaming, as Seton told his story.

"I told you I was a journalist, working in *obscure* areas," he started. "But what I didn't tell you is that I was drawn to the arcane from an early age. I don't suppose you realize the significance of my name?"

Patty had to put the whisky glass down to reply. She had drank a whole two fingers already, hardly noticing it. If she wasn't careful she'd be tipsy in no time, and totally smashed soon after that.

"I haven't heard the name *Seton* before," she replied. "But you're Scottish, aren't you?"

Seton nodded.

"And the family name is an old one. Originally they were Normans, and Templars. The family had been in Scotland since just after the Norman Conquest of 1066. Later one of them, Sir Christopher Seton, married Marjory Bruce, the sister of King Robert I and made the Seton's lineal heirs to the Throne on the maternal side. After his death Marjory married Sir Walter Stewart. Their son Robert became the 1st Stewart Monarch of Scotland as Robert II, making Marjory's first son Alexander Seton a half-brother maternally to King Robert II."

All the names made Patty's head spin.

"It's like the Bible," she said. "Too many *begats*."

Seton laughed. He poured himself another whisky, and motioned with the bottle. Patty refused.

"Go on with the story," she said. "Hopefully you'll get to the point before I fall asleep on you."

Seton got the far-away look in his eye.

"Alexander. He was the first in a long line of Setons to be given the name. And hearing of him as a child put me on the path to where I am now. I discovered that the Seton family long remained intermingled with doings at the Royal Court of Scotland. But they also had a second interest, and one I started to believe was born back in the experiment of 1328. The family has always been seekers of the great secret, practicing alchemy and arcane rituals in the hope of discovering how *The Bruce* was invigorated."

"Now I understand a bit better," Patty said. "It's genetics. You come from a long line on non-sensible people."

Seton raised his glass.

"*Touché*. But the family took it all very seriously. You can see now why I was drawn to the discovery of The *Twelve Concordances*?" he said to Patty.

"Yes," she replied. "I see how you could be. But I still don't see why it's worth killing people."

"It is if the secret has actually been uncovered," Seton said softly.

"You said something like that before," Patty said. "What did you mean? Are you saying there actually is a way of making people stay young?"

Seton nodded.

"And imagine if you were a drug company, and you could develop and market a product that would guarantee at least two hundred years of life for its users? Two hundred years, and possibly even immortality? How much would a company be able to charge for such a drug? How much profit do you think they'd be able to make?

"Put yourself in the mindset of the head of that drug company. What would you be willing to do to get your hands on the secret?"

"Almost anything I imagine," Patty said. "Given how much money there is already in plastic surgery, wrinkle creams and the like. If anyone actually had a *real* way of staving off age, they could name their price.

"Precisely. Now you're beginning to understand."

"But the *Concordances* are nothing but gibberish and gobbledygook," Patty said. "I know, I've read the manuscript."

"Gibberish," Seton said, pouring himself yet another whisky. "Even that word has an alchemical history. The word comes from the name of an Eighth Century Islamic alchemist, Jabir ibn Hayyan, the same man who described the making of the stained glass. His name was latinized as *Geber*. He wrote in a mangled verse that was so convoluted and strange that it coined the word. And since him, alchemists have always hidden their secrets in code."

"You mean all that stuff about pelicans and pheasants actually means something?"

"Well in most texts, the pelican is shown stabbing its breast with its beak and nourishing its young with its own blood. It symbolizes self-sacrifice and the abandonment of worldly things with no thought of consequence. But the pelican is also the name for a piece of apparatus. Double, and even triple, meanings abound. Even after you had deciphered the code, you would still have to struggle through all the possible symbolic meanings to get to the heart of it and find the truth."

"And somebody has?"

"Somebody did," Seton said. "In the Seventeenth Century. The sheaves that were sewn into the *Concordance's* binding are a record of a successful experiment. This time there is no code, no symbolic bollocks. I believe it's a straight telling of how to achieve immortality.

"And somebody wants it so bad, they're willing to kill us to get it."

12

Mike's optimism lasted all the way back to the precinct.

"We're getting somewhere," he said. "I can feel it in my gut."

"Are you sure that's not the coffee?" Sam said, smiling.

"No. I've got the old buzz. We're onto something here. Find the book, and we'll finally get a handle on this case," he said as they got out of the car.

"Certainly looks that way boss," Sam replied. "But I still don't get the situation with Doyle. Has she run off with Seton? Or is she under duress to stay with him?"

"When we find them we can ask her," Mike said. "We've got an APB out on them, and patrol cars staking out the house. They'll surface sometime. But for now, get someone tracing the history of the book. I want to know where Carslyle got it, and when."

When Mike got to his desk he found the Forensics report waiting for him.

He passed it to Sam.

"Check over this for me. I'll get the coffee."

When he arrived back from the machine Sam was just finishing reading.

"The tech boys are baffled," Sam said as she handed him the printouts. "The blood at the Carslyle house matches the sample taken from Doyle's office floor all right. But there's something wrong with it."

"Wrong in what way?"

"That's what's got them baffled. They say the only comparison they have is with blood taken from some athletes who have been on the juice… getting transfusions from people who live at high altitudes to boost their oxygen levels, that sort of thing."

"Or someone on designer drugs?" Mike said softly. "The sort that companies that *Build Better Bodies* might manufacture?"

Sam nodded.

Mike gulped down half his coffee and put the mug on his desk.

"Come on then."

"Where to?"

"Back to Adams Pharmaceuticals. I want another word with Mr. Adams."

"It's getting late," Sam said. "He might not be there."

"He doesn't strike me as the type to stray far from the office," Mike said. "Besides, we've got their security guard's blood tied in with four homicides now. I want to know why."

Sam was quiet as they drove through the dark streets. The further they got from the precinct, the quieter the streets became. Down near the docks the buildings were mostly other businesses, and mostly in the process of shutting down for the night. By the time they reached Adams Pharmaceuticals theirs was the only car around.

"How are we going to play this?" Sam asked.

"We'll hit him with the forensic evidence, and see what he says," Mike replied.

"Remember Mike," Sam said quietly. "We've been asked to take this carefully."

"I'll be gentle."

"And pigs might fly."

They pulled into the car park. The building loomed above them, the windows mostly dark. As they got out of the car they saw, high up, right at the top, that the lights were on in the penthouse.

"Looks like you were right about Mr. Adams," Sam said.

"Let's hope he's in a talkative mood," Mike replied. "I don't think he'd be happy if we took him down to the holding cells."

"You wouldn't," Sam said, shocked.

"I would. I'd probably get a suspension just for thinking about it, but it might be worth it, just to see his face," Mike replied as they walked into the reception area.

The place was in darkness, only a small night-light by the main desk. A bored security guard sat there, his index finger rooting in his left nostril.

"Evening folks," he said. "The building's closed for the night."

"We're here to see Mr. Adams," Mike said.

"Do you have an appointment?"

"No."

"Then you can't see him."

The security guard smiled, triumphantly, as if he'd just won a prize. To celebrate he went back to rooting in his nostril.

"He'll see us," Sam said, and showed her badge.

That got his attention.

"I'll just see if he's available," the guard said, lifting the phone.

"Don't worry. We want to give him a surprise."

"I'm not sure I like that," the guard said.

"I'm not sure I give a shit," Mike replied, and headed for the elevator.

It pinged while he was still ten yards from it. The door opened, and a tall thin man stepped out. Mike recognized him straight away, despite the new white bandage wrapped around his head.

He drew his pistol.

"Ross. Stay right there. We need to talk to you."

Ross dove back into the elevator and the doors started to close.

Mike threw himself forward, slamming a hand on the button, but he was too late. The doors closed on him, and he was left only with a memory of Ross' smile.

"It's going down," Sam called.

"What's down there?" Mike shouted at the security guard.

"The… the executive parking area," the guard said. He couldn't take his eyes off Mike's gun.

"Stairs?"

The guard pointed to the right of the elevator.

Sam reached them first. She drew her gun and covered the door while Mike pushed through into the stairwell.

Red night-lights did little more than cast dark shadows in corners. Mike stepped forward and checked down the first flight. There was no sound, no movement.

"All clear Sam," he called out, and moved forward to the stairs.

Sam followed him as they headed down. The only noise was their footsteps on the stairs.

After two flights they came to a door marked 'Parking'. Mike opened it slowly and peered out.

He looked over a long, low underground parking lot lit by overhead florescent lights. There was still no sound, no movement.

He motioned Sam through and they crept to the side of an SUV for cover.

"Is he here?" Sam whispered.

As if in answer, there was a harsh metallic clang from the other side of the lot.

"What do you think?" Mike said, and smiled grimly.

"NYPD. Come out with your hands up," he shouted.

A shot rang out, loud as a cannon in the confines of the space. Mike rolled to one side and took aim towards where he guessed it had come from. There was a flash of white in the shadows.

The bandage.

Mike aimed for eighteen inches below that and fired.

Damn, missed.

Two shots followed in quick succession, then rapid footsteps on the far side of the lot. Mike poked his head over the hood of the nearest car. A shadow moved.

"Don't move," he shouted. "I've got you covered, Ross. Come out with your hands up."

The only answer he got was another shot. Stone chips flew as the wall behind him took the bullet.

Mike fired.

There was a loud grunt of pain, and Ross staggered from between two cars, holding his side with his left hand. He still had a gun in his right.

"Drop the gun," Sam shouted.

Ross chose not to listen. Mike saw the gun come up as if in *slow-mo*, aimed straight at him.

"Drop the gun Ross. I don't want to have to kill you."

Mike rolled away as Ross fired again. The bullet pinged off the concrete floor less than six inches from him.

He had no choice. In one movement he took aim and fired. The bullet took Ross high in the chest and knocked him backwards, out of sight behind a limousine.

The lot went quiet, leaving Mike with only the ringing in his ears from the shooting. He suddenly remembered to breathe.

Sam came over to join him, shuffling between cars and keeping her head down.

"Are you OK boss," Sam said.

He turned to look at her. Her face was white, bloodless.

"I'm fine. You?"

"I need a clean pair of panties, but apart from that I'm good. Do you think we got him?"

"It sure looked like it. Let's go and see."

They rose, keeping their guns raised.

Nobody shot at them.

They walked slowly to where Ross had fallen.

When they got there they found a pool of blood on the concrete, and a smeared handprint on a limousine.

But that was all. There was no body.

Ross was nowhere to be found.

13

Patty woke up, feeling hot. She quickly became aware that her neck was stiff and sore. She was lying on one of the long sofas, and a heavy duvet covered her from head to toe. She pushed it off her, then immediately regretted it as a cold draft hit her.

It was dark outside, and on checking her watch, she was surprised to find it was just before midnight. Obviously she had fallen asleep, and Seton had found her a cover.

But where is he?

That question was answered when she heard light snoring from one of the rooms in the back.

She rose, stretching and bending to try to ease the kinks in her neck and shoulders. She was no longer tired. In fact, if anything, she felt wired and hyperactive. She walked around the room.

Her gaze fell on the dining table. Seton had obviously been working. The sheaves of paper they'd retrieved at Carslyle's were spread out on the table. Next to them were Seton's cigarettes.

And the car keys.

Patty looked at them for a while.

I could go. Just take them, and get out of here.

Then her gaze moved to the papers. She'd never forgive herself if she left without knowing what was there.

She picked up a page. It had a small number 6 at the bottom. She searched among them, and found that pages 1 to 4 were missing. But page 5 seemed to be the start of a tale. It was written in archaic Scots, but her mind translated as she went, and she realized she could understand most, if not all of it.

She sat, lit one of Seton's cigarettes, and within a minute was lost somewhere in Seventeenth Century Scotland, with a man in pain.

Begin a fast of forty days starting during the full moon of May, drinking only May dew collected with a cloth of pure white linen and eating only a biscuit or crust of dried bread.

I had the room specially built, an eight-foot cube containing a straw mattress. The only break in the monotonous white glare of the walls is a steel door with a flap, the only source of light is a small window in the ceiling, and a six-inch hole in the floor is only a way out for my fluids. When they shut me in, I said a last few words.

"Remember the ritual," I said to them, "I may be delirious but you must stick to the instructions. The rites must be observed."

The last thing I heard before the door slammed and the quiet descended was the soft murmur of assent. I smiled. They had been well trained. They will not fail me.

Not if they value their lives.

My body is failing. Seventy-nine years it has served me well, seeing me through the early battles: the street fighting, the wars in Normandy, the whores in Spain.

But it is failing, eating me hollow from within, the black corruption spreading through the soft tissues like wildfire. Physicians are helpless in the face of the roaring, festering chaos that my body has become. In desperation, I have turned my back on the modern miracles and searched in the past.

In my search for redemption I have spent seven tenths of my fortune and killed many people for their secrets, but what are they when counted against my life? It is imperative that I go on -- there is more yet to be had.

The answer was, as I always suspected, in the Concordances all the time. As I have already written, it took over a year in the doing. But I have it, the black powder, the philosopher's stone.

I will see this thing through. It is a small price to pay for eternal life.

There should be slight bleeding at the seventeenth day.

I have settled easily into the routine: sleeping, the rattle of the door before eating, the slow pace of the sun across the room before sleeping again. There have been no dreams.

I refuse to count the days, refuse to wonder how much longer. I accept the pain and the gnawing in my chest. I even accept the stretching and loosening of the muscles as they shoot complaints of hunger through my system. There will be time enough for indulgence.

I busy myself with thoughts of the future -- the actions I will take in ten, fifty, a hundred years time.

The days melt away in time with my body.

This morning I found the knife and bowl beside my meager rations.

There should be bleeding.

I had discussed the phrase with many 'experts'. They were divided. Some felt that there would be natural bleeding, others that some blood would have to be let out, in the old manner.

I chose to agree with the latter - I do not trust this body to bleed on schedule. That is the reason that the knife is there.

It glinted in the sun as I picked it up, a new thing to look at after over two weeks of white walls and gray steel. The left palm -- that seemed the best bet. The redness welled up, pooling in my hand before I clenched my fist, letting the blood drip sluggishly into the goblet beneath. Squeezing tighter, I forced the redness to flow until the cup was full.

My hand went to my mouth and I sucked at the cut – but only for a moment. I did not want to negate the terms of the ritual.

I wiped my hand on the mattress and held the wound tightly closed until the bleeding stopped.

It was only after eating a biscuit and draining the water, after the knife and the goblet were withdrawn, that the pain came. I fell into sleep to escape it.

The days run on and the dreams increase in ferocity, the terrors of the past coming back to be purged -- the men I have killed, the women I have used and left behind. Time and dream melt and fuse, the passing of day to night becoming blurred until I no longer know if the screams are outside or inside.

The scar of my palm has healed, but other, older scars have been reopened.

On the dawn of the thirty-second day renew the slight bleeding. Take to your bed and remain there until the end of the fortieth day.

The dreams become more vivid and I hold long conversations with the phantasms of my life. In one period of lucidity I have screamed; torrents of soprano screeching until my throat grew pained, beseeching them to let me out.

The walls have stayed white and doors have stayed shut.

The bones of my inner man are beginning to force their way out, the fat and sloth of age melting away. And still the dreams come, nightmares that assault and assail me. I strike out at demons.

This morning I woke with a knife in my leg, the whiteness of the walls now freckled with precious drops of my remaining life.

There was no pain as I slid the steel from the wasted muscle, feeling it grate against the bone as it came. I watched the oozing redness until it stopped and then only then, fell back onto the mattress into a deep and dreamless sleep.

On the first awakening take the first grain of Universal Medicine. A swoon of three hours will be followed by convulsions, sweats and purgings necessitating a change of both bed and linen.

I woke, lucid for the first time in many days, as the cat flap rattled and my food appeared. I feel only a dull throb in the thigh where the knife has been, but I remember the ritual, all of it, off by heart. Thirty-two days gone, only eight to go and the future will be mine.

Along with the water and the biscuit, there was a small piece of tissue paper and, sitting on it, a single grain of the Magi's powder, glinting blackly in the subdued light.

I took the water and the biscuit first, having to force the dry crumbs into my shrunken stomach. I lifted the grain onto one finger and, with no pause for contemplation or retreat, licked it off with my tongue and lay down to wait.

Blackness took me down, away from the whiteness, down into a red hell where I screamed for eternity.

I woke from screams into screams as my stomach convulsed and my insides roiled in a hot flare of pain.

I made it, in a crawl, to the disposal hole just in time as my system voided itself in a stream of bloody slime which clung tenaciously to the walls of the hole before being sucked greedily down into the bowels of the castle.

A thousand blades churn in my stomach, each one nicking off another piece of me. A thousand flames burn in my bowels, each one forcing out a scream and a tear as I squat over the hole listening to my life flow away.

On the next day take a hot bath and a further grain of Universal medicine.

The cat flap clattered as I awoke. Seven days to go and already I am too weak to lift myself into a standing position. I crawled across the mattress to the door, wincing as the cut on my thigh caught on a rough piece and dragged the scab open.

A bowl of hot water and a towel was placed beside the food. I used most of the water to clean up the reeking mess by the disposal hole, sending the sodden towel down after the rest. Then I washed.

I ate the biscuit slowly, relishing every crumb, and washed the second grain down with the last of the water.

I believed myself ready for whatever came next. I was wrong.

Blackness came slowly, sneaking in around the corners of my vision, eating into the white room until I was left alone and naked and weak in the all-enveloping dark.

I felt my stomach move, writhing with a life of its own, a life which spread across my torso, wriggling and spasming as it made its way to my throat.

I tried to scream but my voice was blocked by the crawling mass of corruption. I gagged and coughed and it left me in a thick stream, my sickness made flesh.

It lay there before me, coalescing into a mannequin, a black slimy parody of myself.

It spoke.

"Like father, like son."

And it cackled in a deep bass voice, a laugh that propelled me once more into wakefulness.

I woke with my head over the disposal hole, having lost all sense of time and place. I coughed, a stream of yellow bile falling into the sucking hole and watched dumbstruck as tiny blobs of red splashed the white, throwing me back into dreamless blackness.

I have just woken again to feel bruises on my body, and soft pain from the wounds on my head. There are marks on the door -- my efforts to escape, my body trying at the last to betray the ritual.

The last grain is placed on its paper beside the last of my food.

I am nearly there.

On the thirty-seventh day take the third and last grain. A profound sleep will follow during which the hair, teeth, nails and skin will be renewed.

I am light-headed and my body is so thin that a slight breeze will knock me over, but my mind is clear and there are only three days to go. The end is in sight.

This morning I took the last in one gulp, the water, the biscuit and the grain.

My wrinkles are gone, smoothed out into new flesh, new skin. The hairs on the back of my hand are thick and strong.

It is done.

14

As Mike expected, Adams was sitting at his desk when the elevator doors opened. They walked into the penthouse. Adams didn't seem surprised to see them as he motioned them to the seats they were in earlier.

"To what do I owe the pleasure?" he said. "As it's late, I'm assuming it's something important?"

Mike wasn't in the mood for preamble.

"When was the last time you saw your man Ross?"

"Last night," he said. "When I sent him after Seton."

"Not since?" Sam asked.

"No," Adams replied. "Should I have?"

"Enough playing around Mr. Adams," Mike said. "We've just seen him in your parking lot downstairs."

"Was he OK?" Adams said.

"He was. Now I'm not so sure," Mike replied. "He's got at least two gunshot wounds in him."

Adams didn't flinch.

He's good, Mike thought.

"Shooting my people now are we?" Adams asked.

"I never said we did it," Mike replied, and smiled.

Adams smiled back.

"I should hope not. Otherwise I'd have to call my friend the Commissioner and tell him you're wasting your time chasing the wrong man."

"We're not so sure," Sam said. "Ross's blood has now been found at the scene of four homicides. As of now, he's a suspect."

"You have my word," Adams said. "He's after Seton, nobody else."

"Convince me," Mike said softly.

"It might take a while."

"We're not going anywhere," Sam said.

Adams sat forward in his chair, and looked straight at Mike.

"What do you know about the drug trial Seton volunteered for?"

"Only what you told us earlier."

"So, nothing then. Forgive me, but you'll need a little background into stem cells. They're used by our bodies to help to repair damaged tissue. It has long been thought that a combination of drugs could trick the body into sending its repair mechanisms into overdrive and speed the healing of organ and bone damage.

"When we tested it, the bone marrow of treated mice released 100 times as many stem cells. The release of stem cells by the bone marrow is a natural part of the repair process—different types are sent to replenish tissue depending on the nature of the injury.

"We hoped that by releasing extra stem cells, as we were able to do in mice in our study, we could potentially call up extra numbers of whichever stem cells the body needs.

"The test subjects were given firstly a growth factor drug -- substances that already occur naturally in the bone marrow, then our new drug called Methusol.

"And at first, the results were encouraging. Both endothelial and mesenchymal cells were released at a much greater rate. The patients showed increased resistance to infection, and seemed to be both stronger, and faster than before."

"Let me guess," Mike interrupted. "Shit happened?"

"As you so colorfully put it, *shit happened*. The metabolisms of the subjects started to run too fast for their bodies to handle. Instead of repairing them, we gave them cancer, a cancer so ravenous that it ate them up even as it made them stronger. They were all dead within a week, burned alive from the inside out. All except one."

"Seton?"

"Yes. Alex Seton. With him, the drug seems to have worked. But it had *unfortunate* side effects."

"The paranoia you mentioned earlier you mean?" Sam said.

"Yes. That, and a propensity to violence. Which is where our Mr. Ross enters the story."

Adams pressed a button on his desk. A picture on the wall slid up to reveal a large plasma screen behind it.

"You asked for proof that Ross is after Seton," Adams said. "Well here we have his motive."

He pushed another button and a video started to replay.

Seton lies in a hospital bed, hooked up with numerous tubes and monitors. He stares at the ceiling, and looks catatonic. That all changes when a nurse walks into picture carrying a syringe. Seton moves, almost too fast to follow, grabbing the syringe from the nurse and backhanding her against the wall. The nurse falls in a heap to the ground while Seton starts to untangle himself from the machinery.

The door opens, and Ross runs in. He grabs Seton, trying to get him back into bed. Seton is too strong. He shrugs Ross off. And stabs the syringe into the man's neck.

Seton leaves out of shot while Ross falls slumped against the bed.

"You see," Adams said as the painting dropped back down over the screen. "With Ross, this is personal."

"He got a dose of the drug?"

"No," Adams said. "All he got was a tranquilizer."

And there was the lie. Mike saw it in his eyes, and in the way the man suddenly moved his gaze to a point over Mike's shoulder. Mike let him have it. As long as Adams was talking, they were getting information. They could sift for the truth later.

"Ross begged me to let him go after Seton," Adams said. "And I know the man. He would no more kill than I would."

Well that's not much of a testimonial now, is it?

"And Seton? What form did his paranoia take?"

"He has delusions that he is descended from a group of Templars," Adams said. "He thinks there is a conspiracy to keep a great secret from the people, and he means to break that conspiracy."

"What's the conspiracy?"

Adams smiled.

"I don't know. It's a secret."

Mike planted the bomb carefully.

"It wouldn't have anything to do with *The Twelve Concordances of the Red Serpent* would it?"

Adams laughed out loud.

"That? That's just some fourteenth century Scotsman's idea of a joke. They didn't have much to smile about back then."

"But you *have* heard of it," Sam asked.

"Seton talked about little else after we started giving him the drug. He became obsessed with it. But it's been missing for many centuries. It's just something he uses to feed his fantasy, to justify what he does. I'm telling you detectives, Ross is on the side of light in this one. I've told you already, and you've seen the evidence now. Seton is homicidal. He must be stopped."

"Maybe we should just have a look around the building," Sam said. "Just to make sure Ross is not still on the premises."

Adams stood.

Looks like we're dismissed again.

"That I cannot allow," Adams said. "We are engaged in many current trials, all of which are commercially sensitive."

"We could get a warrant?" Mike said.

"You can try," Adams said, and smiled. Mike knew what he was saying. This man had more friends in high places than either cop.

Many more.

15

Patty read through the whole thing again. Just as she was finishing, Seton walked into the room, rubbing at his eyes.

"Good," he said. "You've read it. That'll save time."

He got the whisky bottle from the cupboard and poured two large ones.

"No more for me," Patty protested, but her heart wasn't in it. She took it, and sipped while Seton talked.

"What we've found is the *result*. Obviously the four missing pages contain the actual process for making the stuff."

"What *stuff* are we talking about exactly?"

"You've read it. The universal medicine, the elixir of life, the philosopher's stone... whatever you want to call it. The thing that every alchemist in history has searched for."

"I thought that was the means to turn lead into gold?"

"No. That's merely a nice by-product. The main point of the great mystery was to find enlightenment, and eternal youth."

"And you're saying somebody actually did it? The writer of these papers?"

Seton nodded.

"It *could* be fiction?" Patty said.

Seton took a while before answering.

"I have it on good authority that it's not," he said finally.

"What authority?"

Again he took a while in replying, as if wondering how much to tell her.

"Family history," he said finally.

He moved to her side and picked up his cigarettes. He offered her one and they both lit up.

Seton sat on a sofa and showed no signs of continuing.

"Come on then," Patty said. "You can't leave it there."

He took a long sip from his whisky.

"It comes from another Alex, or rather, Alexander Seton. He was, like the others before him, a seeker after the truth. And he nearly got there on his own. He is one of the few who successfully managed the transmutation of lead into gold. And that was his undoing."

"Come on," Patty said. "If someone had managed that, then the whole world would know of it."

"Would they?" Seton said softly. "Or would whoever you told the secret to want to keep it for themselves?"

He stared into space for a while before continuing.

"Alex's sin was pride. He was only a poor man from a small town in Scotland, yet he was invited to grand palaces and mansions all over Europe. They were all amazed by his transmutations. All were desperate to find his secret. Alex was also smart. He knew that if he ever told anyone, they would have no reason to keep him alive.

"So for three years he traveled, and lived the high life. He wooed Countesses, ate at the highest tables, and dressed in frippery and finery. But he was too cocky.

"Christian II, the young Elector of Saxony, heard of Seton's alchemical success and invited him to his court. Seton had a new young bride at the time, and was reluctant to go, but Christian was insistent, and offered a large sum of money, enough to keep Seton in style for many years. So, fool that he was, he went.

"It soon became evident to him that Christian II had only invited him for the purpose of learning his secret, but Seton flatly refused to reveal it.

"In the end the Elector ordered him to be imprisoned. He was subjected to the vilest tortures, but still he refused to talk. Only when he was so close to death that he could hear angels singing did Christian relent. Seton was finally released. He returned to Scotland, a broken man. With the last remnants of his wealth he brought a fellow alchemist to his home. There he finally shared his secret.

"He had found the *Concordances* in a family vault. Found them, and used them, as far as the transmutation of lead to gold. He only lacked the final revelation.

"And that came from the other alchemist. They worked together for many years, and had many failures. But finally they made a breakthrough. Between them, they had completely decoded the Concordances. Seton undertook the rest of the experiment, that you have read here tonight."

The story had ended too abruptly, leaving too many questions.

"So what happened next?"

"He came to a bad end," Seton said. "Like most of the family. But his story survived. It gets told at family gatherings… the Seton who nearly made good."

He laughed. Patty had never met anyone who found humor in so many different places.

"And you've made it your quest to find out how he did it?"

"Quest. I like that word," he said, smiling. "No. I've made it my quest to stop anyone else from doing it again."

"But why?"

"Can you imagine how boring immortality must be?" he said, and laughed again. "People should learn to live in the now. They spend all their time thinking about past glories and worrying about the future. Meanwhile all the moments of spontaneity and beauty they'll ever have in their lives are flitting from the future into the past without being noticed.

That's why there are so many grumpy assholes in the world."

This time Patty laughed.

"See," Seton said. "Now you're getting into the swing of it. But there's a serious side. Old Alex may have found the secret. But everyone else who has tried since has died in the attempt. If any drugs company tried to replicate it, they'd end up killing far more people than they help. The great secret is not just a physical change... it's a spiritual change. If your spirit isn't ready, you will die. That's why Alex eventually had his papers sewn up inside the Concordances. He didn't want the deaths on his conscience."

"But not all of the papers were sewn up apparently?" Patty said.

"No. I'll admit, that's got me baffled. I was always under the impression that all twenty sheets were there. If four were held back, then it probably happened right at the start, back in the seventeenth century."

He jumped out of his seat as if he'd been given an electric shock.

"Come on then," he said. "Time to get moving."

Patty sat and stared at him.

"It's the middle of the night."

"What better time for fugitives from justice to be about their nefarious activities?"

"You are so strange."

"Thank you," Seton replied. "Now come on. We've got a long way to go."

"Where are we going?" Patty said as she stood.

"You don't have to come if you don't want to," Seton replied. "But the answer lies in Scotland. So that's where I'm headed. I'm going home."

16

The elevator door slid closed leaving Mike with the memory of Adams' predatory smile.

Sometime soon, I'm going to make sure that smile disappears.

"Well that didn't get us very far," Sam said.

"It got us in," Mike replied. He reached out and hit the button to stop the elevator at the next floor down.

"What are you doing boss?" Sam said as the elevator slowed.

"What I told Adams. Having a look around for our suspect Ross."

"Can I just remind you that we don't have a warrant?"

"At the moment, I don't care," Mike said.

Sam had *that* look in her eye again.

"We'll just have a quick look around," Mike said. "Something stinks, and I won't sleep until I know more than Adams wants to tell. Have you got my back?"

The door *pinged* and opened. Mike stepped out into a darkened hallway. He turned back and held the door open.

"Third floor for haberdashery?" he said.

Sam sighed and followed.

"You do know, if we're seen, that we'll be off the case quicker than shit off a shovel?" she said.

Mike nodded and let the elevator door close behind them.

"I get kind of ornery when I get shot at. It brings out the worst in me," he said.

"Now that I can understand."

Mike heard the elevator descend then silence fell around them. They walked slowly along the corridor. All they found was offices, all locked up for the night.

"Let's try down one floor," Mike said.

They tried two more floors before they found any sign of activity. As they went down an interior stairwell they saw light from under the next door down. They moved forward slowly and peered through the small round window.

They looked out onto a long dormitory. As far as they could see patients lay asleep in three rows of beds. Several white-coated figures moved among them, taking notes from readings on monitors.

"How many trials did they say they were running?" Sam whispered.

Mike backed away.

"Maybe this was a stupid idea," he said.

"Finally, the penny drops," Sam replied. "Let's get out of here. It's late. We can approach it again in the morning with clearer heads."

Mike nodded and they headed back to the stairwell.

They'd only gone down one flight when they heard rapid footsteps. A door slammed somewhere below them.

Mike drew his gun.

"It might just be security?" Sam said.

"Best not to take any chances."

They kept going down, slower than before. The next floor proved to be another admin level, but when they went down one further they saw light beneath the door, and a flickering shadow as someone moved around on the other side.

Mike crept carefully towards the small window.

"Boss. If we're seen…" Sam whispered.

Mike ignored her and stepped forward.

Across the corridor from the door was what looked like an operating theatre. Two doctors worked frantically on someone lying on a gurney. All Mike could see of the person was a flash of white bandage around the head.

Ross.

"Cover me," he said, and without waiting for a reply, stepped out into the corridor.

Nobody paid any attention to him. The doctors, if that was what they were, kept working frantically on their patient.

Mike stepped into the operating room. There was a lot of blood, but he recognized the thin face and chiseled features of the security guard. He was almost beside the gurney when one of the white-coated men turned around. He saw Mike's gun and immediately backed off, hands raised.

Mike took out his shield.

"NYPD," he said. "I need to know this man's status. He's a suspect in a serious crime."

The white-coated man quickly regained his composure.

"I don't care who you are," he said. "Get out of here right now. We're trying to save this man's life."

"He's dying?"

"Get out."

Sam arrived and pulled at Mike's arm.

"Come on. Let them do their thing. We know where he is. It doesn't look like he's going anywhere."

Mike put his gun away and backed off. They stood in the doorway watching the men work on Ross.

"You're right, he's not going anywhere," Mike said. "But I want to get a watch put on him. I don't want him vanishing on us again."

"We can do that from the car. Let's go. You look all in."

In truth, the day was starting to catch up on him. He'd been tired to begin with, and for the last few hours had been running on coffee and fumes.

"Nothing a few beers wouldn't cure," he said, turning to leave.

"I've got some in the fridge at my place?" Sam replied, smiling.

Mike didn't get a chance to reply.

He heard a yelp of surprise from behind him. As he turned, there was a crash of metal on metal as the drip feed unit hit the floor. By the time Mike got fully turned his gun was only half out of the holster.

He was too late to stop Ross.

The man got out of the bed as if it was on fire and threw himself straight at Mike, hitting him in the midriff and knocking him to the floor. Mike's gun got knocked out of his hand and slid away. After that he was too busy trying to keep from being pummeled to think about retrieving it.

Ross knelt over him, throwing punches that felt as heavy as hammer blows where they hit Mike's shoulders.

"You shot me," Ross screamed, and hit Mike again, catching him on the jaw. Blackness started to eat in at the edges of his sight. Another punch caught him on the side of the head, and he heard ringing again. Mike tried to roll away, but Ross was too heavy.

"You shot me you bastard!" Ross shouted, flecks of bloody saliva spraying over Mike's face. He was bent so close that Mike could feel the heat of his breath. Ross was running hot, *very* hot. It was like standing too close to a hair dryer.

Ross threw another punch that rocked Mike's head to the left and brought pain all up that side. The blackness encroached further, and Mike knew he only had seconds left before he would be glad to just slip down into it.

Suddenly the weight on him lifted and Ross stood up.

"Freeze," he heard Sam shout.

Ross stood over Mike. A foot came up and kicked Mike, hard, in the stomach, forcing him to curl up in pain.

Sam fired a shot into the ceiling.

"I said freeze!"

Ross didn't give her time to lower the gun. He threw himself at her. Mike saw Sam dive out of the way and get her gun pointing in the right direction, but Ross barreled past her and out of the door, his hospital gown flapping. The last Mike saw of him was a bony white ass as he went out the stairwell door.

"Get after him," Mike shouted hoarsely.

Sam took a step towards Mike, concerned.

"Get after him Sergeant. I'll be OK."

She turned and ran out of the room.

Mike got slowly to his feet. His gun was on the floor about six feet away, but when he bent to get it he almost toppled over. The room spun, and he got the same dizzy feeling as if he'd tried to lie down after a skin-full of whisky. His gun seemed to recede away from him down a long tunnel.

The gurney looked awfully tempting. He could just lie down, just for a little bit, until the world stopped spinning. It was the thought of Sam chasing Ross down the stairs that stiffened his resolve and got him moving.

He reached out an arm that seemed impossibly long and finally managed to pick up the weapon. He swayed slightly as he straightened up, but managed to persuade the room to stay on an even keel.

One of the white coats moved towards him, but Mike pushed him away.

"You two. Don't go anywhere. We'll need to talk to you later."

On the second attempt he managed to get his legs moving and stagger out after Sam.

He reached the stairwell without throwing up. He considered it a major achievement. The gun felt as heavy as an iron rod in his hand, and it shook as he lifted it in front of him. He hoped Ross wasn't feeling too frisky.

One more blast of that hot breath will probably blow me over.

At the top of the stairs he stopped to listen, but all he could hear was the sound of his own labored breathing.

"Sam!" he called.

"Down here boss," she said from somewhere below. Even at a distance, he heard the pain in her voice.

Despite his dizziness he took the stairs three at a time.

He found her slumped in a corner by the door to the parking lot and knelt down beside her.

"If he's hurt you, I'll kill him," Mike said.

"He got the jump on me as I went through to the lot," she replied, holding her side. "I think he's cracked one of my ribs."

"Did he get your piece?"

"No," she said, lifting her hand to show the gun was there.

"Where is he?"

"Off and away I think. I heard an engine a few seconds ago."

Mike opened the door. There was no sound.

He crept out slowly. Nobody shot at him.

At least that's some good news.

He took his time circling the lot. The place was empty. By the time he got back to the door, Sam was standing there, gun in hand. She winced as she spoke.

"Anything?"

Mike shook his head.

"Let's head back upstairs. At least we'll be able to get a doctor to look at you."

Sam groaned, and leant on his shoulder the whole way. Mike swayed twice, and almost took the two of them backwards down the stairs but between them they made it back up to the operating room. Mike was surprised that the men in white coats were still there.

"Got a sick lady here," he said as they walked in.

He let them take Sam off him, and leaned against the nearest wall to keep upright.

The men moved quickly to help Sam over to the gurney. It had been cleaned up quickly since they left, and there was now no sign of blood.

Or evidence, Mike thought.

One of the men prodded Sam in the side and she let out a yelp of pain.

"Sorry," he said.

He touched around her side for a minute.

"Doesn't look like there's anything broken. But you're going to have some nasty bruising. Do you need anything for the pain?"

Sam shook her head.

"Yes please," Mike said. He pushed himself off the wall, then fell back towards it again.

Now it was his turn to be manhandled by the doctors. They flashed lights in his eyes, checked his pulse, and declared him fit, if not well. One of them gave him two pills.

"Strong stuff," the doctor said. "Don't drive after taking them, and be close to a bed, as they'll knock you out for a while."

Mike looked from one white coat to the other.

"So. Care to tell me what was going on earlier? This isn't an ER, I know that much. So how come you treat gunshot wounds?"

The men looked at each other.

The nearest started to speak, but was interrupted by a voice from the door.

"I'm afraid that's something you'll never know the answer to Lieutenant."

Mike knew who it was before he turned. Adams stood in the doorway.

"What, you don't think we have more security than the guy in the lobby?" Adams said, and smiled. "I warned you off chasing Ross. Now here I catch you running around my offices harassing my doctors… without a warrant. I do believe the Commissioner will be *most* interested in what I have to tell him."

"I'll get a warrant," Mike said. "And I'll be back."

"I won't be holding my breath," Adams replied. "Now, do I have to get you escorted off the premises, or will you leave peacefully?"

The day finally caught-up with Mike, and all the tiredness and pain turned into rage. He balled up his fist and stepped forward. He wasn't sure whether he would actually throw the punch, but Adams reacted as if he would. The old man stepped back.

"Mike," Sam said softly.

That's all it took. The rage left him as quickly as it had come. He turned back to Sam.

"You OK to move?" he said.

Sam stretched, winced, then stood.

"Nothing a few beers won't cure boss," she said, and managed a smile.

"Come on then. I've got a bad taste in my mouth that needs to be washed away."

17

"I can't go to Scotland," Patty said as Seton led her from the house and out to a garage.

"Why not? It's a great place to visit. Full of history, friendly people and scenery that will knock your socks off."

"I don't mean I *can't* go. I mean I don't have my passport on me," Patty said

"That's OK," he replied. "Neither have I."

"Then how…"

He tapped the side of his nose and smiled.

"Trust me. It's what I do. Just go with the flow."

Patty looked at the car they'd driven in the night before. The rear window lay in glittering fragments in the back seat.

"It's a bit chilly for al-fresco driving," she said.

He tapped his nose again and opened the garage door..

"Mi'lady's carriage awaits."

Inside was a huge pickup truck, bright red and with enough chrome to dazzle passing drivers.

"So, we're going to be travelling inconspicuously," she said sarcastically.

"I keep this here for the winter months when the weather gets bad," he said. "But the one we came in is even more conspicuous. The police will have us on camera by now. We need a new mode of transport, and this is what's available."

Patty stood to one side smoking another of Seton's cigarettes while he got the truck out of the garage and replaced it with the other car. He helped her load a suitcase into the back beside his own. She'd packed it full of clothes from the closet without really looking at them.

Her mind felt split in two… half wanting to cut and run, the rest intrigued by the puzzle, and keen to get to the answer. It was Seton's charm and smiling manner that was tipping the balance at the moment, but the way she felt it could tip the other way in a second.

"So, what happens if we find these papers," she asked as Seton put the car in gear and drove off.

"We destroy them, of course."

"Of course," she replied, almost to herself. "But if we do that, how do we prove to the police that we're innocent?"

"I'll cross that bridge when I get to it," Seton said. "That's too far ahead to be worrying about. Let's just concentrate of getting out of the country first."

"And how do we do that? They'll be looking for us."

"Yes. They will."

"You don't seem particularly worried."

"Worrying solves nothing," he said. "Besides, I have a plan. But I need to get back to the city before I can do anything. That's going to take a while. So, relax, enjoy the scenery. There's a bit of the planet you've never seen before out there, and you're missing it."

"And you're missing the point."

"Am I? Am I really? I'm currently happy. How about you?"

Patty laughed.

"That's because you're too stupid to know any better," she said.

"That's as may be," he replied, and drummed a little rhythm on the steering wheel with his palms. "But I'd rather be happy as often and for as long as possible. Is that a bad thing?"

"I never said it was. But I need to know where we're going, what happens next. Stuff like that. Like where the next thug trying to kill us might be now. You know, unimportant stuff like that?"

Seton smiled.

"I try not to think that far ahead."

"Well, just look where it's got you," she said.

"Yes, just look."

He waved his hand at the view beyond the windshield.

"Just *look*."

She looked.

The car's headlights lit up the road ahead. The roadside to the left dropped away to a rocky shore where stunted conifers huddled above the water's edge. The sea glistened, a deep blackness that looked almost like a polished stone and the moon danced on the water like oil on a hot griddle.

She sat and let the scene sink in. Neither of them spoke for a while.

"Now you're getting it," Seton said quietly.

Patty dragged her gaze away from the view.

"Yes. It's pretty," she replied. "Stunningly so in fact. But it doesn't solve my problem. Our problem. Where are we going."

Seton sighed.

"You're going to keep asking until I tell you, aren't you?"

"Damn right mister," she said. "If you wanted a mute companion, you picked the wrong *doll*."

"Ah, I doubt that very much," he said, and smiled.

She hit him on the shoulder with a balled up fist, none too lightly.

"OK, OK, I'll tell," he said. "Just stop hitting me."

Patty smiled, and showed him her fist.

He laughed.

"We're heading for my house in the city where I have a couple of, let's say, non-legal passports stashed away for times of emergency. We'll get them, get on a plane, and head for Scotland. How does that sound?"

"It sounds like the start of a plan, but…"

He raised a hand.

"Is there anything you're going to say that will change the fact we're heading for my house?"

"No, but…"

"That's what I thought," Seton said. He turned on the radio. It was tuned to a classical station. Soft violins filled the car with sound. "Relax. Enjoy the ride. You might never be this way again."

He passed her a cigarette. She refused. Any more and she would be in danger of regaining a habit that had taken her *far* too long to get rid of the last time.

She watched him light up.

"Are those part of your *No Worries* attitude," she said.

Again he laughed.

"I could get hit by a bus tomorrow, or live till a ripe old age. I don't know. But I'm damned sure I'm not going to deny myself anything on the off chance it might bring the end closer."

"*Life is but a passing shadow, a poor player who struts and frets his hour upon the stage then is heard no more*," he quoted.

This time it was Patty's turn to laugh.

"*A tale told by an idiot?*"

"Ah, you know the Bard," Seton said. "And it's a fitting quote, for we will be travelling close to Glamis if all goes well."

"And if all goes badly?"

He sighed.

"Let's just get to my town house first, and see what happens."

Seton was right about one thing. Watching the scenery go by kept her in the now, kept her from thinking backwards, or forwards. Twice she caught glimpses of white-tailed deer as their rumps flashed in the lights. And once Seton had to slow and stop as a mother escorted two calves across to a pond.

Patty was actually disappointed when they turned off the country road and into the busy traffic on the main route back.

"Now comes the fun bit," Seton said. "Now we get to be sneaky."

"And that's what you call fun?"

"Well, admittedly there are other things I'd rather be doing," Seton said. "But in the absence of a hot tub and some champagne, this will have to do."

"Mr. Seton," Patty said. "Are you flirting with me?"

"Constantly my dear," he said. "Haven't you noticed? I must be slipping. And call me Alex."

Patty realized that she'd started to blush, and turned her head aside.

"Do you think the police will be watching your house?" she said, quickly changing the subject.

"I would hope so," Seton replied. "Otherwise they wouldn't be doing their job. But there's a hidden back entrance, and if they haven't found that, then I should be able to get in and out without being seen."

"Should?"

"Well, if everything was a certainty, life would be no fun, would it?"

"But a lot less terrifying."

"I terrify you?"

She laughed.

"I've never met anyone less terrifying in my life."

He put on a mock-crestfallen face.

"Don't tell me you *want* to be terrifying?"

"Well, it's better than being cuddly," he said.

"Oh, I'm not so sure about that," Patty replied.

"Ms. Doyle, are *you* flirting with *me*?"

Patty blushed again.

He smiled, drummed the steering wheel, then he started singing at the top of his voice.

> *"There was a young lady from Brest.*
> *Who had an enormous chest.*
> *You could balance a city,*
> *On each of her titties,*
> *And hide a small hill in her vest."*

Patty found herself laughing out loud.

"Where did you learn *that*?"

"It's an old family in-joke," Seton said. "Alex, the alchemist, was once married to a lady from that city. It's said he wrote it just after she ran away with a courtier while Alex was being tortured. Part of his revenge is that we sing it as loudly and as often as we can."

He drummed the wheel again.

"Are we having fun yet?"

Patty smiled.

"I think we're getting there. I'll keep you posted."

Dawn was just coming up as they entered the city. There was a lot more traffic around.

A kid in the back seat of a passing car pointed at their truck and the occupants turned and looked at them. Suddenly Patty felt vulnerable. She sat down low in her seat, so far down she could barely see out of the window.

Seton rapped on the windshield.

"Tinted windows," he said. "I doubt if anyone can see any details."

"But they will as soon as we stop. Shouldn't we have some kind of disguise?" she said. "Carslyle had plenty of clout, and the cops will be out in force looking for us."

"What did you have in mind?" Seton asked. "A moustache and a pair of glasses?"

"It's not funny," Patty said.

"Yes, it is," he replied. "Just about *everything* is funny if you look at it the right way."

"Including the fact that just about everybody in the State is looking for us?"

"Yes," Seton said. "All that activity, and here we are, still free. I imagine we're top the *Most Wanted* list right about now. But it's not the first time I've been a fugitive. You get used to it after a while."

Patty slumped down further as a 4x4 passed them and the driver stared in at her.

"I doubt I ever will."

"Just stay close to me," Seton said. "I'll keep you out of trouble."

"Yes. Like *that's* been working so far."

Seton smiled.

"As I said, all that activity, yet here we are, still free."

He drummed on the wheel and sang the ditty about the *Lady from Brest* again.

"You get to value freedom once you've had a spell in captivity," he said.

What the hell does that mean?

Seton didn't elaborate, and Patty didn't ask.

I might not get an answer that I like.

He pulled the car off the highway not long after they entered the city and parked in an alley next to an abandoned warehouse.

"Best walk from here," he said. "It's not far. We'll leave the suitcases. We'll be back for them later."

Before they'd gone a hundred yards Patty wished she'd worn something a bit more sensible than the cowboy boots. They were fine for standing around looking pretty in, but hopeless for anything else.

"How far did you say it was?"

"About ten minutes walk," Seton said looking down at the boots. "Or twenty at a hobble."

She resisted the urge to take off a boot and pound him over the head with it.

He led her down several side roads and alleys. She noticed that he always kept off busy streets, always leaving them plenty of places to run if spotted.

"You've obviously done this before," Patty said.

Seton smiled.

"I *told* you I was sneaky. I'm a journalist. It comes with the territory."

"I've never met a journalist like you before."

"That's because there are no journalists like me," he said. "Now come on. We're nearly there."

He led her through a small area of urban parkland. It hasn't been tended for a while, and they waded through knee high grass. They passed an abandoned roundabout and swings in a play-area slowly sinking into disrepair.

"Quiet now," Seton whispered as they came to a long iron fence. "If they're watching this way in, they'll be around here somewhere."

They crept forward slowly. They weren't challenged. They approached a gate. The gravel path on the other side led to a tall imposing red brick house.

"You live here?" Patty whispered. "Journalism must pay better than I thought."

"It does if you're good at it," Seton said. "Come on."

The gate was locked, but Seton opened it with a key from his pocket and together they went quickly along the path to a tall oak door.

"Nearly in," Seton said. "Now be quiet. They're unlikely to be in the house itself, but they'll be watching. And they may be listening."

Patty stood back as he opened the door with a different key and slowly pushed it open. The hallway beyond lay in darkness.

They moved inside, and Seton shut the door behind them. At first it was so dark that Patty couldn't see, and panic rose inside her. Seton took her left hand.

The very act calmed her. His hand felt cool, and his grip was strong.

"Just move slowly," he whispered. "I'll lead. There's a flight of stairs ahead, six steps."

"OK," Patty replied, and gripped his hand as he moved away. Together they went slowly up the steps.

"I'll need my hand back," Seton whispered as they reached a level landing at the top. Patty realized she'd been holding on so tight that her fingers hurt when she released them.

"Stay here," Seton whispered. She heard a loud click, then a door swung open. Light poured through, suddenly blinding her.

Once her eyes adjusted she looked out over a large room. Torn up books lay scattered on the floor, alongside overturned bookshelves and a badly busted laptop computer. Seton was already across the room, crawling under a heavy wooden desk.

Ignoring what Seton told her, she stepped into the room. She picked up a book and read the title: *Apologie Compendiaria Fraternitatem de Rosae-Cruce Suspicionis et Infamiae Maculis Aspersam Abluens.*

Seton turned, saw what she was doing and started waving frantically at her.

"What?" she said, and immediately covered her mouth.

Seton pointed at a point over her shoulder. She turned... just in time to see a bookcase swing closed over the concealed doorway they'd come through.

It fell shut with a loud bang.

Over Seton's shoulder Patty could see out of the front window. A cop got out of a car and head up the driveway, unholstering his pistol. In the car another cop was on the radio.

"Time to go," Patty whispered. "The cops are coming."

"I'll just be a second," Seton said from under the desk.

"I don't think we've got that long," Patty said as the first policeman reached the front door.

"Got them," Seton said and stood up, holding a pair of small, red documents.

He ran for the bookcase and started to pull it open.

"Freeze," a voice said. The policeman stood in the doorway, pistol raised and pointed at Seton.

Patty didn't stop to think. She threw the book. Her shot was a lucky one. It hit the cop's gun and knocked it out of his hand.

Seton stepped forward and hit the cop on the jaw. It didn't seem that powerful a punch, but the cop crumpled and fell, eyes rolling up in the sockets.

"Dr. Fludd would be most displeased." Seton said, kicking the book to one side.

"What?" Patty replied. She still couldn't quite believe what she'd done.

"I'll tell you later," Seton said. Over his shoulder Patty saw the second cop heading for the house.

Seton dragged her through the opened doorway, and pulled the bookcase closed behind them.

18

Mike woke with a smile on his face for the first time in many months.

He rolled over and faced Sam.

"Good morning," she said softly. "Still want that beer?"

They hadn't got as far as the beer the night before. They'd got back to Sam's place and Mike wanted to check out her bruising. Sam had lifted her shirt, one thing led to another, and here they were… smiling at each other across a pillow.

Even the remnant headache from the industrial strength painkillers couldn't dampen his spirits.

"No beer needed," Mike said. "I can think of something better."

He reached for her. She moved to put an arm around him, and groaned in pain.

"Sorry tiger," she said. "I've stiffened up. I need a hot bath."

"I can give you a rub?" Mike said hopefully as she rose out of the bed.

"No. That'll just lead to trouble. We need to get into the precinct in half an hour. You rustle up some coffee. There are some bagels in the cupboard. See if you can toast them without burning down the kitchen."

He lay there for a few seconds after he left.

"Are you up yet?" she shouted from the shower.

"Yes dear," he called back sarcastically. But the banter felt natural. More than that, it felt good.

He got out of bed and stood, too fast. The room span and suddenly he felt light headed and weak. He stood still for several seconds until the room stopped.

Getting too old for this shit Mikey, he thought, and the dark depression reared its head again. But Sam started to sing in the next room, and suddenly he was smiling again.

To his own surprise he managed to toast the bagels, find some cream cheese spread, and get the coffee brewed. After that he just had time for a quick shower before he joined Sam back in the kitchen. She smiled at him.

"I would have given long odds yesterday against this happening," she said.

"Me too," Mike admitted. "But I guess helping damsels in distress brings out the best in me."

She smiled.

"Call me a damsel again and I'll have to break your arm."

"Fair enough," Mike replied. "What about *dame*? Is dame good?"

She threw a bagel at him that stuck spread-side down to his cheek before sliding off. She came round, sat in his lap, and licked the cream cheese off.

"I suppose a quickie is out of the question?" Mike said as she stood up.

"You suppose right. Get with the drill boss. We've got bad guys to catch, and the day is a-wasting."

Mike's good mood lasted all the way back to the precinct, and for all of ten seconds after he got there.

"The Captain wants to see you Mike," the desk sergeant said as they walked into the foyer. "He said to tell you to get your butt up to his office as soon as you got in, if not sooner."

"Well that can't be good."

"I'd say that's an understatement, but don't quote me on that," the sergeant replied.

"He's in a bad mood?"

The desk-sergeant nodded.

"He took a call half an hour ago that's got him antsy. You know what he's like when he's looking for someone to chew on?"

Mike knew only too well.

And I bet I know who made that call.

"Better go and face the music I suppose," Mike said. "Get a collection going for me. I might be out on my ear in ten minutes."

He was headed for the stairs when Sam called after him. She held a note in her hand and waved it at him.

"We need to go boss. It's Collins at the stakeout," she said. "Seton's surfaced."

Mike turned and headed back towards the door.

"Sorry. I'll have to stand the Captain up. I hope he didn't spend too much time getting ready for me."

"What shall I tell him?" the desk sergeant said.

"Tell him what you've always wanted to tell him."

The desk sergeant laughed.

"No thanks Mike. I want to keep my job."

"Don't we all," Mike replied, and followed Sam out onto the pavement.

"So what's the situation?" he asked.

"All I know is what it says here," she said. "Suspects Seton and Doyle spotted but escaped apprehension."

Escaped apprehension. There's far too much of that going on in this case.

When they got to Seton's place they found Collins sitting on the doorstep holding an ice pack to his chin. His partner stood beside him.

"The little guy packs a mean punch," Collins said ruefully.

"You lost him?"

"We lost him," Collins' partner said. "Though God knows how. I got into that room only ten seconds after Joe, and they were already gone."

"There's a lot about this case that doesn't make sense," Mike replied. "It's nice to see our batting average isn't improving."

Collins looked downcast.

"We do have something on tape though," he said. "That's how we knew they'd got into the house."

"Let's hear it," Mike said.

All four of them got into the parked car and Collins got ready to play back the recording.

"Where was the bug?" Sam asked.

"In the light fitting. And here's where we picked up something."

Collins ran the tape.

"*What?*" a female voice said.

It was followed by a loud bang.

"*Time to go,*" the voice whispered soon after that. "*The cops are coming.*"

"*I'll just be a second,*" a man replied.

"*I don't think we've got that long.*"

"*Got them,*" the man said.

"*Freeze,*" another voice said. There was the sound of a scuffle then they heard Collins' partner say, "*Joe? You OK?*"

Collins stopped the tape,

"That's it?" Mike said.

Collins nodded.

"What did he mean, *Got them*?" Sam asked.

"He was holding two red documents, about yeah size," Collins said, holding his hands apart.

"British Passports?" Mike asked.

"Could be."

"Must be," Sam said.

Mike got out of the car.

"Put out a call to have the airports watched. Find out what his passport number is and get it blocked."

Minutes later he was back in Seton's front room, staring at the large map of Scotland.

"That's where he's headed," he said to Sam. "That's where the answer is. My spidey sense is tingling."

"I don't think the Captain's going to sanction a trip. Do you?"

"Let's go see," Mike replied.

It turned out the Captain wasn't ready to sanction anything except warning Mike and Sam that a suspension was hanging over them. They sat across the desk from a red-faced man Mike barely recognized, while words like *gross misconduct, dereliction of duty* and *final warning* were bandied around. They were ordered to drop the whole Adams Pharmaceuticals side of the case and focus on Seton, and only on Seton.

"Tell me Captain," Mike said when they were dismissed. "Just how far up your ass does Adams have his hand?"

Sam dragged him out of the office before he said something he *really* regretted.

The morning went downhill fast from there.

He got a call from the desk sergeant that Collins was here to see him. He met the officer in reception.

"Hi Lieutenant," the officer said. He now had a livid bruise rising on his jaw.

"What can I do for you officer?" Mike asked.

"Detective Ross said you wanted a word with me."

"Who?"

"Tall guy, thin face, pale? Said he was working an angle with you? He took the tape and told me to come and see you."

"The tape? From Seton's place."

"That's right. Did I do something wrong?"

No. I did.

Mike's disgust with himself led him to speak too quickly, before he'd thought about it.

"Apart from letting two suspects con you on the same day, no."

Suddenly Collins looked like he might burst into tears, and Mike felt like something you'd scrape off your shoe in a hurry.

Congratulations Mikey. You just won the thoughtless shit of the year award. Again.

He put a hand on the young officer's shoulder.

"Don't worry son. The fault's mine. I didn't realize how devious a bastard I was dealing with. But I do now."

"Not quite boss," Sam said from behind him. "Detective Ross also checked out the evidence from forensics. About ten minutes ago."

"The blood?"

"Yep. He took the blood from both crime scenes, along with the reports, and the photograph of him entering the crime scene. He just walked in, claimed to be a detective, and they handed it over."

"Well, that phone call the Captain took from Adams might have something to do with it."

"That it might," Sam said. "Although it doesn't do to say it too loudly. Besides, however it was done, we've got nothing left on him."

"That's what *he* thinks. We'll just find something else," Mike replied.

"But the Captain said…"

"I heard. I was there, remember? We'll keep it under the radar, but I want both crime scenes gone over again. Hair, fibers… anything you can find on Ross. And I want it now."

Sam gave him a mock salute.

"Aye, aye sir. I'm on it."

Mike headed for the stairs.

"What are you going to do boss?" Sam called after him.

"Make a call that you don't need to know about," he said.

And I'll show Adams that he's not the only one with friends in high places.

19

All the way back to the pickup Patty jumped at shadows, seeing policemen in every car, every window, behind every tree.

This is not me. I don't assault officers of the law.

But it seems she did. The memory of the book flying across the room kept coming back to her. What surprised her most was that she'd done it on pure instinct, with no thought between seeing the gun and the throw.

I chose a side. I just hope it's the right one.

"So," Seton said as they approached the lane where they'd parked. "How does it feel to be a felon?"

"I threw a book at a cop," Patty said, as if saying it would somehow wind back time, make it go away.

Seton lapsed into his bad American accent again.

"You're a bad 'un right enough. It's the chair for you for sure," he drawled.

Patty couldn't help but laugh.

"See. That wasn't so bad, was it Mrs. Hannay."

"What?"

"Mrs. Hannay," he said, holding up the passports. "We're going to have to make you a brunette, but I think you'll pass."

"What *are* you talking about?"

"Our way out. As of now we are Mr. and Mrs. Dick Hannay, travelers returning to Scotland after an extended stay in the Colonies."

"Mr. and Mrs?"

He smiled.

"I though it for the best. I had another passport for a *David Balfour*, but I didn't think I could get you to grow a moustache... at least not overnight."

Again she was forced into a laugh.

"But seriously, you have forged passports available when you need them?" she asked.

"Over the years they've come in very handy. Especially when you're a wanted felon, on the run with a beautiful blonde, with dark forces bent on your destruction. A little light disguise and an assumed identity are just what we need at this point."

"Surely they'll be watching the airports very closely," Patty said.

"Yes. But mostly in this country."

He got into the pickup and lit up a cigarette. He turned to Patty as she got in the passenger side.

"Tell me, have you ever been to Canada?"

Patty surprised herself by falling asleep as soon as they left the city and got onto the highway. She woke when Seton started drumming on the steering wheel, and singing a song she almost knew.

"*I'm on my way, from misery to happiness again, ah ha.*"

She was slumped far down in the seat, and had to push herself upright, bringing a new complaint from her neck and back.

I can hardly remember the last time I slept in a bed.

Indeed, the last thirty-odd hours seemed to be the only thing she did remember. Her life had never before been so vivid, so all encompassing.

And, God help me, I'm enjoying it.

Seton noticed she was awake.

"Sorry," he said. "I forgot myself."

I know how that feels.

"What I wouldn't give for a bed right now," she said in reply.

"I'll see what I can do," Seton said.

They were driving on a long straight stretch of quiet highway, with nothing to be seen but conifers on either side.

"You have to get us out of the country first."

"Oh, you don't have to worry about that," Seton said.

"I think we do," she replied. "They'll be watching all the customs points, and the passport shows a brunette, and this, this… thing you're driving isn't exactly inconspicuous."

Seton laughed.

"No. You *really* don't have to worry about that." He waved his hand at the view through the windscreen. "Welcome to Canada."

"I slept through Customs?"

He looked sheepish.

"Well, technically, there were no customs. Just two guards and a gate. All I needed was the right application of knowledge and charm. Those, and money, are a lethal combination at any time."

"You should have warned me," she said.

"Why? You'd only have got worried. My way, you looked exactly the way you were meant to… tired and washed out after some serious holidaymaking."

"You still should have warned me," she said. She tried to put some real annoyance in her voice, but it was just so damned hard to dislike Seton for any length of time.

He turned to her.

"If it's any consolation, getting out of Canada is going to be a lot harder than getting in."

"You'd better let me see that passport then," she said.

"It's in my jacket in the back."

She rummaged around in his jacket pockets. Firstly she came up with his cigarettes and lighter.

"Ah... my savior," he said gratefully as he took them from her.

The passports were in an inside pocket.

The picture on his at least looked like him, but hers was of a heavily made-up brunctte.

"You'd better find me a pharmacy," she said. "We've got some make over work to do."

"Oakley doakley ma'am," he said, and gave a mock salute.

She looked at the picture again, then the rest of the passport. It was an UK citizens' passport, dated some eight years before, in the name of Anne Hannay.

"Who was she?" Patty said, waving the picture in front of Seton.

He lit a cigarette and took a long puff before replying.

"My wife," he said softly.

"What happened to her? Too much happiness?"

She regretted it as soon as she said it, but it was too late to take it back. Seton's eyes took on a sadness she hadn't seen there before.

"She died," he said, and a tear ran down his cheek.

"Shit. I'm sorry," Patty said. "You said ex-wife and I just assumed..."

He wiped the tear away, and smiled at her.

"No need. You weren't to know."

"I'm sorry anyway," Patty said. She reached over and took a cigarette. She had just got it lit when Seton started to talk.

"Somebody like me has no business getting married," he said. "I'm too feckless, too swayed by the mood of the moment, always wanting to be chasing rainbows and slaying dragons. I never thought I'd find anyone the same.

"Then Anne found me, on top of a mountain near Banff. Up there, you feel close to Heaven, almost touching the sky. She helped me reach it.

"Together we followed wherever our noses took us, and I was happy, for a time. Then, one day, in the middle of nowhere, she complained of feeling dizzy. Three days later she was dead. An infection of the blood they said."

He stopped, and stared out the window, puffing on his cigarette before continuing.

"And that's why I went to the company. I needed to find out if they were on the right track, if what they were doing might save a life, save another man like me the pain I went through."

The sudden lurch into the present caught Patty by surprise.

"Company? You mean, the same *Company* who's trying to kill me?"

"Not just you," he said, and the smile was back. "Me too. I know too much."

"More than I do, that's for sure," Patty said.

"Well here's a starter," he replied. "What do you know about stem cells?"

Patty sat quietly while Seton explained the research going on at Adams Pharmaceuticals.

"And *that's* why they're interested in the *Concordances*?" she said. "They think it holds the answer to perfecting their wonder drug?"

"Maybe," Seton replied. "But I believe with Adams it's a personal thing. He's an old man, and he refuses to go quietly into the night. He wants to live forever."

"Don't we all?"

"Well, actually, no. There's the boredom factor to consider for a start, and the fact that you'll have to watch everyone you love or call a friend die, and…"

"OK. I get the point," Patty said. "But you have to admit the idea is enticing."

"It's enticing all right," Seton said. "Especially to men like Adams."

Patty sucked smoke. It was disgusting how quickly she'd slipped back into the habit. She stubbed the butt out angrily in the car's ashtray.

"How did you know to go there in the first place? She asked. "And how…"

He tapped the side of his nose again.

"Trade secrets," he replied, and would say no more.

They drove in silence for a while. Conifers began to give way to warehouses and drive-through coffee shops, and soon they drove through a strip of shops and small malls.

"Civilization," Seton said. "Food or pharmacy first?"

"Pharmacy," Patty said. "The sooner I get incognito the happier I'll be."

When they pulled into the parking lot of the largest mall, Patty realized that the pickup truck was not so garish, or out of place, as she'd imagined back in the city. Row after row of them lined the lot, in all colors.

Seton saw her looking.

"Welcome to the big country," he said. "If you haven't got a truck we don't give a…"

"I get the picture," Patty replied.

When she got inside the mall, she found everything about it was equally as large. Back in the city she was used to her neighborhood, to small, individual shops in cramped premises. Here they'd had room to spread out, and they'd taken full advantage of it.

I'll never find anything.

She spent nearly an hour in the pharmacy, and met Seton back at the car. He was putting bags of groceries in the back. She realized as she walked towards him that she had not once thought of running, or calling the authorities, since they'd left the city.

Looks like I'm in for keeps.

"So what now?" she asked Seton.

"A couple more hours driving," he said. "Then we find a motel to hole up in so I can arrange our passage out of the country. Do you want to drive?"

Patty shook her head. " Hell, I don't even know where we are, never mind where we're going."

Seton laughed.

"I completely forgot that I hadn't told you. We're now in New Brunswick," he said. "Heading north towards Moncton. Are you sure you don't want to drive? It's just one highway, all the way."

Patty shook her head.

"Not this beast. It's too big."

"In this country, your transport can never be too big." Seton said as they got into the pickup and drove off. "Let me tell you a story about a truck, a blizzard and a long, long night in the Canadian Rockies."

The story took a while in the telling, but by the end they were both roaring with laughter.

He pulled the truck into a motel parking lot.

"Happy yet?" Seton asked her softly.

20

Mike paced in his office.

Ross's gall in *raiding* the precinct for the evidence had him raging, at the Captain, at the forensic team, but most of all, at himself, for taking his eye off the ball at the wrong time.

You should have done something Mikey.

He wanted to punch something, but settled for throwing a coffee mug against the wall. When it bounced off and landed back at his feet he knew that today wasn't going to be his day. He was about to chase up the team on their progress on finding Seton and the woman.

But I did that only five minutes ago.

So he paced, his mind racing, trying to figure an opening that would give them a way into the case, or at least stop the case from running away from them.

"You'll wear out the carpet," Sam said, arriving with more coffee. "You should sit down."

He took a cup from her. The bitter liquid threatened to scald his throat on the way down. He put it down on the desk to cool and stood by the window.

"A penny for them?" Sam said.

"I'm waiting for a call," he said. "I put out word with Jimmy Drago that I'd pay for info about our *Detective* Ross, especially info as to where we can find him."

"Jimmy Drago? You can't trust him."

"We went to school together," Mike said softly. "And he owes me. I did him a favor. A big favor, that never made it into a report. Nothing you need to know about."

"And nothing I should be mentioning around anyone from I.A.? Is that it?"

Mike nodded.

"As I said. He owes me. And he knows everything that's going on in this town, or knows somebody who does. He'll come through."

"He's a crook," Sam said quietly.

"I know that," Mike replied. "But he's *my* crook. I know him."

He'll come through. He has to.

Mike started pacing again.

"Well, if we're waiting," Sam said, and sat down. "I've got some ideas to run past you."

"Shoot," Mike said.

Sam shook her head.

"Sit down first. You're making me dizzy."

Mike sat, and picked up his coffee.

"OK. What's on your mind," he said.

"It's the Doyle woman," Sam said. "The more we find out about her, the less I like our theory."

"Which theory is that," Mike said, smiling. "The one Adams is trying to feed us, or the one we don't have yet?"

"It's just that as far as we can determine, she's lived a quiet, dull life. People like her don't just suddenly get involved in plots to murder colleagues and abscond. Hell. If she wanted the book, all she had to do is put it in her bag and walk out with it. You've seen how crap their security was?"

Mike nodded.

"I've been thinking that as well. But she's obviously with Seton voluntarily. It was her that threw the book at Collins."

"Yes. I know. There's something going on here we haven't got a handle on."

"There's a *lot* going on here we haven't got a handle on."

He lifted the files that Adams had given them and tossed them over to Sam.

"See if you can make anything of these," Mike said. "My brain's had too much. Any more and it'll be leaking out my ears."

While Sam read the files Mike sipped his coffee and stared at the phone, willing it to ring.

It stayed quiet.

Sam examined the small tear in the corner of Ross's file that Mike had spotted earlier.

"You're right. There was definitely at least one more sheet here."

"Yeah. But what was it? Was it a medical record? Personnel file?" Mike said. He banged hard on his desk. "Come on Jimmy, ring! Give me something to go on."

The phone still stayed quiet. Mike finished the coffee, got up and started pacing the floor again.

"Mike," Sam said softly. "It'll come when it comes. You know that. It's part of the job."

"And the part I never liked," Mike said. The thought of a drink grew in his head again, but he pushed it down.

"I wish I knew where that bugger Ross was hiding."

Someone coughed.

Officer Collins stood in the doorway.

"I can't tell you where he is Lieutenant. But I can tell you where he's been."

Five minutes later they were watching a video on a television that Sam wheeled in from the main office.

"It was thinking about how Seton disappeared that did it," Collins said as he put a tape in the machine. "I wondered whether there were any security cameras in the area, given that the occupants are all well off."

He got the tape started.

"And we got lucky. The next door neighbor has a twenty-four hour cam running. There's nothing for today… just us going in. But I went back a couple of weeks. And found this."

The scene shows the street outside Seton's house. A digital timer shows that it is seven o'clock in the morning, 13 days previously.

Seton comes out of his house, turns his back to lock the door. A tall, thin figure steps up behind him and covers Seton's face with a cloth. Seton immediately slumps in the tall man's arms.

Collins stopped the tape and zoomed in on the thin man. He didn't look as pale as they'd seen him, but Mike was getting to know the face well. It was Ross.

"I knew Adams was lying," Mike said, almost shouting. "I knew it."

"And that's not all," Sam said.

She showed Mike the tear in Ross's record. Then she picked up Seton's record and took a staple out, releasing the separate pages.

"Maybe it wasn't Seton they were experimenting on after all," she said.

She showed Mike the medical record they'd been told was Seton's and held it next to Ross's record.

There was a small tear in the corner of each.

It was an exact match.

21

Patty came out of the washroom nearly an hour after she'd gone in.

"I thought you'd got lost in there," Seton said. "I was about to send in a rescue mission."

He had his back to her. He turned as she closed the washroom door, and his mouth fell open.

"Now, *that* is what I call a makeover."

The hair was the most drastic. She'd cut it to a short bob, and dyed it a dark brown. She'd worried that it might look false, but the dye did what it said on the tin, giving her *a natural look that's full of life*. She'd also spent a lot of time on the makeup, particularly around the eyes. A coat of red lipstick completed the look.

She handed Seton the passport and he checked her against the picture.

"How did I do?" she said.

He couldn't take his eyes off her.

"You could almost be her double," he whispered.

It looked like tears might not be too far away. To save him embarrassment Patty went to the small kitchen area. Someone had been cooking. Rather, it looked like someone had been throwing food around with abandon. The oven was on, but she wasn't sure she wanted to see what was in it.

"Did you sort out the travel arrangements?" she said.

He cleared his throat before replying.

"We're on a flight from Saint John first thing in the morning," he said. "We have to change in Iceland, but that's all the better. It's about a three-hour drive, so we'll have to get on the road really early."

"Anything on the news about us?"

He managed a laugh.

"No. They don't care for much news in these parts. It's wall to wall hockey and football. That's Ice Hockey, and American Football."

He came and stood next to her and opened the oven door.

"Dinner's ready dear," he said with a smile.

This time it wasn't out of a tin. She discovered that Seton was a good cook, given the right ingredients. In this case it was salmon, with rice and fresh vegetables. There was even a pudding, and a glass of wine each. It felt almost too civilized for the motel room.

Every so often she'd look up from the table to find Seton looking at her. And once, there was sadness in his eyes.

"You really do look like her," he said. "Maybe this disguise will work after all."

"Of course it will work," Patty said, with more conviction than she felt. "But for it to be effective, you'd better start calling me Anne."

He jerked, almost as if he'd been shot.

"I'm not sure I can do that," he whispered.

I'm not sure you can afford not to," she replied. "Trust me, I'm a pragmatist."

That got her a small smile.

"Aye. I'd noticed. There's not many would be so calm after the experience you've had."

Patty put down her cutlery.

"You know," she said softly. "I haven't thought about… about them. Jill, George, Mary. They're dead. And I haven't mourned."

"You've been a bit busy," Seton said.

Suddenly she was crying again.

Seton came over and held her tight. She clung to him, like a drowning man suddenly finding a lifejacket.

After a minute she pushed him away.

"Any of that wine left?" she asked, wiping her eyes. "And a cigarette? I think I need a cigarette."

She left the table and headed for the washroom. She stood there for long seconds, hands on the washbasin, staring into eyes that she did not recognize. The makeup had run, but she wasn't ready to repair it. Not yet. Her hands shook too much to even think about it. Guilt had hold of her, and it wasn't about to let go any time soon. But it wasn't guilt about what had happened.

I should feel more, she thought. *Why don't I feel more?*

What she felt was excited.

This stuff doesn't happen to people like me.

But it seemed it did. Thirty-six hours ago she'd been plain Patty Doyle, living a life of routine and order. Coffee from Starbucks on the way to work, donuts from George in the mornings, a sandwich from Joe's Eatery and flirting with John, a stockbroker from the next building over. Then back to her desk, a lemon tea in mid afternoon, and home to a quiet apartment, soap operas, and a book before bedtime.

Five years.

She'd thought herself happy. Now she knew better. She hadn't been happy. She'd been comfortable. But she'd never been happy.

Until now.

Standing in front of a mirror, a refugee from justice, Anne Hannay smiled. And she meant it.

When she finally left the washroom, she found Seton sitting at a cleared up dining table. He had the *Concordances* open in front of him. Next to him, beside the empty seat, sat a full glass of wine, a cigarette, and his lighter.

"It's time we talked about this," he said, pointing at the book. "Unless you're tired?"

She sat and lit the cigarette.

"I won't sleep, not till we're safely out of the country."

Seton nodded.

"Anne was the same."

She put a hand over his.

"Anne is the same."

He smiled sadly, then picked up the book to show her the first illuminated diagram.

It was titled MALAGMA, and showed a fiery red serpent eating the world which was depicted as a shining golden disc.

"Strictly speaking," Seton said. "This isn't part of the process at all, rather, this picture is a symbolic representation of the whole process. Malagma is Latin, meaning Amalgamation. The whole process, the quest if you like, is to amalgamate the soul, the microcosm, with the universe, the macrocosm."

"Sorry," Patty said. "You've lost me already."

Seton laughed.

"I thought I might. Fourteenth century symbolism was obscure even then."

He thought about it for a short while.

"Do you know anything about Zen?"

It was her turn to laugh.

"Only from re-runs of *Kung Fu*."

"Well, Grasshopper," Seton said. "Everything is one, and one is everything."

"*I am he as you are he as you are me and we are all together?*" Patty said.

"Yes," Seton replied. "We are the egg men. All together in one huge womb that is the Universe, the *macrocosm*. Alchemists were convinced that mercury transcended both states, both above and below, both life and death. It came to symbolize the transformation required to reach illumination and eternal life."

"Illumination?"

"Let's not get ahead of ourselves," Seton said smiling. "I just wanted you to get some idea what we're getting into. We're looking for the code-breakers notes. It won't do us much good to get bogged down in the code itself."

He turned the page.

CALX was the heading. The pictures showed a young man, bound to a burning wheel by hands and feet in a figure X. He was smiling.

"*Calx* is Latin for Lime," Seton said. "In this case, it means, calcination, or the process of purifying by heating. If you burn a body hot enough, it goes black, then, if you burn it even hotter, the ash turns white. Similarly, if you heat limestone, you'll produce a white powder that the Romans called *Calx Vita* or quicklime. This was considered a magical material, for, if you poured water on it, it gave out heat. Effectively, giving the heat back to the giver."

"And now I'm lost yet again," Patty said.

"This one's easy," Seton replied. "Look at the picture. Fire purifies. It's also a code that says, in effect, make quicklime, or something like it that will give heat back to the giver. And, beyond that, it symbolizes the fact that the adept must purify his soul before continuing. Wheels within wheels yet again."

He tapped at the picture.

"This is from Greek mythology. *Ixion* was punished by Zeus. He tried to seduce *Hera*, and for his presumption was bound to a perpetual wheel of fire. But Ixion had seen the face of the goddess, and although in eternal pain, was also eternally happy. That's something else there's a lot of in the *Concordances*; duality. Everything can be seen from two angles. Everything has at least two meanings."

He turned the pages quickly.

"Number five is an easy one."

It showed a great serpent going into a deep dark cave.

"*PREGANS*, or Impregnation. In this case, impregnating one substance with the seed of another to produce something else again."

"Which is?"

Seton laughed.

"That's why we need the code-breaker's notes. We could be here for eternity otherwise."

"OK," Patty said. "I understand why the notes are important. But that doesn't help us with where they are. And I don't understand how the *Company*, as you call them, will know any more than us."

Seton had a faraway look in his eye. He shivered, and shook his whole upper body, as if shucking off an old skin.

"Well there's one thing for sure," he said. "They can hardly know anything less."

He drank a long swig of his wine.

"Now, let's talk practicalities. We need to get our story straight at the airport."

22

Jimmy Drago finally called at seven-thirty that evening, by which time Mike was close to climbing the walls. Sam was down in the bowels of the building somewhere, chasing up forensics on their rework at the crime scenes, so Mike was left to stare at the telephone and try not to think about booze.

Last night with Sam had been the first night for months that he's woken feeling rested, even calm. Sam was good for him. He knew that. A part of him, a big part of him, might even be growing to love her. But the booze had been a lover for a lot longer, and had a tight hold.

A very tight hold.

He had started young. His dad, his uncles, his granddad, and his mother had all been drinkers. Fighting Irish from a long line of fighting Irish. Rebel songs, maudlin nights around pianos in smoky bars, and laments to the auld country. That was what Mike took from his childhood. That, and a thirst for beer that never seemed to be quenched. The beer wasn't the problem though, apart from the damage it had done to his waistline over the years. No, beer he could handle. He knew his limits, and could stick to them with beer.

It was the whisky chasers that were starting to kill him, little bit by little bit.

A wee half-and-half.

That's what his granddad had called a half-pint of beer and a whisky. And that's what Mike had taken to as his poison of choice when he got settled in a bar.

A man's not a man if he can't take his whisky.

His father's voice this time. That's what Dad had said when, on Mike's fourteenth birthday, he's plonked Mike down on a barstool and introduced him to the uisque beatha.

The water of life. That's a joke.

Nowadays, when Mike looked in the mirror, he could see his Dad starting back at him. Dad died of cirrhosis of the liver at fifty-two.

Not too long to go now, Mike.

Which brought him back to thinking about Jimmy Drago.

Mike had known Jimmy most of his life. Even at eight years old Jimmy had been big. He'd learned early that bulk meant strength in the pecking order that existed in the school. Unfortunately, picking on a young Mike Turner was a *big* mistake. What Mike had lacked in bulk, he more than made up for in temper. He'd pounded Jimmy's face into the dirt, and then helped the big lad home so that he could apologize to Jimmy's ma for ruining his school clothes.

From that day on they'd been friends, not as close as some, closer than others were. They met up about once a month for booze and pizza, yakking about the good old days and both gently pumping the other for information, neither really caring much about any that they got. And if recently, Mike had been more interested in the booze than the pizza, Jimmy pretended not to notice.

Mike knew that Jimmy was running cons, big ones. But it wasn't drugs, wasn't prostitution, and nobody got dead, so Mike turned a blind eye. In return, Jimmy sometimes passed on some info Mike could use.

Things had been on a steady keel until a couple of months ago. Jimmy turned up in the bar with a face that looked like raw beef that was going off. Someone had pounded on him, and hadn't stopped for a rest.

Jimmy didn't want to talk about it, but as the beer, then the whisky loosened him, he told Mike about a small time tobacco smuggling ring, a gang boss, and Jimmy's *bit of cream from the top*.

Jimmy had been siphoning off some, actually a lot, of the profits. The boss found out, and was now leaning on Jimmy. And leaning hard by the look of it. Jimmy told Mike there would be nothing the cops could do.

He'd been wrong about that. Gang bosses weren't the only ones that knew about *cream*. Mike had a word with some of the officers in the precinct. Two days later the gang boss was locked up in a small room with the vice squad heavies. Jimmy moved in, took over the whole operation, and now it was the cops who got the cream off the top. Everybody was happy.

Except Mike. Yes, he'd done a friend a favor, but it left a bad taste in his mouth. *Cream* from crime always did. Maybe Jimmy's phone call would sweeten it a bit.

But only if he calls.

Mike nearly jumped when the phone actually did start to ring.

"How's things Mikey?" Jimmy's voice said on the other end.

"Better for hearing from you big man," Mike replied. "I hope you've got something for me?"

"No pleasantries Mikey? Maria is fine by the way, and the kids haven't seen Uncle Mikey in a while. Michela will be 21 in two months. How about that, Mikey? Have you even *thought* about a present yet? You're her godfather furchristssake. And…"

"Jimmy," Mike said softly. That was all it took.

"OK, OK. I was getting to it. I've found him."

"Where?"

"In the JFK parking lot. Section F, Row 2. He's sitting in a red sedan. He's been here for fifteen minutes now. I think he's waiting for someone."

"You're on him yourself? Jesus Jimmy, this guy's a killer. Don't go near him. We'll take it from here."

"What do you think I am, stupid or something?" Jimmy said. "I'm sitting here waiting for the cavalry. Where the hell are you?"

Mike was already on the move. He left the room in a hurry, shouting for Sam.

"Where's the fire boss?" Sam said.

Mike pushed the car as fast he dared, weaving through traffic and running red lights where it looked safe.

"Jimmy's not big on waiting," Mike said. "He's not known for his good sense either."

"We've got other cars heading that way," Sam replied. "Maybe…"

"*Maybe*," Mike said. "*Maybe* never won any prizes."

He narrowly avoided hitting a security van, and scraped his right wing along the side of a parked car.

"Neither did getting both of us killed," Sam said.

"It's not us I'm worried about."

They reached Section F ten minutes later. Mike had to slow to avoid ramming an SUV that decided to reverse from a parking bay into his path.

Instinct, anger, distraction… later he was never sure what caused him to do it. He hit the horn, hard.

And three cars down, a white face looked up. Ross looked out of the windshield of a red sedan, straight at Mike.

Mike saw Ross throw the sedan into gear and try to do a wheel-spinning reverse out of the parking bay. It didn't get far, slamming into a vehicle that came out of the sedan's blind spot and boxed him in. Mike saw Jimmy Drago smile behind the wheel of a SUV. The big man reversed, then rammed forward again, squeezing the sedan tighter into the parking area.

"That's enough Jimmy," he whispered. "That's enough."

Jimmy didn't listen. He rammed the sedan once more, then got out and approached it. He carried a tire iron.

"Oh Jimmy," Mike whispered. "What are you doing?"

Mike and Sam were still getting out of their car, still drawing their guns, when they heard the double pop of Ross's pistol. Jimmy fell to the ground, the tire iron clanging on the concrete.

Ross squeezed out of the battered sedan.

"Jimmy," Mike shouted, and started to run. Ross let off two more shots in his direction and Mike felt one tug at his shoulder. He fired back, but only took out the windshield of the next car in the row. Ross turned and ran.

As Mike knelt beside the big man, Sam ran past him.

"See to Jimmy," she shouted. "I'm on him."

Jimmy was clutching at a wound in his left shoulder.

"I'm OK Mikey," he said hoarsely. "Go catch the bad guy."

A squad car pulled up. Mike showed his badge.

"Get a medic here, on the double," he said. "And call for backup. We've got an armed suspect, and he's running."

"Now you owe me one," Jimmy called out as Mike ran to follow Sam.

She was almost a hundred yards ahead of him, and running hard after Ross. Mike couldn't keep up. He stopped, breathing heavily, his heart thudding in his chest.

Enough of this running shit.

He turned back and ran for the car, all the time watching Sam, trying to gauge where Ross might be going. As far as he could tell he was headed almost straight for the fence that ran along Runway Two.

Mike had to reverse around two static cars, and by the time he got straightened up, he'd lost sight of Sam.

Hold on. I'm coming.

Tires squealed as he hit the pedal, and several cars, just cruising looking for a space, had to get out of his way fast.

As he got close to the fence he saw Sam running ahead of him. Ross was little more than a speck in the distance, and getting further from Sam with every stride.

He's like a damned cheetah.

Mike pulled up beside Sam and she jumped in.

She sat and wheezed, gulping in air as Mike took the car off the road and onto the grass, following the line of the fence.

"Where the hell is he headed? There's nothing out here for miles but more fence."

Sam was too out of breath to answer.

"He…" she coughed, then started again. "He had a cellular phone. He was using it just as I started chasing him."

"By spotting him we changed his plan. He must have been waiting for something. Now he's been flushed out, we might get some more company. Are you OK?"

"Nearly. I'm getting there."

And finally, they were catching the running man.

Ross must have heard them coming. He turned, and fired a shot that glanced off the bonnet of their car.

"Got you now," Mike shouted as they closed in.

But he'd spoken too soon. Ross turned to face the fence, then climbed up it, scampering over the top like a kid in a playground and dropping down on the other side to land lightly on his feet.

"Shit… that fence is nearly twenty feet high."

Ross was already running off across the airfield. It looked like he had a target in mind, a small executive style jet that had its rear door open with a stepladder leading to the runway.

"That's all right," Mike said grimly. "We're not going over it."

He reversed the car nearly fifty yards, then gunned the engine, straight at the fence.

"I don't think this is a good idea Mike," Sam said.

Mike didn't get a chance to reply. They hit the fence, hard, rocking them in their seats. At first Mike thought they were just going to bounce off it, but their momentum carried them through. A chunk of bent and mangled fencing fell on the car, bounced on the hood and raised cracks across the windshield before falling off with a screech.

Something caught under the back wheels. Metal screamed and the car's back axle sounded terminally broken.

But we're still moving.

Somewhere in the distance a siren started to wail.

"I think we pissed somebody off, boss," Sam said.

"I'm just getting started," Mike replied, and gunned the accelerator.

Ross reached the jet while they were still a couple of hundred yards short. Someone gave him a hand up into the plane and the stepladder was pulled up.

As they pulled level with it, the plane started to taxi off.

"We've lost him," Sam said.

Ross leaned out of the plane's open door and waved at them. Behind him they could see Adams standing at his shoulder, a big smile on his face.

Mike banged his hands on the steering wheel in frustration as the jet raced away from them. It was just taking off when the sirens got *much* louder.

Airport security descended on Mike and Sam in force, and their day went from bad to worse.

23

Seton left Patty alone with the luggage on the Saint John airport concourse as he went to pick up their tickets. His *disguise*, if you could call it that, was a pair of glasses and a baseball cap.

"These, and my natural shyness, will make sure I'm not remembered," he said as he left.

She watched the crowds milling around her. Most were obviously holidaymakers chasing the sun. Fathers dressed like teenagers shepherded their families into long snaking checkout queues. Children screamed blue murder, pensioners fretted and teenagers flirted with anything that moved. But nobody paid *her* any attention. She felt like leaping around and shouting.

Hey, over here. I'm a fugitive on the run from justice.

But even then, she'd just be one more frazzled person among many. Most of them looked stressed already, and their holidays hadn't even begun.

"Excuse me Miss," a man said at her side. "Do you know where the check-in for the Paris flights is?" He only came up to her shoulder, and looked almost as round as he was tall. His head looked to have been placed askew on his shoulders, like a snowman just starting to melt in the sun. Sweat ran down his forehead, which was hardly surprising, given that he pushed a trolley piled high with suitcases and overnight bags.

"I've been around this damn place three times now," he said. "And I'm about ready to give up and go home."

"Sorry," she said. "We're going to Venice."

"Ah, Venice," the little man replied, and burst into *O Solo Mio*. His high floating tenor filled the concourse, and people stopped, stared, and stayed to listen. He carried the song all the way through to the end, and got a spontaneous round of applause from everyone in listening distance.

He nodded to Patty and tugged at an imaginary forelock.

"Once more into the breach," he said, and pushed at the trolley, taking two attempts to get it moving.

"Not quite what I meant when I said '*Keep a low profile*'," Seton said when he returned. He waved tickets at her. "But I got them. Come on, the check-in is open… the sooner we get through security and out of the public areas the better."

Security proved trickier than they'd hoped. Something in Patty's satchel aroused suspicion as it went through the X-Ray machine.

"Could you open your bag please Miss," the guard said.

Patty opened it, and handed it back to him. He took out the *Concordances*, opened it and studied some of the pages.

"You do know," he said finally, "There's a law against taking antiques out of the country without declaring them."

"Yes," Seton said beside her, much too eagerly. "I can explain."

"Please darling," Patty said to Seton in the nearest she could muster to a British accent, and putting a hand on his shoulder. "Let me handle this. You go on through. I'll just be a second."

"But," Seton said. "I can…"

"No," she said firmly. "Please Alex. Don't make a scene. Trust me. I'll handle this."

He looked at her, smiled, and nodded.

"I'll be just through the door. Shout if you need me."

Once Seton had gone she leaned closer to the guard and whispered conspiratorially.

"It's a fake," she said. "But he thinks its real. I can't let him know though. It would break his heart."

The guard looked at the book and back to her.

"Look," she said. She lifted it and tore the front page out. "Would I do that if it was real?"

She gave him her best smile.

"Can't you just let it go. I'm trying to make the old man happy."

The guard smiled back.

"I'm sure you're good at that," he said.

"Not that you'll ever get to find out," she replied and took the book from him. "But maybe, if I'm back this way, I'll look you up."

She left him grinning.

"You did *what*?" Seton said ten seconds later.

"Shush," she replied, and hurried him away from the security area. "It was the only way to get it through," she whispered.

Seton grinned.

"I knew you were the right girl for the job. But please… don't destroy any more of it."

Patty put the loose leaf back in the book and placed the whole thing carefully in her satchel. "Cross my heart," she said, again in her British accent.

And hope to die.

As they walked along the terminal corridor, she noticed that Seton was more alert, focused even.

"Problem?" she asked.

"No. Just being careful. By now the Company will know we've left the country. And if the cops are anywhere near smart, they'll have figured it out as well."

"But we could be going anywhere," Patty replied.

Seton shook his head.

"The *Concordances* history is well known. Anyone who's after us will know that we'll eventually turn up in Scotland. But we have an edge. We know exactly where we're going. They don't," he said, and looked all around again. "Which is why I'm being careful. I'm guessing they'll have all the airports watched."

"So there is a problem."

"No, just a distraction. A problem would be if the wing fell off the plane."

"Would *that* worry you?"

"That would depend on whether we were in the air or on the ground," he said, smiling.

He led her to a waiting area.

"I'll get us some coffee," he said. "Stay here, and don't talk to any strange opera singers."

She did as she was told. She sat and watched the well-ordered drill of airport technicians outside the waiting room as planes came and went. The staff moved like ants in a hive. Each had their own job, each was almost oblivious to what else was going on.

Just like us in the office.

And once more it all rushed back to her. She forced it away, hard. Sometime soon she'd have to grieve, but the middle of a busy airport wasn't the place for it.

Patty jumped as someone moved, too close to her.

"Sorry," Seton said, handing her a paper mug of coffee. "You were miles away."

"Not far enough," she said.

Not nearly far enough.

She gulped at the coffee, wishing it were whisky, and suddenly thinking about a cigarette.

"So when's the flight?" she said.

"We should be boarding within the hour," Seton replied.

"Good. Maybe then I can relax."

"Maybe we both can."

She smiled at him.

"It's not as if you need to. You're the most relaxed man... the most relaxed person I've ever met. You're permanently relaxed."

He laughed.

"No. I'm permanently *trying* to relax. There's a difference."

For the first time she noticed he was carrying a newspaper.

He saw her looking.

"We made page four," he said quietly. "There's an old picture of me, but all it says about you is that the police want to talk to you *'to determine your involvement'.*"

"What do you think they'd say if they saw you now?" he said with a smile. "You seem to be getting into your role."

She finished off the coffee.

"I would say I'm pretty involved now," she said, looking him in the eye.

He looked back.

"I'd say we both were."

She broke the stare first, but looked back again.

"I'm not her," she whispered.

He took her chin in his hand.

"I know," he said, and kissed her softly on the lips. It was over in a second, but the memory stayed for a lot longer.

They held hands as they boarded the plane. It didn't feel like an act.

They had a double seat near the back of the plane on its own. Patty sat nervously through all the pre-flight preparations, expecting at any moment that the authorities would come aboard and frog-march them out.

It wasn't until they were out on the runway that she started to relax. The engines roared and they started to accelerate. Then, just as quickly, the engines wound down and they slowed.

Patty looked around. Panic started to grow, but Seton stroked her hand.

"Don't worry," he whispered. "I doubt it's got anything to do with us."

And to prove his point, the Captain came over the public address.

"Sorry about that folks. A flock of geese chose the wrong moment to check out the airfield. We'll be on our way again in a few minutes."

He was as good as his word. Three minutes later they once more accelerated along the runway and this time the plane took off without any hitch.

Patty also remembered to breathe, but her hands had begun to shake, and suddenly she felt boxed in, claustrophobic.

Seton took her hand.

"Are you a bad flier?"

She *nearly* laughed.

"No. I'm a bad fugitive. How can you live like this?"

"It's in the genes," Seton said. He stroked the back of her hand, softly, and kept doing it while talking to her. "We Setons have always had a colorful lifestyle. Take my Uncle George for example. He was a fugitive for a long time. Not from justice though. George was running from cuckolded husbands. There was this time…"

Soon Patty was so engrossed in Seton's story that she forgot to be worried, and by the time he got to the part where his Uncle George was being chased down the Royal Mile with his trousers round his ankles she was almost fully relaxed.

She fell asleep with her head on his shoulder, and when she woke she found him staring into her eyes.

"Not too shabby for a bad fugitive. You slept like a baby."

He paused, then continued.

"You screamed, you bawled and I had to change your nappy twice."

She hit him on the shoulder, but she couldn't keep the smile from her face.

He handed her a coffee that was still hot.

"They came round ten minutes ago, but I didn't want to wake you."

She sipped at it gratefully, and looked out the window. They were travelling over a large expanse of open sea.

"Where are we?"

"The Captain announced the start of the descent just before you woke. We'll be landing in Iceland soon."

"Do we disembark?"

He nodded.

"And we have to get on to another plane for Glasgow."

She looked into his eyes.

"If I didn't know better, I'd say you were starting to worry."

"And if I didn't know better, I might agree with you," he said. "We're going to have to get really sneaky from now on."

"Sneakier than using forged passports and disguises to flee the country?"

"Much sneakier," he said. "This is going to be fun."

24

The Captain kept them waiting all night. They sat in Mike's office and drank endless cups of coffee.

"So what do you think boss?" Sam asked at one point. "Are we still cops?"

"Until the cantankerous old bastard says otherwise," Mike replied. "I hate all this *regulations* crap."

"Maybe shouldn't have been a cop then," Sam said softly, and Mike had to laugh.

"Maybe not. But it was either that or go down the Jimmy Drago route."

And I used to know which one I preferred.

"Is Jimmy OK?" she asked.

Mike nodded.

"The bullet was a through-and-through. It won't stop him bitching about it for years to come though. I'll be buying his whisky for him for a while."

"Will you?" Sam said quietly. "And will you still be drinking it with him?"

"Ask me again in the morning," Mike said. "At the moment, whisky sounds like too much of a good idea."

The night passed at a snail's pace and at some point Mike fell asleep in his chair.

The results were predictable.

He woke with the taste of stale coffee in his mouth, a full bladder, and a back that felt like it had been smashed against a wall a few times, then jumped on by a team of wrestlers.

Sam sat in the chair opposite. She looked up from a book in her lap.

"Nothing like a good night's sleep?"

"You're right. That was nothing like one."

He stood up and went to stare out of the window. From here the whole city looked asleep, and the reinforced windows kept out enough sound to maintain the illusion. But Mike knew otherwise. Bad things were happening out there. Bad things were *always* happening out there.

"We should be out there," Mike said angrily. "Going after those bastards."

"I know," Sam said quietly. "But maybe we shouldn't have destroyed that nice fence at the airport?"

Mike grinned.

"Most fun I've had all year."

Sam grinned back.

"Just let me know the next time you want to try it again. I'll be sure to be somewhere else."

"I'll take the blame," Mike said. "We'll say you tried to talk me out of it."

"I doubt if the Captain will let you get a word in," Sam said.

And she was proved right when they were finally called into his office.

The Captain's face was an even deeper shade of red than before. And the words he slung at Mike and Sam this time were venomous, with real poison in them. Words like *suspension, forced retirement*, and *indefinite leave*. That was just the beginning. After twenty minutes of abuse Mike and Sam were finally allowed to leave. But their badges and guns stayed behind with the Captain, along with the remnants of their careers.

"That went well," Sam said as they left the precinct into the early morning sunlight.

Mike just grunted.

"Want to join me for a beer to wash away the bad taste?" she said.

"What I want to do is pound the bastard Ross' face into the concrete of that runway."

"Well unless you've got a pair of wings handy, that'll be tough."

Mike breathed deeply, and shucked the last remnants of the night away.

I'm not a cop.

That still didn't sit right with him. But his next thought made him feel slightly better.

The regulations don't apply any more.

"Actually," Mike said after a few seconds. "I was thinking more along the lines of a holiday. Want to join me?"

She linked an arm in his.

"Where are we going. Somewhere warm I hope?"

"Not unless Scotland has moved south," Mike said.

"Scotland?"

He nodded. "That's where Seton has gone."

"We're not cops any longer Mike," Sam said.

"That's why it has to be *off the books*," he replied. "But nobody else is going after them. And if Seton is there, that's where Ross and Adams will be."

"Then that's where we should be as well, don't you think?"

"Yes. But it's a big country. We need to narrow down the search. Come on. I've got an idea."

Twenty minutes later they were at the door to Seton's house. There was no sign of any stakeout, but there was a hatching of crime-scene tape across the doorway.

"Shouldn't Collins and his partner still be here?" Sam asked.

"The Captain took them off the case," Mike replied. "And I'm guessing the brass just want the whole thing quietened down for a while. We should be safe enough."

He tried the door.

It was locked.

He ripped the crime-scene tape down, balled it up and threw it aside.

"Give me some room Sam. This is a big-assed door, and I'm not as young as I used to be. I'll need a run at it."

"Mike," Sam said, putting a hand on his arm. "If we do this, we become the criminals."

"And if we don't, Adams and Ross get away with murder," he said.

"Just being the voice of reason," Sam said. "It's not that I'm disagreeing with you. We're in this together."

"Together it is then," Mike said.

He kissed her on the lips then gently moved her aside.

He took a short run up, put his full weight behind it and shouldered the door. It hurt like hell, but the door gave, just. Sam joined him, and together they managed to push it open. They stood in the doorway for several seconds, but there was no movement from any of the neighboring houses, not even the twitch of a curtain.

So much for Neighborhood Watch.

Once inside, he led Sam through to the front room and stood her in front of the map.

"This is what I came to see. There's a pattern here, an order of some kind." he said. "But I couldn't see it before."

He squinted, putting the map out of focus, but still no pattern emerged.

Sam stepped forward. She touched some of the colored pins and examined the map more closely.

"I recognize some of the place names," she said. "Especially the gold pin ones. Iona, Kirkwall, Dunblane, Paisley. They're all cathedral towns."

"How the hell do you know that?"

Sam smiled.

"Strict religious upbringing, remember? That, and the fact that I did some reading up on Seton's conspiracy theories while you were snoring in your chair last night. They are also all places that had Templar connections... or so the book said."

"More Templar shit," Mike said. "That's all we need. And it still doesn't get us anywhere."

"Not very far, I'll admit that," Sam said, and moved closer to the map.

"Here's something though," she said. "In Carslyle's papers we found a bill-of-sale for the *Concordances*. He bought it from a book dealer. Right here."

Her finger stopped on a red dot near Edinburgh.

Mike moved up and stood at her shoulder so that he could read what it said.

"Linlithgow," he read. "There's our starting point."

25

Night was just starting to fall as the flight to Glasgow took off from Iceland.

"I must have slept longer than I thought," Patty said. "But it shouldn't be night already, surely?"

Seton laughed.

"No. It's just that Scotland moved closer while we were in the air. You're forgetting the time zone difference. We're going to be jet-lagged for a few days I'm afraid."

The three hours they'd spent in the airport terminal had gone uneventfully. Patty spent most of it watching Seton. There was something about him that reminded her of a predator; a big cat, or maybe an eagle. It was in his eyes, and the way he noticed everything that was going on, while all the while appearing casually disinterested. He also had the same sense of fun she'd seen in animals at play; all needs met and content to just *hang out and chill.*

She sat sipping coffee and guiltily smoking another of Seton's cigarettes while he checked the perimeter. If you weren't actually watching him, you'd think he was just another little man, walking the waiting area, passing time idly. You wouldn't notice that he checked out all the entrances, or that he had a good close look at all the people in the hall sitting alone.

Even as he made a phone call his eyes were always watching.

"All clear," he'd said on his return.

"Who were you calling?"

"Just making some arrangements for transport in Glasgow," he said. "Nothing you need to worry about."

"I won't even bother asking," she said. "You're not *really* a journalist, are you?"

"My secret is out," he replied. "I have written journals, but no, I'm not a journalist. I'm a researcher. Most of the time."

"In what field?"

"I think you've guessed that already? I dabble in esoterica… and before you ask, that's got nothing to do with kinky sex."

"Pity," Patty said smiling.

She got a smile back.

"Mostly I hunt down weird stuff. I'm a bit of a history geek."

More than a bit, Patty thought.

For the rest of the time before their flight he told stories, about the history of Iceland, with diversions into bloody sagas that told of revenge, redemption, and love lost, only to be found again. He was a natural storyteller, and had Patty captivated.

And now that they were safely on the plane, he was at it again. Patty was in the window seat, and Seton leaned right over her to look out of the window.

"Look," he said. "A fire wurm."

A fissure in the land below glowed red; a thin line of lava belched orange flares into the sky.

"The dragon is breathing," Seton said. "Can you imagine, millennia ago, when the first wanderers came to this place not long after the ice retreated? Can you imagine what they thought of the heat that chased the ice away and heated the water? They made it a god."

He looked down at the rapidly receding line of fire. Patty watched his eyes. They twinkled with excitement and delight. She struggled to find the right word to describe them, then realized it was one she hadn't heard used in a while. But it fit Seton perfectly. What she saw in his eyes was *joy*.

He caught her looking.

"It's a volcano," he said by way of explanation. "You don't get to see them very often."

"Is there anything that doesn't fascinate you?"

He sat back in his seat and took her hand.

"No," he said. "But if it makes you feel better, I'm not too fond of cats?"

Patty looked out the window again, but they were now over sea, and darkness was falling fast.

"I do hope you've got a plan in mind," she said.

"A particularly cunning one," he said. "We find who sold the manuscript to Carslyle, and see if he knows what happened to the missing four pages."

"That's it?"

"Unless you can think of anything else we should be doing?"

Patty shook her head.

"Well, at least it has the value of simplicity in its favor."

"Just like me," Seton said, and smiled.

"So how do we find this dealer? I take it he won't be legit?"

"I doubt it," Seton replied. "But luckily I know most of the shady operators who would be both interested, and capable, of the deal."

"Now why doesn't that surprise me," Patty said.

They sat in silence for most of the rest of the flight, but he didn't let go of her hand, even after he fell asleep and started to snore loudly. The woman in the aisle seat gave her a pitying glance, but Patty found comfort in the sheer banality of it. It gave her something normal to hold on to in a world that was threatening to eat her up and spit her out again.

Besides, it's been a long time since I was as near a man as this.

She held his hand tighter, remembering John. They'd been high school, then college sweethearts. Completely inseparable for nearly six years, she'd have done anything for him. And he idolized her… or so she'd thought. Right up until the morning she left work early feeling flu coming on. She'd meant to curl up in bed. But it was already too crowded, what with John and his secretary being in there already.

Five years. Five long years.

She'd got used to being alone, losing herself in her work and simple pleasures. But the last two days had woken something she'd thought was dead. What she felt now, wasn't guilt, wasn't worry.

She looked down at Seton once more.

I should wake him up and tell him, she thought. *I've got there now. I'm actually happy.*

Seton woke as they were starting their descent into Glasgow.

"How long has it been since you were last home?" Patty asked.

He got a faraway look in his eyes.

"I haven't had a home for a long time. But if you mean back here, in Scotland, it's been a few years. But I don't expect it to have changed that much."

The plane bounced twice on landing to welcome him back.

"Home is the sailor," he said softly.

They taxied slowly to the terminal. Seton still held Patty's hand.

"Hold back and let everyone else off first," he whispered in her ear. "I want to see if anyone is paying special attention to us."

As he drew away he nibbled lightly on her earlobe.

"That reminds me," he said. "By the time we get out of the airport it'll be time for breakfast. Then we'll find out whether you're a porridge or kippers type of person."

"*Porridge* or *kippers*?"

He nodded.

"You can tell a lot about a person by what they order given only those choices," Seton said.

"But I don't like either," she protested.

"Doesn't matter," he replied. "It's the choice that counts."

"In that case," she said. "I'll have…"

Seton held up his hand.

"No. This is important," he said, smiling. "But it has to be done at a breakfast table if it's to be done properly. We'll find out later."

The people around them started to disembark. Patty noticed that Seton was watching them all very closely.

"Do you think we've been followed?" Patty said softly.

He shook his head.

"No. Not on *this* plane anyway. But there might be someone looking for us, either here, or in the terminal building. It's time for some of that sneakiness I mentioned earlier."

He waited until the last person left the plane before he got up.

"Looks like we're OK so far."

He took her arm.

"Welcome home Mrs. Hannay," he said as they stepped off the plane. He kissed her on the cheek. "I wish I could have brought you here under better circumstances. But needs must."

She kissed him back.

"Just in case you haven't noticed, you're doing just fine."

By the time they got into the long soulless corridor that led down to the center of the terminal Seton had that predatory, watchful look back. Patty tried to see things through his eyes. But all she saw was a nearly empty corridor.

"What are we looking for?"

"Not just looking," Seton said. "Listening, tasting. It could be something small, or something big. But there'll be something to tell us."

"Tell us what?"

"Whether it's safe to go through customs or not."

The public address system chose that moment to shout into life.

"*Would Mr. and Mrs. Hannay inbound from Reykjavik please report to the security office at passport control?*"

"I guess that's a '*No*' then?" Patty said.

Seton smiled.

"That's why it helps to have a backup plan," he said. He took her by the arm and led her to a service exit.

No members of the public beyond this point.

"Come on. This is where we get off."

"What about our luggage?" she said.

"That's getting seen to."

Seton pushed the door open. An alarm went off in the ceiling above them, its wailing screech loud enough to cause pain.

"Now will you get a move on?" Seton said.

They ran down the stairs and emerged out onto the taxiing area at the side of the terminus. A small truck came straight at them and Patty turned back, heading for the stairs again. Seton stopped her by taking her arm.

"Don't worry. It part of the plan."

The truck came to a stop beside them and a very hairy man stuck his head out the window.

"Taxi for Mr. Hannay?" he said, and cackled like a cartoon witch.

"Get in," Seton said, pushing her into the passenger side seat. He climbed inside after her. It was so cramped that she was wedged right up close to the hairy driver. He smelled like he hadn't washed in weeks.

He must have noticed her discomfort.

"Excuse the whiff missus," he said. "But you've cadged a lift wi' the shite wheecher."

His accent was so thick that she only caught every second word, but even then she only understood half of them. She turned to Seton, who was laughing into the back of his hand.

"We've hitched a ride with the van that empties the plane's latrines," he explained.

"Aye. Was that no' whit I said?" the big man replied.

"You have to excuse the lady," Seton said. "She's American."

"A Yank eh? Well let me tell you, I ken a wee bit aboot Yanks. Did ye ken that…"

He drove them along the side of the main terminal all the while keeping up a line of chat she couldn't follow.

She tuned out his voice, but couldn't do anything about the smell. Thankfully Seton wound down the window on his side, but that only helped marginally. Breathing through her mouth didn't help either, bringing a thick, cloying, taste to the back of her throat.

"You call this a plan?" she said to Seton.

"One of my best," he replied. "Nobody looks twice at a toilet cleaner."

"Aye," the man beside her said. "Ma wife calls me *The Invisible Man*. Mind you, that could be because I'm never in the hoose when it's time to do the cleaning. And I don't mind the smell. It actually comes in handy in the pub… I can get a clear space at any bar in toon."

He laughed loudly.

They drove out of a service entrance onto the main road outside the airport.

"Have a guid nicht," he said as he left them on the pavement. It was after three in the morning local time, but the place bustled as people vied to get on buses or get into cars and cabs.

Seton handed her a cigarette and they lit up gratefully.

"Do you think he always smells like that?" she asked.

"Only on the good days," Seton replied, and suddenly they were both laughing.

"Best get going," he said when they finished their cigarettes.

"Our luggage?" she asked again.

"Either it's being held by the security people, or the backup plan worked and it'll catch up with us," Seton replied.

He hailed a cab. "In the meantime, let's go see a man about some breakfast."

The cab dropped them off outside a bar nearly half an hour later.

The Twa Dugs the sign said, and showed two greyhounds standing side by side. There was a faded notice in the window.

"This is a bar. That means we sell alcohol. We may also sometimes sell you a packet of crisps or a mutton pie and beans, but we do not guarantee to have any food on the premises. If you want food, I suggest you go to a restaurant. But if it's booze you're after, come on in, we've got plenty."

"Classy joint," Patty said.

"You'd be surprised the people that have been here at one time or another," Seton replied.

There were no lights on in the bar, but when Seton rapped on the window the door was opened almost straight away. A portly, gray-haired man showed them inside.

A long mahogany bar ran the length of the far side of the room, high stools spaced along its length. In the main bar area sat an array of tables of different shapes, sizes and ages, some Formica tops, some mock burnished copper, some scratched and stained wood. The chairs stacked on the tables were the same mish-mash, plastic, pine and padded leather. Along the three walls ran a leather bench, ticking escaping in places, other rips badly patched with black tape. The wallpaper had at one time been floral flock, but was now stained yellow with nicotine and the windows, ornately inlayed with adverts for long defunct breweries, looked like they hadn't been cleaned in living memory.

The man who'd showed them in stuck out a hand

"Alex. Good to see you again. Fancy a beer?"

Seton shook the offered hand.

"Maybe later George," he said. "Thanks for getting us out of the airport."

"Nae problem," George said. "And your luggage shouldn't be far behind you. I had a lad wait at the carousel like you asked."

Seton nodded.

"He might have a long wait. Security could decide to have a look at it when we fail to turn up."

George shook his head.

"He's got it already. He rang in just before you got here. He said the place was in an uproar."

"That would be my fault then," Seton said smiling.

"And not for the first time. Remember when…"

Patty sensed this was not going to be a short conversation. She cleared her throat loudly and the men went quiet.

"You two know each other then?" she said.

George looked her up and down.

"You were right," he said to Seton. "She is Anne's double."

He stuck out a hand.

"George Dunlop," he said. "Any friend of Alex is a friend of mine."

"Check your purse after shaking hands with this one," Seton said laughing. "And your knickers. George can have both off you in seconds."

"Rubbish. I believe you hold the record for relieving a wench of her panties," George said. "One night in the back bar. Remember?"

Seton grinned.

"I remember she was *really* ugly."

"You shouldn't have drunk so much whisky," George said, laughing back.

Patty sat down at a table.

"If there are stories to be told, could I have a drink?"

"A lady after my own heart," George said, and winked at her.

He returned a minute later with a whisky bottle and three glasses.

She sat back and enjoyed the show as the two men talked.

It was obvious that they were old friends. Casual acquaintances would never get away with the level of insults that they casually threw at each other.

"So, let's get this straight…" Seton said.

"That's funny. That's just what you said to the lassie involved," George interrupted.

Seton roared with laughter.

"At least I was capable," he said.

"That's not what she told me," George replied.

They laughed loudly, then drank a couple of measures of whisky that would have floored Patty if she'd even got close enough to smell them.

George suddenly looked serious.

"This trouble you're in Alex. Are you sure you can handle it?"

Seton nodded.

"We've got it under control."

That's news to me, Patty thought, but kept it to herself.

"All I need to do is get to Linlithgow in the morning," Seton said.

"You're going to see Wee Tam?"

"That's the boy," Seton said. "He's the reason we're all in this trouble in the first place."

"If you need anything," George said. "Money, some boys to help with the muscle… anything. You know you just have to ask?"

Seton clasped George on the shoulder.

"I know," Seton said. "We'll be OK. But if I get into trouble, I'll give you a call."

"Trouble? You mean, like that time you stole the polis man's troosers?"

And off they went in another round of anecdote and insults. As more whisky flowed, George's accent got thicker and she started having trouble following him. Seton on the other hand seemed to remain clear headed and lucid, despite having put away at least as much whisky as his friend.

George was in the middle of a long and very crude story about a nun and a Great Dane when there was a knock at the front window.

"That'll be your luggage now," he said. He stood, rather unsteady, and made for the door.

All Patty heard was a small muffled pop. There was a thud as George's body hit the floor.

They had no time to react as Ross walked into the bar and pointed a gun straight at Seton.

26

Mike squirmed uncomfortably in the cramped seat.

"How much longer?" he asked Sam.

"Another three hours or so," she replied.

The woman who was sitting on Mike's right shifted in her seat again for maybe the fiftieth time since take-off, and her thigh pressed heavily against Mike's leg. He sighed loudly and shifted sideways, but all that did was give her more room to move even further towards him.

"Sorry," Sam said. "It was the earliest flight we could get. I didn't know it was a people crammer."

Crammer is right, Mike thought. Pack them in as tight as possible, and don't feed them. That seemed to be the airline's philosophy. The fact that they were cheap meant they got plenty of customers, but that didn't mean Mike had to like it.

"Maybe this was a mistake," he said.

Sam leaned close to him and kissed him lightly on the cheek.

"What you need is some distraction."

Mike smiled, but it was a struggle.

"Let's talk business," Sam said. "Do we have a plan?"

"Beyond talking to the dealer in Linlithgow? No."

"What about our suspects? Do we still fancy Seton and Doyle for any of the murders?"

Mike shook his head.

"I can't see it. I think they stole the book, sure. But Ross did the homicides. I'd stake my life on that."

Sam agreed.

"But there's still something going on we don't understand. Why did Ross abduct Seton? And what about that tape Adams showed us? What the hell is that all about?"

Mike stretched his back as much as he could.

"We'll know when we find Seton," he said. "And I suspect, when we do that, Ross won't be far away."

The decision to make the trip had been surprisingly easy. And even the finances weren't a big problem. Not yet anyway, although Mike wasn't looking forward to his next credit card bill.

He'd tried to talk Sam out of it.

"You've got a long career ahead of you," he said. "This is only a suspension. You should serve it out quietly, grovel to the Captain a bit, and you'll be back in no time."

"No can do boss. I'm not letting you out on your own in Scotland. *The home of whisky*? Sounds like a place you might not come back from to me."

Mike had smiled.

"I'll take the pledge if it will stop you from making the same mistake as me?"

She shook her head, and kissed him softly.

"You're stuck with me Mike, get used to it."

Mike smiled at the memory. His good mood lasted just as long as it took the large lady to move in her seat again.

"I need to stretch my legs," he said, and got Sam to move so he could get out. The constant reverberating hum of the engines was starting to get to him, sounding like a roaring lion inside his head. He pushed at the small of his back, trying to stretch out the cramp, then walked up the length of the plane and back.

His head was full of theories, but none would mix with any of the others. He still believed that Seton and the woman had stolen the book, possibly to blackmail Carslyle. For some reason the drug company were after the book, and Seton. At every turn people were trying to hoodwink him with bullshit, smoke and mirrors.

Over thinking never solved a case.

He knew that from long experience. Cases got solved by old-fashioned legwork. Catch the perpetrator and get a confession. That was the game they needed to play now. The fact that the bad guy seemed under the influence of a drug that made him strong and fast only made the job more important than ever.

Ross was their target. But he was not the only one. Mike wanted to take Adams down. Mainly because he hated rich men who used the police force as their plaything, but also for that overconfident grin he'd seen as the jet took off.

I'll see that grin wiped off his face. It might cost me my job, but it'll be worth it.

27

"You're looking well," Seton said sarcastically as Ross walked towards them.

The white bandage around his head looked soiled and matted with dried blood. He was still pale, but now his face shone with a gray sweaty pallor, and the gun was far from steady in his hand, but it kept pointing almost straight at Seton.

Patty couldn't take her eyes off the gun, but Seton seemed totally calm and relaxed.

"We need the book. And what you found in it," Ross said. His voice trembled and shook, and there was a watery rumble from deep in his chest that spoke of something badly broken inside him.

"I'm sure you do," Seton said. "But we would be stupid to bring it with us, don't you think?"

"And you would be stupid not to," Ross replied. "We both know it's vital to what we're after."

Seton laughed.

"I've no idea what you're after," he said. "But this is Glasgow. Most things can be had if you've got the money. I suggest Paddy's Market down at the Barrows. They cater for the *exotic* down there."

"Enough of these games Seton," Ross said. "I'm tired."

"You look it. Come and sit down," Seton said. "Have a dram. Let's settle this like Scotsmen."

He lifted the whisky bottle and poured himself a large one. He motioned towards Ross.

"Come on man. This stuff is the water of life. It'll perk you up no end. Get some color back in those cheeks. You could do with some, if you don't mind me saying so?"

Ross didn't move.

"The book?" he said.

"I've told you. I don't have it," Seton replied.

Ross turned and pointed the gun at Patty.

"Last chance," he said to Seton.

Patty was about to reach into her satchel for the book when Seton threw the whisky bottle at Ross. The man dodged the bottle and it smashed harmlessly against the wall behind him, but Seton was already out of his seat. Ross let off a shot that took a chunk out of the table in front of Patty and showered her hand in splinters.

Seton dived for Ross, trying to get in below the gun again. This time he was too slow. Ross brought the butt of the gun down, hard, on Seton's head. A sickening *crack* echoed around the bar.

Alex. Oh Alex.

Seton fell, unmoving, at the man's feet. Ross kicked him, hard, but didn't raise a grunt.

He stepped over the body and once more pointed the gun at Patty.

"Are you as stupid as him?" he said.

Patty shook her head.

She reached into her bag and took out the *Concordances* and the sixteen loose papers.

Ross came and stood over her as she laid them on the table.

He kept the gun on her as he counted the loose pages.

"Sixteen?" he said. "There should be more."

"Don't ask me," Patty said, as calm as she could manage. "I'm just the carrier pigeon. He does all the thinking." She pointed at where Seton lay unconscious on the floor.

Ross wasn't convinced.

"Show me what's in the bag," he said.

Patty opened the bag up and showed him there were no more papers in it. This close up she noticed that Ross looked greasy, and he smelled, a rancid acidic odor, like stale sweat, but nothing she'd ever smelled from a human being before.

Ross seemed confused as to what to do next. He lifted the loose papers and put them in his inside pocket, then took the *Concordances* in his left hand. He started to back away.

The loose page that Patty had torn at the airport chose that moment to slip out of the Concordances. It wafted in the air, drifting to the floor. Ross instinctively bent to catch it.

Just as instinctively Patty shoved the bar table away from her, hitting Ross on the top of the left leg and setting him off balance. Patty pushed again, harder, and Ross fell away to one side.

The gun hand started to come up again. Patty stepped forward and kicked him in the balls as hard as she could. This time there was a grunt. She stamped hard on the hand around the gun, and felt fingers crunch under her foot.

Ross looked even grayer now. He lay on the floor, moaning as Patty took the gun away from him. She raised it, pointing it in his direction.

"Get the *Concordances*," Seton said behind her.

She bent over Ross, keeping the gun aimed at his face. He didn't put up any fight as she took the book. She put it on the ground beside her and reached for the loose papers he'd put in his pocket.

His hand grabbed her by the wrist and started to squeeze. She aimed the gun at his face.

"Let go. Let go, or I'll shoot you."

"No, you won't" Ross said, and squeezed harder.

He was right. She couldn't shoot him. But she didn't have any qualms about causing him some pain. She smacked the gun across his nose. Blood flowed immediately, and Ross let go of her arm.

But in the same movement he grabbed the gun back from her and rolled away across the floor.

Patty picked up the *Concordances*, shoved it in her bag and ran. Seton was still getting to his feet groggily. She grabbed his arm and hauled him towards the door. They had to step over George's body, but didn't have time to stop and check whether he was alive or dead.

A shot took out the big window at the front of the bar, then another hit the doorjamb ahead of them.

Patty ran out into the street, half-dragging Seton along with her.

28

Mike and Sam emerged from the airport into a Glaswegian summer day. The heavy sky overhead was slate gray and flat, and the air was heavy with moisture you could almost chew. Mike started to sweat as soon as they left the terminal heading for the hire car.

They'd discussed the plan of action on the plane. It boiled down to something very simple.

Hire a car, go to Linlithgow, find who had sold Carslyle the book, and hope that Seton, or Ross, or both, turned up.

Step one had been easy. All it took was another hefty hit on Mike's credit card, and they had the use of a car for a week. It was only when Mike went to get in it that he realized things weren't going to be quite so simple.

The steering wheel was on what he thought of as the *passenger* side. Once he got round behind the wheel, he got another shock. It was a manual shift, five gears and a reverse.

Sam saw his confusion and laughed.

"I haven't driven a stick since the tractor on Uncle Joe's farm. I was sixteen."

Sam laughed again.

"It's over fifty miles to Linlithgow," she said. "Don't get us dead."

Mike took a few practice trips round the airport car park to get used to the vehicle, but it was going to take him a bit longer to get used to being on the wrong side of the road. What with that, the different road markings and traffic signals, and the general weight of traffic, it took them nearly an hour to reach Glasgow itself. Once there, they got stuck in a tailback that was going nowhere fast.

"We get off on the M8? That's what the guy at the hire car desk said?"

"Yes," Sam replied. "Get on the M8 and stay on it till you get to the Linlithgow turnoff, that's what he said. If we hit Edinburgh, we've gone too far."

"I think we've already gone too far," Mike muttered.

He stared out at the queue of traffic. It was four lanes wide and snaked away from them in a long curve that headed up a hill and out of sight.

If I wanted to sit in traffic, I could have stayed at home.

"Any idea how far to the M8 junction?"

"Yes," Sam said and smiled. "I come this way every day."

Mike hit the steering wheel in frustration.

Sam turned on the car radio.

The first station was playing a truly terrible version of "Your Cheating Heart" sung in a Scottish accent. She tried another, and got a news report.

At first Mike didn't listen, being too busy trying to contain his frustration. But something caught his attention.

"Turn it up," he said.

The Scottish tones of the broadcaster were strange to the ear, but the news was all too familiar.

"Police are investigating the shooting of publican George Thorpe in the early hours of this morning. In a brutal and seemingly unmotivated attack Mr. Thorpe received a bullet wound in the chest, but is in a stable condition in the Southern General Hospital. He is believed to have described his assailant as a tall pale American man. Police are warning the public to be on the lookout, as this man is considered armed, and extremely dangerous."

Mike and Sam looked at each other.

"It's too big a coincidence," Sam said.

"Agreed," Mike replied. "What say we get off this road and head for the hospital? Maybe this Thorpe will be able to tell us something."

"What about the plan?" Sam said as he pulled out onto the hard shoulder and started to reverse back to the previous exit.

Cars honked and people rolled down their windows to shout abuse.

"I was never big on planning," Mike said. "I never had much talent for it."

"No," Sam said as someone else honked loudly as they passed. "Your special talent is pissing people off."

It took them a while to find their way to the Southern General, through a circuit of one-way systems, road-works and rush-hour traffic, but finally they drove into the large parking area in front of the main building.

"I know you're not big on plans boss," Sam said. "But how do we get to see this guy? There'll be cops crawling all over him."

Mike smiled, and produced a badge from his pocket.

"Well, we're cops aren't we?"

"I thought you left that with the Captain?"

Mike grinned.

"He got the replica. I had one made up years ago."

"Funny you should say that," Sam replied, and also took out a badge. "Looks like planning is our forte after all."

The badges got them through reception and onto the ward where George Thorpe was being treated, but there they hit a wall.

He was a policeman and at least six foot two tall. He looked like he ate rottweilers for breakfast. His face was beet root red, and he was breathing heavily, like a bull before a charge. His suit, shiny at knees and elbows, was a full-size too small for him, and he looked like he'd burst if he kept breathing too energetically. The corridor shook and Mike could feel himself inwardly cringe as the cop approached them. If he'd said '*Fee-fi-Fo-Fum*' Mike wouldn't have been surprised.

"I've told you bastards already," he said. "Nae reporters."

Mike showed his badge.

"Lieutenant Mike Turner, NYPD." he said.

"Aye," the big cop said belligerently. "What about it?"

"We're here on a case."

"Aye," the big cop said, more belligerently, and louder this time. "What about it?"

Mike knew when a pissing contest was coming. Usually he managed to avoid them, but this time he wasn't in the mood.

"We're here on a case," Mike repeated, louder than before, and stared at the big man.

"So am I. And I was here first. So bugger off hame, there's a good Yank."

Mike could feel the red rage coming down. All the frustration of the last few days were about to come down to a knock down fight with a Scottish cop.

This could get messy.

Luckily Sam knew the signs. She stepped in between the two men.

"We're here to see your victim," she said. She touched the Scotsman's arm, and smiled. From that moment, the big cop was lost. Mike backed away and left her to it.

"We think we're after the same man as you are," she said. "Tall, pale American? Possibly with a head wound?"

"I'm nae saying anything," the cop said, but Mike had seen the reaction to the head wound statement.

We're on the right track.

"At least tell me your name big man," Sam said, and smiled again.

He took his time, but seemed to come to a decision. He smiled back at her and gave her a hand to shake.

"Detective McCall," he said. "Jock McCall, from Partick CID."

"There. That wasn't hard, was it?"

That got Sam another smile.

Go girl, Mike thought. *He'll be eating out of your hand in no time.*

"We've come a long way Jock," Sam said quietly. "We'd like to see the patient. As a favor? One cop to another?"

McCall looked from Mike to Sam.

"Tell me what you know, and I'll see about letting you in to talk to Thorpe."

Once more Mike left the talking to Sam.

"It started with a triple homicide," she began.

She laid out the story. She missed out the parts where they got kicked off the force.

That was probably for the best.

McCall never took his eyes off her all the time she was speaking.

"Ross you say? A security guard?" he said when she finished.

Sam nodded.

"He works for Adams Pharmaceuticals. I'm sure they'll provide you with all the details."

McCall believed her.

Why wouldn't he? When she smiles like that, anyone would believe her.

He was still reticent about letting them in to see the patient though.

"The docs say he needs plenty of rest. We really shouldn't disturb him."

Sam had an answer for that. Mike knew from bitter experience that she had an answer for most everything.

"Tell him we're friends of Alex Seton's," she said. "If that doesn't get his attention, then we've come to the wrong place anyway."

"I'll go and ask," the big cop replied. He took his time dragging his eyes off Sam before heading off along the corridor.

"You Jezebel you," Mike said, and Sam laughed.

"The Mendoza charm is a powerful thing," she said.

"Don't I know it."

"It took its time working on you though."

"Sorry," Mike said. "I'm slow on the uptake."

"I'm just glad you got there eventually."

The big man was already coming back along the corridor. He seemed to fill it.

"I can give you five minutes with him," he said. "But no more. He's hurt bad. He had open chest surgery just a couple of hours ago, and he's no' happy."

"Neither would I be after that kind of operation," Mike said.

"That's no' what I mean," the big man replied. "Somebody broke the big old window in his pub. He's really no' happy."

They noticed that as soon as they entered the room. Thorpe was hooked up to monitors tubes and drip bags. From his expression he was just about the most miserable thing that Mike had ever seen. There had been a whipped dog in an animal rescue center that came close, but Thorpe had even that beat.

"Mr. Thorpe," Mike said from the doorway. "We're from the NYPD. We'd like to ask you a few questions about the attack."

"More bloody Yanks," Thorpe said. "This day just gets better and better."

A doctor approached them. Mike already knew all the moves. The doctor would say "OK but only for a minute" or "It's touch and go. The next few hours will be crucial" or "It could be minutes, it could be days... you never know with these cases." The policemen usually get to say nothing. They just stand around and chew the scenery in frustration.

Not this time.

Mike strode forward, ignoring the medic completely. Sam completed the maneuver by intercepting the doctor as Mike went to the bedside.

"We're here to help Alex Seton," Mike said. "And to catch Ross."

"He's the lanky streak of pish that shot me?" Thorpe said. He coughed, then winced as pain hit him.

"You'd think they could have been a wee bit less careful wi' the morphine," he said. "Or at least let me have some whisky. I had some earlier, but it's worn off. Getting shot does that to a man. Hae you ever been shot?"

Mike nodded.

"Twice. Hurts like a son of a bitch."

"That it does," Thorpe said. He looked at Mike, appraising him.

"You know Alex?"

"Never met him," Mike said. "But we know that Ross is after him, and we want to get to him first."

"He's a hard wee bugger to catch," Thorpe said, and laughed, then winced again. "Remind me no' to do that."

"Mr. Thorpe," Mike said softly. "About Seton?"

"He can look after himself."

"But what about Miss Doyle?"

"The brunette? She's what you Yanks call, a tough cookie. I wouldnae worry about her."

Mike filed the *brunette* part away for reference.

"Mr. Thorpe, if I wasn't a patient man, I'd think you were stalling."

"And if I wasn't a *patient* I might get out this bed and kick your arse out the door," Thorpe said. He coughed again, and his face screwed up in pain. "I thought you were going to remind me no' to do that?"

He sighed.

"This man Ross, what's he done?"

"Four murders that we know of, along with kidnap, attempted murder and fleeing the country. And he's pissed me off."

Thorpe smiled.

"I can see that. And that I can understand," he said. "Alex and the lassie are on their way to Linlithgow. There's a dodgy book dealer they want to talk to… name of Tam McGuire."

"And Ross?"

Thorpe laughed and winced.

"Last I saw was him running out after Alex. Well, staggering more than running. He was holding his balls as if they were going to fall off."

Thorpe laughed loudly at the memory, then started to cough. Blood came up.

The doctor finally got away from Sam's charms and pulled Mike away from the bedside.

"That's enough," he said. "This man needs to rest."

Thorpe laughed through the pain.

"What *this man* needs is a drink. Come back and tell me the story when you're done," he said to Mike. "I've always got some single malt ready for a good story."

Mike smiled back.

"I've taken the pledge," he said. "Otherwise I'd take you up on that."

"It's a shame to see a good man going to waste," Thorpe said, and laughed so hard that more blood came up.

"That's enough," the doctor shouted. "I want this room emptied. Right now."

He bundled them all out.

McCall stopped Mike and Sam from going much further than the door.

"I want you two to remember this is a Partick CID case," he said. "You don't have any jurisdiction here. And we don't need any John Wayne cowboy shit."

Sam nodded.

"We know that Detective. We won't get in anybody's way. But we'd like to come along for the ride. I presume you *will* be going to Linlithgow?"

"That's outside *my* jurisdiction," he said, and laughed. "It'll take time for me to get permission. But I can't stop a pair of tourists from visiting the old Palace in the meantime can I?"

Sam laughed.

"No. I don't suppose you can. And we promise there'll be no cowboy tactics. If we find Ross, we won't move without contacting you first."

"Just don't tell my Chief I know about this," McCall said. "He'll have my balls for breakfast."

Mike clapped the big man on the shoulder.

"Get him to call my Captain. He had mine yesterday, scrambled."

Five minutes later Mike drove out of the Hospital Car Park.

"So. How do we get to Linlithgow again?" Sam said.

29

Patty sighed as they got into their seats on the 12:15 train from Queen Street to Edinburgh.

"At last, I can relax a bit."

Seton took her hand.

"Just a bit," he said. "For about forty minutes."

She closed her eyes, and tried to calm herself. The previous six hours were a blur. She'd dragged Seton from the bar and ran, with no idea where they were going. Seton was moving on instinct, legs working but brain somewhere else, and Patty had no plan, just to run, as far and as fast as possible.

And that they had done, stopping only when Seton started to buckle at the knees. They'd been on the outskirts of a park, and Patty half-dragged half-carried Seton to a bench in a secluded corner.

And there she'd sat, with Seton's head in her lap, as night became day.

He'd almost woken once. He looked up at her, and smiled.

"Anne," he said, his eyes wet with tears.

"Shush dear," she replied, and stroked his hair until he slept again.

Several times he muttered in his sleep, words that sounded Latin, but made no sense to Patty.

Solutio, materia prima, sublimatio, volate. Solutio, materia prima, sublimatio, volate.

But all she had to do to calm him was stroke his hair and he regressed back to sleep.

She had no idea how long they sat there. There was no appreciable dawn, just a lighter shade of gray. She twitched every time someone came into view, but most were people in their way to work.

Work. I remember that.

She'd been living in Seton's Now Time for so long that she'd almost forgotten her previous life... her real life. Sitting here on a park bench in another country, the office seemed very far away. But all she had to do was close her eyes and she could see. They were still there, just behind her eyes. She suspected they'd always be there.

She chose to stay awake, cradling Seton's head.

An old lady passed, pushing a shopping trolley full of empty bottles.

"Too much bevvy?" she said.

Patty was flummoxed, and chose the standard city option of ignoring street people. But this one wasn't to be denied. She came and sat next to Patty at the end of the bench.

"I asked," she said, loudly, as if talking to someone she though might be a bit slow. "Has he had too much bevvy?"

She was lined and weather-beaten, and her clothes had been patched so often they looked like a quilt made by drunken dwarves. Grime had embedded itself in all the wrinkles and folds in her skin, and she smelled, of lavender and mothballs.

"Some folk jist don't ken how to look after themselves," she said, and cackled. "No' like me. I never touch the stuff, and I'm as fit as a fiddle." She coughed loudly, wheezed and hawked up a lump of phlegm that looked disgustingly solid as it hit the path in front of them. "You don't have a fag do you hen? I'm gasping."

Seton shook in Patty's arms. She looked down, worried he might be having a seizure, but to her astonishment found he was trying to hold in laughter.

He sat up and gave the old woman a kiss full on the lips.

"My princess, you have awoken me from my slumber," he said. "Permit me to bestow upon you a great gift. Guard it wisely, and it will bring you great joy."

He handed the woman a pack of cigarettes, stood, took Patty's hand and led her away.

"Like I said," the old woman shouted after them. "Too much bevvy."

Seton was still laughing as they left the park.

"Are you OK," Patty asked.

"I'm as fit as a fiddle," he said in a close approximation of the old woman's voice."

That got Patty going, and they were both laughing as they hailed a cab.

"Ah, young love," the cabbie said as they got in. "Where to folks... is it a walk on the beach or a romantic breakfast?"

"Queen Street station," Seton said. "And breakfast is a great idea. I could eat a horse."

"Funny you should say that," the cabbie replied as he pulled away, and launched into a long story about an Indian curry house, a racehorse and a dodgy bookmaker. Seton laughed at all the right places, but the man's accent was so strong that Patty only caught half of it.

Not that it bothered her. She was too interested in the sights out of the window. Glasgow was a bewildering mixture of old sandstone buildings intermixed with modern monstrosities of glass and metal. The area they were currently driving through consisted of a row of restaurants intermixed with small ethnic shops and newsagents, and it seemed like every race on earth was represented in less than twenty yards of pavement.

The shops soon gave way to more of the tall sandstone building, the street so narrow that it felt like they drove through a canyon. Patty felt strangely at home. If she squinted slightly, these could almost be streets that she knew.

The cabbie chose that moment to wax lyrical

"See this place? I love it. But see these folk?"

He waved his hand at a crowd of people leaving a subway station.

"For these people, the Glesga I know is a foreign country. They visit it during their working hours, but they only see what is on the surface, what the city lets them see. They don't remember that all around them is a dark, old lady, brooding and cold. She mostly lets herself show at nights, in the bars, around the docklands, and in the vast cemeteries which mark where all her children lie sleeping.

"Some of them might occasionally catch a glimpse of her, in the face of a drunk, in the hands of a beggar. But they soon forget her once safely home and locked into their hooses with their soap operas and reality shows and their TV dinners and boxes of Australian wine.

"Cabbies are never allowed to forget her. And neither should you."

"I think we met her already," Seton said, and laughed again.

The cab dropped them off outside the station.

"In case you hadn't noticed," Patty said. "We've lost our luggage. And if I don't get a change of clothes soon, you'll smell me before you see me."

Seton took her by the arm.

"Then my lady *shall* go to the ball. Let's go shopping."

Patty quickly found that Glasgow had a thriving shopping center, with a surprising number of big name designer shops. Equally as surprising was the fact that Seton didn't seem to mind spending money on her.

"Get what you need," he said. "My credit cards are at your disposal."

She limited herself to several sets of underwear, a woolly jumper, a pair of sensible walking boots and a heavy waterproof jacket. When she met up with Seton he was already wearing new boots and a similar waterproof.

"Great minds think alike," he said.

They bought a travelling bag for the underwear for both of them.

Seton looked up at the large clock hanging from the ceiling in the shop.

"Time we were getting moving," he said.

They had arrived at the railway station at 12:05. Seton had got tickets and hurried Patty through onto a train that was getting ready to depart.

Now they sat, side by side, going backwards into the future.

Patty opened her eyes. Seton was staring at her.

"Are you *sure* you're OK?" she asked him.

He knocked on his forehead with his knuckles.

"Sound as a bell," he said. "I just needed some sleep."

"I'm sorry about your friend," Patty said.

"Me too," he said, taking her hand. "But I'm pretty sure he was still breathing, and he's a tough old fart. We'll have more time left to tell stories I think. But what about you? How are you doing?"

She didn't have to think about it. She covered their joined hands with her other one.

"I'm fine. I was worried about you though."

"Now that's one worry I'll allow you. There was no sign of Ross while I was out?"

"No. We lost him after getting out of the bar. I guess I slowed him down."

"For a while anyway."

"And another thing," she said. "You talk in your sleep."

"Nothing incriminating I hope?"

"That depends. Does *Solutio, materia prima, sublimatio, volate* mean anything to you?"

"Ah. Maybe it was incriminating after all," he said, almost to himself. He squeezed her hand.

"Let's have another look at the *Concordances* shall we?"

Patty let go of his hand and rooted in her bag.

"Shit. I forgot. Ross got the loose papers."

"All sixteen of them?"

She nodded. She took the *Concordances* from her bag and put it on the small folding tray that came down from the seat in front of them.

"Not a problem," Seton said. "It's the missing four that are the important ones. But forget that for now. You want to know why I was spouting Latin?"

He took the book and opened it.

"*Solutio*," he said and pointed at a picture. It showed a tall figure with two faces, one old, one young. The young one looked over a winter scene, the old one over summer. The bottom half of the figure seemed to be melting into a deep black pool, but both faces were smiling.

"I've seen this figure before," Patty said.

"Yes, in stained glass, at Carslyle's place. I don't know whether he knew the significance, but I'm betting he did."

"What significance?"

"That this is one of the main steps in the great journey," he said. "The male and female principals are subsumed and dissolved by oil of mercury, the last vestiges of the old removed, preparing the way for the new."

Patty laughed.

"Nope. Didn't get that either."

"Think of it as melding the psyche into one un-conflicted whole?"

"Be at one with yourself before you can be at one with the world?"

Seton laughed.

"Very good Grasshopper. Let's see how you do with this one."

He turned the page again.

"*Sublimatio*," he said. "To transfer into the Macrocosm and leave the world behind."

The picture showed a white dove rising out of the same black pool as before.

"That one I do get," Patty said. "Rising to a higher consciousness?"

"Or something similar," Seton said. "Or it could be more prosaic, meaning simply, *Be prepared to leave the things of your old world behind*. Then again, and more appropriate to our current quest, it is quite probable that it's a metaphor for another chemical process, one which sublimates the oil of mercury releasing the essential spirit of the elixir of life."

Patty laughed.

"All of this is making my head spin."

Seton joined her in laughing.

"For that you'll need *Ritus exorcizandi obsessos a dæmonio*."

"Just keep me away from green pea soup and I'll be OK," she replied.

They sat for a while in comfortable silence.

Seton took her hand again.

"Things could get a *bit* exciting from here on in," he said.

"Oh good," Patty replied. "I've been getting a bit bored. Nobody's tried to kill me for at least six hours."

Seton gave her a peck on the cheek.

"That's my girl," he whispered.

Patty didn't get a chance to reply. The train pulled into Linlithgow Station and she had to hurry to get the *Concordances* back into her satchel.

Two minutes later they stood outside the station, blinking in a sudden burst of sunshine. Suddenly it felt much warmer.

"There's a saying round about here," Seton said. "If you don't like the weather, just wait for five minutes."

Patty raised her head, letting the heat soak into her face. The air also felt fresh, a slight breeze bringing with it the smell of new-mown grass. She had such a sudden memory of childhood that the nostalgia of it threatened to bring a tear to her eye.

"Make the most of it lass," Seton said. "It could be the last sunshine we see all day. Maybe all week. Look."

He pointed to a range of small hills that could just be seen beyond the town.

"There's another saying. If you can't see the hills, it's raining."

"And if you can see the hills?"

"Then it's going to rain."

They were still laughing as she took his arm and they walked down a small hill to a town that reminded her how far she was from home.

A large red sandstone Palace dominated the far side of a small cobbled square, looking like something from a fairy tale; a fairly stolid, sensible fairy tale where castles were big square and slightly dull. Around the square were small shops and bars. The place was nearly empty of people.

"Now I feel almost at home," Seton said. "Come on. Let's got and see a man about a book."

She wasn't really surprised when Seton led her into another bar. It was as deserted as the streets around it. They were the only customers apart from a crumpled, disheveled figure in one corner. The man waved at them. Seton made a drinking motion with his right hand, and he held up an empty beer glass in response.

"Do you know him?" Patty asked.

"He's the reason we're here," Seton replied. Patty carried their overnight bag while Seton carried three large glasses of beer and they went and joined the man.

"Bitter and Twisted… your favorite," Seton said as he put the beer down.

"I like my beer the way I like my women," the man said, and laughed. And at that Patty's whole view of him changed.

At first glance he looked like a down-and-out, but he was clean… and clean-shaven… and his clothes, though old and frayed at collar and cuffs, were washed and newly ironed. But it was the smile that did it. His whole face got involved and his grin lit up the room. The laugh that followed was deep and melodious.

"Patty Doyle, meet Tam. Tam is an expert in rare books, among other things" Seton said.

The man laughed again. Patty suspected he did that a lot.

"I'm his mole in the underworld… just call me Deep Throat."

"More like Deep Pockets," Seton said laughing. "When was the last time you bought the beer?"

The man smirked.

"When was the last time you brought me any information?"

"Touché," Seton said. "But you'd better get the moths out of your wallet. Show him what we brought Patty."

She took out the *Concordances* and laid it on the table.

The man's smile came back full beam.

"Good. There are stories to tell. We'll need more beer."

Although Patty had drunk no more than the top inch of her pint, both Seton and the man McGuire were already near the bottom of theirs.

She declined when McGuire offered her a drink.

She watched the man stand, somewhat unsteadily and begin a stagger to the bar.

"Does he always drink so much?" she whispered to Seton.

Seton watched McGuire with affection.

"Aye. He says he drinks to forget."

"Forget what?" she asked.

"I can't remember," McGuire bawled in her ear. His booming laugh followed him as he wobbled towards the bar.

"How do you know him?" Patty asked.

"Oh, we go way back," Seton said, but he was being cagey.

Patty didn't get time to press further as the man came back quickly with two more beers.

Seton had a mouthful of his before talking.

"Let's cut the crap Tam," he said. "You know why I'm here."

Tam sipped his beer and wiped foam off his lips. He nodded towards the *Concordances*.

"You got that from Carslyle I presume?" he said.

"Aye. And we need what was inside…"

"I didn't touch them," McGuire said. "I left them all there."

"You left sixteen there," Seton said. "There were twenty."

Tam took another gulp of beer.

"Nope. There were only sixteen."

"Look Tam," Seton said. "I know you did a great job of sewing it back up again, I saw it. But you and I both know there were twenty sheaves in there when it was first stitched up. You had proof of that."

"I thought I did," McGuire said. "But I swear Alex, there was just the sixteen."

"And?"

McGuire suddenly looked shifty.

"You always were crap at poker, Tam" Seton said. "And what?"

"What's it worth?"

"Keeping your name out of the Carslyle murder inquiry for one," Patty said.

"And keeping in my good books for two," Seton said. "Don't forget how much business I've put your way over the years."

McGuire sighed.

"Best get me another beer," he said to Seton. "Then I'll show you."

Seton left to go to the bar.

"Have you known the wee man long?" McGuire said.

"Seems like a lifetime," Patty replied. "But no. We only met recently."

"Well don't be fooled by the front," McGuire replied. "He's a hard wee bastard. It disnae pay to mess with him."

Patty smiled sweetly.

"I knew that already."

Seton returned from the bar.

"My ears were burning. You weren't telling any tales about me were you Tam?"

McGuire took the beer and swallowed nearly half of it before putting the glass down.

"That would take a while Alex. It's no' as if there's no' plenty stories to tell."

It was Seton's turn to look shifty. Patty realized there was something going on she wasn't privy too, some secret these two shared.

Maybe I'll get lucky, she thought. *Maybe they'll get drunk and tell me.*

Seton got back to the subject.

"Fess up Tam. What have you got?"

McGuire sighed.

"I had a feeling somebody would be coming for this," he said. "And I'm glad it's you."

He took a plain white envelope from inside his jacket and passed it to Seton.

Inside was a single sheet of faded parchment written in a tiny crabbed hand. Patty read over Seton's shoulder, translating as she read.

> *The maister has gone, leaving me to settle his affairs. I cannot allow this terrible calumny to befall another man of God. I will respect the maister and leave his testimony in-*

tact. The sixteen pages have been sewn here in the Concordances and will be hidden deep in the family vault.

But the great secret cannot be allowed such a resting
place, which might be disturbed in years to come. Yet I
cannot bring myself to destroy these four pages that caused
the maister so much grief and suffering. So I will hide
them, in places that only the maister's family might find
them later, in the hope that another may come with the
strength of will to succeed in the great Arcanum.

His faithful Servant
John Samson

In this year of our lord sixteen hundred and forty, in the
land of the guid folk.

Seton laughed.

"Samson. That auld bugger."

"You've heard of him?" Patty asked.

"Oh yes," Seton said. "And I've got a good guess as to
where to go next."

30

It was late afternoon by the time Mike drove off the motorway and down into Linlithgow. It felt like they had only just survived the journey.

"I thought the drivers in the city were bad," Sam said. "But some of these here should be charged with *reckless endangerment.*"

After an hour of dodging cars speeding by like bullets Mike had to agree.

Linlithgow calmed him down. The place was nearly empty and devoid of traffic. Mike parked in the shadow of the Palace.

"This is more like it," Mike said as they got out of the car.

"What first boss?" Sam asked.

"Find McGuire," he said. "You look for a telephone directory, I'll ask around. Meet back here in ten."

She gave him a mock salute and headed off along the pavement.

Mike took a look around. Scouting out information was the same anywhere, whether it was on city streets or here in a rural town. You went where people's tongues were most easily loosened. Experience, and his nose, led him to the nearest bar.

Like the streets outside, the bar was near empty apart from one old man in the corner nursing a half-pint of beer through the afternoon. The room echoed as he walked across the floorboards. From the outside it hadn't looked like much, just a plain frontage with the pub's name, *The Three Marys.* But inside it was a marvel of baroque paintings, leather sofas and tall brass beer fonts that had Mike salivating before he even got near the bar.

"Quiet today," Mike said as a barman came over.

The man smiled sadly.

"It's like this most afternoons sir," he said. "Folk just haven't got the money these days. It'll pick up later when the commuters start coming back from Glasgow and Edinburgh. What can I get you?"

Mike flashed his badge.

"NYPD? Is that real?"

Mike nodded.

"Do you know Andy Sipowitz?" the barman said, and laughed loudly. The sound echoed in the silence. "Sorry, I couldn't help it. I think I'm going stir crazy."

"It's enough to drive a man to drink, right enough." Mike said.

The barman shook his head.

"Not me sir. I see what it does to people, day in, day out. It turns good men into bad men, and bad men into psychopaths."

"A philosopher as well are we?"

He got the echoing laugh again.

"Just like all barmen, great at listening, terrible at talking. Are you here on business?"

"Yep. I'm looking for a book dealer. Name of Tam McGuire?"

"Wee Tam? You just missed him. He had company for a while. When they left, he stayed for a couple more beers. He'll be home sleeping it off by now."

"Company? A tall thin man? Pale faced, high cheekbones?"

"No. A couple. A wee Scots guy and a stunning brunette. She was one of you. An American I mean."

A minute later Mike was back out on the pavement and running towards where he'd last seen Sam.

The address the barman gave them led them to a cul-de-sac at the edge of the town center. A small semi-circle of modern houses ringed a patch of grass that hadn't seen a mower in recent years. To Mike's eyes the houses all looked far too small, too close together.

Why buy a detached house where you're less than three feet from your neighbor?

"Do you think Seton and Doyle are with him?" Sam asked.

"Not according to the barman," Mike said as they walked up the drive. "He said they left earlier. But keep frosty, we might get lucky."

"I wish I had a piece with me."

"Me too," Mike said. "But I'm working up a righteous anger at getting dragged around, and something to hit would do fine right about now."

He walked up to the front door, and was about to knock when the door fell slightly ajar.

"Shit. *Now* I wish I had a piece."

He put a finger to his lips, and Sam nodded back as he stepped inside. He moved quietly down a thickly carpeted hallway. At the far end a door lay open.

McGuire wouldn't be drinking any more beer. He sat slumped over a desk, with blood pooling on the floor at his feet. Someone had added a new smile below his chin.

Mike felt for a pulse. The man was dead, but still warm.

He motioned to Sam that she should take a look around. He bent and had a closer look at the body.

Someone had done a number on McGuire. His face was puffed, skin broken at nose and lips. Two of his fingernails had been violently torn off, and a chunk of his left earlobe was missing. It looked like it had been bitten.

There was something else there too, a gray, slimy substance that felt greasy to the touch. Mike couldn't identify it, and from the smell coming off it, he wasn't sure he wanted to try.

Sam came back.

"Anything?" he asked.

"Nope," she said. She looked down at the body.

"Same M.O. as the guy in the first triple?"

Mike nodded.

"I'm betting it's that bastard Ross," he replied. "And what do you make of this?"

He drew his finger along some of the gray residue and let Sam smell it. She pulled away as if stung.

"That's just *nasty*," she said. "What the hell is it?"

Mike didn't reply. He kept staring at the body, as if an answer might be forthcoming.

"I'm guessing Ross wanted to know what McGuire told Seton," he said.

"And I'm guessing he got what he was after," Sam added.

Mike checked the contents of the desk, but all that was there was writing paper and old worn pencils. He banged his fist on the desk, setting the pencils rolling.

"I didn't come this far for it to end here,"

Sam put a hand on his shoulder.

"Neither did I. But we need to get out of here. This is a crime scene, and we're corrupting the evidence just by being here."

Mike nodded.

They backed out of the house, cleaning up anything they'd touched on the way.

They walked into *The Three Marys* two minutes later.

"Did you find Tam?" the barman asked.

"You were right," Mike said. "He's out of it."

Mike ordered two beers.

"The couple he was with earlier. Any idea where they went?"

The barman looked up over the top of the tall font. He took a long time thinking about it.

"They got me to order them a cab," he finally said. "Listen, I don't want to get involved, and I don't want to get anyone into trouble. "

Sam stepped forward.

"They're in trouble already," she said. "That's why we need to find them. We think they're in danger."

Mike kept quiet and sipped at a beer. Sam was better at the softly-softly approach. Besides, the beer was tasty. And seductive. He put the glass back on the bar.

"Please?" she said.

The barman sighed.

"I only remember because it's a fair way away and the cab fare is going to be huge. They went to Falkland, over in Fife. The wee Scottish guy said something about needing to pay a visit to an old friend's grave."

31

"Look," Seton said, pointing out of the cab window. "Can you see Robert Donat?"

They were crossing a long suspension bridge over a wide estuary that gleamed golden-yellow in the fading light. Four hundred yards away a dark red cantilevered rail bridge spanned the narrowest point of crossing. A commuter train crossed slowly along its length.

"Folk pass across that every day without thinking," the cabbie said. "Ninety eight good men died building that thing. And they spend millions of pounds every year in upkeep on it. It's a scandal in this day and age. Nearly everybody has a car."

"Ah," Seton said. "But there's still magic and romance in train travel."

The cabbie laughed.

"Clearly you've never been on one of them," the cabbie said, waving his hand in the general direction of the train. "At this time of night they'll be packed tighter than sardines, all sweaty and tense after a hard day at the office, and some kid will have his personal stereo turned up too loud, and some other kid will be screaming its head off. And then there'll be a signal failure, and you'll be stuck for an hour, with the heating on full blast and the windows shut. Magic and romance right enough."

"I think I'll stick to thinking about steam trains and carriages with long empty corridors and little compartments," Seton said.

"Aye, dream on mister," the cabbie said. "You should move with the times. All that stuff went out with the dinosaurs."

"That's exactly what I am," Seton said. "A dinosaur."

The cabbie laughed.

"At least let me get you where you're going before you eat me."

It took another forty-five minutes to get to their destination, and by that time it was nearly dark. The cabbie let them out onto a cobbled street outside yet another bar. Old stone buildings lined this side of a wide road, a winding line of them that ran away into the gloom at the far end.

Seton paid the cabbie what seemed to Patty like an excessive amount of money and they were left alone on the pavement outside the bar.

The other side of the road was dominated by a huge gray stone building. Its leaded windows looked like dead black eyes staring back at Patty, and she felt a shiver in her spine.

As they stood at the kerb, it started to rain, a fine mist that felt cold and clammy and almost alive as it wrapped itself around them.

"Best get inside," Seton said. "This stuff will have you drenched in two minutes."

He led Patty into the bar. He got them both a beer and while Patty sat by a fire trying to get warm, Seton got them a room for the night. He came and sat beside her. He offered her a cigarette that she took gratefully.

I'll give up once this is all over. And if this is never all over, at least I'll be happy.

She stared into the fire for a while before talking.

"So. Are you going to tell me what we're doing here?"

"We're here to find the four missing pages," Seton said. "Samson told us they were here, *in the land of the guid folk* or Falk-land as it came to be known. Samson was the servant during the great experiment. Afterwards, he was supposed to sew all twenty pages up but, as you've seen, he held four back. He hid them *where the family would find them.* And that's here, in Falkland."

"Why here?"

"This was the summer home of the Stewarts back as far the Fifteenth century. Samson was one of their men, as were the Setons. I have family buried all around here. And so did Samson. The clues will be here somewhere."

"So what's first?"

He held up his glass.

"Beer. Then maybe another."

"Don't you take anything seriously?"

"That's the wrong question," Seton said. "I take *everything* seriously. Just not at the same time as you do."

He turned so that he was facing her.

"Everything has a natural rhythm," he said. "The Earth spins once a day, goes around the sun once a year. The moon goes round the earth every 28 days. Your heart beats in a rhythm particular only to you. Everything has its drumbeat and everything contributes to the dance. You've just got to know when to lead and when to follow."

"Well I've been doing plenty of following," Patty said.

Seton took her hand.

"That's because you're not listening to the drums," he said. "You're too busy watching all the other dancers. Let me show you a trick."

He took a pocket watch from his jacket and let it hang on the length of its chain. It hung straight down, unmoving.

"Put your hand below the watch," he said. "Palm up."

She did as he asked.

The watch started to move. First it swayed from side to side then slowly started to spin in a circle that widened until the watch rotated slowly above her hand.

"Take your hand away," Seton said.

Again she complied.

The watch stopped moving and went back to hanging dead on the end of the chain.

"Now you try it," he said, handing her the watch.

She took it from him and held it by the chain. The watch hung dead until Seton put his hand under it, whereupon it immediately started to spin in a circle.

When Seton took his hand away, the watch went dead again.

Patty examined the watch.

"You're doing it again," Seton said. "Looking at the dancer rather than the dance."

He took the watch back and held it over his beer. It swung in a much wider circle this time.

"Everything has a beat. Even the beer," he said.

"I think I've heard of this," she said. "It's dowsing, isn't it?"

He shook his head.

"Not quite. A dowsing rod responds to electromagnetic fields. This is more of a mechanism for accessing innate rhythms. Your unconscious makes slight adjustments to your muscles in response to the rhythms, and these are amplified and turned into rotational movement by spin vectors being produced in your fingertips. The same as dowsing, but different, if you get my meaning?"

"No," she laughed. "But its always fun trying to get there. Let me try again."

She took the watch from him and held it by the chain, letting it still before putting her hand under it.

"It will also answer questions," Seton said softly. "Your unconscious knows a lot more than it tells you, but you can fool it and get an answer using the pendulum."

"How?"

"Just let it hang and ask a question you know the answer to," he said. "It will respond with either a yes or no, true or false."

Here goes nothing.

"Is my name Patricia Doyle?"

The watch started to swing, slowly at first then gathering momentum until it swung, in a tight three-inch circle."

"OK," Seton said. "You're a *clockwise positive*."

"What?"

He pointed at the watch.

"Clockwise spin for a true response. Try again, with a false this time."

He reached out and stopped the watch. It hung dead on the end of the chain again.

"This is just a stupid parlor trick. It has to be," she said.

Even before she'd finished the sentence, the watch started to move, side to side at first, then settling down into a tight three-inch circle. A tight counter-clockwise circle."

Patty laughed.

"That doesn't prove anything."

"No. But it is *indicative* of something. To quote the Bard again, *This is wondrous strange*. It gives me hope, that there is more to life than just blood and flesh, that there might just be a point beyond staying alive as long as possible."

"I don't know about that," Patty said. "As you said, if it's anything, it's just your unconscious mind finding an outlet."

Seton looked wistful.

"Maybe. But why not ask it some questions that there is no way you know the answer to either consciously or unconsciously? See what happens then. Would you think it *wondrous* if you started to get some truth from the great beyond?"

Patty looked down at the watch.

"The truth is, I'm afraid to ask," she said quietly.

"Me too," Seton replied, and took the watch away from her.

He put it away in his pocket and stood.

"And now my rhythm says its time we were moving. Come on. Let's get dressed for an adventure."

Twenty minutes later after a quick wash and change they were once more out on the pavement, but this time they were better dressed against the elements, both of them wearing their new boots and waterproofs. It was still raining, and fog draped across the buildings like a muslin shroud. The vapors hung around the old-fashioned style streetlights, giving them an orange glow that looked both eerie and warm simultaneously.

"So, miss worry-boots," Seton said, smiling. "Have you been listening to the beat? What do we do now?"

She smiled back.

"Let's go pay our respects to your family and friends shall we?"

Seton took a flashlight from his pocket.

"Capital idea. And one I had myself. I borrowed this from the cellar in the hope you'd agree with me."

He took her by the arm and led her down the street.

"Is the weather always like this?" she asked, huddling against his shoulder.

"No. Sometimes it gets windy as well," Seton said. He was still laughing at that as they walked the length of the main thoroughfare. At the foot of the street they turned onto a busier road while keeping the Palace itself to their left. Walking the perimeter wall soon brought them to another junction that led away from the main road and down a heavily wooded pathway. Seton made sure no one was watching them and took Patty by the hand.

"This way," he said. "It's time to get sneaky again."

The trees hemmed them in here, but at least they kept the rain off. Seton lit the flashlight and they danced around small puddles and muddy ruts. Soon the path came to a halt at a high, iron, gate. The wall on either side was over fifteen feet high.

Seton switched off the flashlight and started to climb the gate. He turned when he was five feet off the ground and looked back at Patty.

"If you don't want to come…"

Patty stepped forward and grabbed the cold metal.

"I haven't done any climbing since I was ten," she said.

"It's just like riding a bike," Seton said.

"I never learned that either," Patty replied.

She needn't have worried. The climb was remarkably easy, and with Seton encouraging her every step she was up and over the top before she knew it. She even jumped down on the other side, landing softly in a soft area of wet grass, but overbalancing and falling sideways. She lay there giggling.

Seton jumped down beside her and helped her to her feet. He wiped a small wad of mud from her cheek.

"You're starting to look disreputable Ms. Doyle."

"You say that as if it was a bad thing," Patty replied. They both laughed again then went quiet quickly when they realized where they were.

Seton took out the flashlight and panned it around.

They were on the edge of a graveyard. The stones stood tall like sentinels all around, the torchlight gleaming off damp moss.

"This way," Seton said, and headed off down a left-hand path. "If I remember rightly the Samson plot is over here."

"Remember rightly? How long ago was it you were here?"

"Some years ago," he said, taking on a far away look. "It was daylight then. The place was full of sunshine and the smell of flowers. A piper played a pibroch, and everyone wept. I was at the funeral of an old friend. Not a memory I want to revisit too often. But at least it means I can remember my way around."

They wound through some well-tended pathways. Patty caught occasional glimpses of names and inscriptions on headstones.

"Mark the perfect man, and behold the upright for the end of that man is peace."

"Here lies Andrew the Miller, gone to grind for the architect of all."

"Remember friend as you walk by, As you are now so once was I, As I am now you will surely be, Prepare thyself to follow me."

"Doesn't this creep you out at all?" Patty whispered.

"No," Seton replied. "I take comfort in the history of places like this, in the lineage and family lines, all here together at the end. It's something I'll never have. Ah… here we are."

He stopped in front of a tall rectangular stone and shone a torch on the inscription.

"Here lies John Samson. Faithful servant as above, so below."

"We seekers are all climbing Jacob's ladder."

"The truth is in the steps taken."

"I never noticed before," Seton whispered, almost to himself.

"Noticed what?"

Seton shook his head.

"The clue was here all the time. *Jacob's ladder.*"

He grabbed Patty's hand.

"Come on. We have to go inside."

"Inside?"

"Into the Palace itself. I know where he's hidden the papers."

She pulled him back towards her.

"We can't do that."

He pulled against her.

"Why not? Are you balking at a little breaking and entering after what we've been through the past few days? Come on. The drums are beating."

Breaking and entering. He makes it sound like a child's game.

But she let herself be led as he took her through the graveyard and past a well tended herb garden to the back wall of the Palace itself.

"How do we get inside?" she asked.

"Trust me," he said, and winked.

Eventually they reached a large oak door.

Seton felt all around its rim and checked with the flashlight around the lock. He took a small leather pouch from his pocket and opened it to reveal a small set of tools.

"Do you always come prepared for burglary?" Patty asked.

"I forgot the big bag marked SWAG though," Seton replied and turned back to the door. "This won't take long. Keep yourself amused for a bit."

Illegal immigrant, absconder from justice, what's a little burglary to a master criminal like me?

She looked out over the garden and the graveyard beyond. The rain had eased off and the mist rolled unimpeded. It hung, a foot off the ground, and crept slowly towards them, like a living carpet. Suddenly Patty felt cut off from all reality. Time had gone, the twenty-first century just a distant memory as she stood, somewhere in the past, in a graveyard, in the dark.

Like many before her in similar situations she felt the cold shiver of dread.

"Hurry up," she whispered.

"Getting the heebie-jeebies?" Seton asked.

"No. Getting cold," she answered.

Seton started whistling. It took her a little while to realize what it was, then she started laughing.

"*Ghostbusters*?"

Seton smiled.

"It got your attention, didn't it?"

He turned a long metal implement in the lock. There was a click, too loud in the still night. He turned the handle, and the door swung open.

"We're in. Come on."

The door opened directly into an old kitchen area. Patty would have liked to stop and marvel at the butler's sinks, copper pans and huge butcher's blocks, but Seton seemed to know where he was headed and dragged her through to a corridor beyond.

It was lined in huge oak panels. Rank after rank of dignitaries frowned down on them from faded portraits and the black glass eyes of long dead animals followed their passage from high mounts.

"Isn't there *any* security in this place?"

"At the front door and on most of the windows," Seton said. "But none once you get inside."

"As far as you know."

He nodded.

"As far as I know. So best make it quick, don't you think? If we've tripped any silent alarms, the cops will already be on their way."

She held tight to his hand as they hurried up a stairway wide enough to take six people abreast.

"You do know where you're going?" she whispered.

He didn't reply. He led her into a library of tall book-stacks. That wasn't what caught her eye though. Three small steps led up to a huge bay window. A streetlight shone through stained glass, lighting it from behind.

"*And behold a ladder set up on the earth, and the top of it reached to heaven: and behold the angels of God ascending and descending on it*," Seton said. "Genesis, chapter twenty-eight, verse twelve."

The window did indeed show a ladder stretching from a pastoral, farming scene up to a glowing heaven. Cherubic angels ascended and descended on the steps. Beneath the ladder a man lay watching, his head resting on a stone pillow.

"And just to show you just how much all is intercon-nected," Seton said. "The very stone that Jacob rested his head on found its way to Scotland and was used as a seat for the crowning of the old Kings, since the time of Ken-neth MacAlpin, the first King of Scots. The Stone of Destiny they call it."

"More fairy stories?"

Seton laughed again.

"We could go to Edinburgh Castle, hang the watch over the stone and ask it for ourselves if you like?"

"Let's stick to one impossible quest at a time shall we. Where's the clue?" Patty said, stepping closer for a better look at the window. "I don't get it."

"It's another metaphor," Seton said. "It symbolizes the great journey, from the Microcosm below to the Macrocosm above. But the clue isn't in the ladder. In fact, it's not even on the window."

He knelt, and at first Patty thought he was about to pray. Then she saw him take a penknife from his pocket. He started knocking with his knuckles on the boards of the steps up to the window.

The truth is in the steps taken.

She knelt down beside him.

"It's that easy?" she asked.

"Old Samson was no Leonardo, that's for sure," Seton said.

One of his knocks came back hollow. He started to work around the board with his penknife.

32

Mike and Sam arrived in Falkland in thick fog.

"They *do* have summer here don't they?" Sam asked.

"It reminds me of the Maritimes," Mike replied. "We went on holiday up there when I was a kid. We had two weeks of this gray shit. And that was in July."

Sam shivered.

"But I bet it was warmer than here. This is a dismal country."

Mike snorted.

"Yeah, but think of the history."

"I would if I could see it."

The journey from Linlithgow had turned into a minor nightmare. They'd got stuck in commuter traffic trying to get across the Forth Bridge and had sat in a queue for well over an hour. In that hour Mike went through the gamut from murderous rage to boredom and back again.

"We should have stayed in *The Three Marys*," he said. "I could handle more of that beer."

"No. You couldn't," Sam said quietly.

No. She's right. I couldn't.

McGuire's body was never far from his thoughts. All his cop instincts told him he should have called it in, started the paperwork and got the force of the law onto the case. But that would only give Ross time to escape.

And that bastard is not getting away. Not this time.

Once they got across the bridge things didn't get much better. The fog had come down like a steel door falling, and traffic almost came to a halt. What with that, and them getting lost twice on side roads that led to places neither of them could pronounce, Mike was not in the best of moods as they parked in Falkland's main street.

The light of a nearby bar looked far too inviting.

"Let's have a look around," Mike said.

Sam agreed. She surprised him by coming round the car and taking his arm.

"It wouldn't do to look too much like a pair of NYPD cops, now would it?"

As they walked up the street Mike found that he was actually enjoying the walk, despite the clammy fog and incessant drizzle.

The town was quiet, not a single person to be seen. But it reeked of history, all narrow alleys, cobbled lanes and houses that had no square edges on any of their corners. A couple of the older buildings had thatched roofs, and a plaque on the side of another said it had been built in 1596.

That's before the Mayflower, Mike thought. Back in the States, they thought history was something that happened before the Civil War, something you rarely encountered.

But here it's real, and tangible.

When they came to the Palace itself Mike ran his hand over a wall, imagining all the people it had seen walk past over the long years.

"Penny for your thoughts?" Sam said.

"Just thinking," Mike said. "About Adams, and his longevity drugs. Do you think you'd like to live for hundreds of years? To see buildings like this one here get built, and be around long enough to see them crumble into ruin? Would it inspire you? Or would you become depressed that the works of man, seemingly so sturdy and strong, will all, eventually, be no more than dust in the wind?"

Sam laughed.

"You do need a drink after all," she said. She gave him a kiss on the cheek. "Come on. It's obvious we won't get anywhere out here. Let's schmooze the locals."

He tried not to appear too eager as they stood at the bar, but the thought of a cold beer had him salivating. To distract himself, he tried to engage the barman.

"Have you seen our friends?" he said. "A small Scots guy and his wife, a brunette?"

The barman eyed him suspiciously over the beer font.

He knows I'm a cop.

"I wouldn't know sir. What did you say their names were?"

"Seton," Mike replied. "Mr. and Mrs. Alex Seton?"

The barman put two beers in front of Mike.

"Sorry sir. We've got no one of that name staying here. Maybe you should try Covenanter up the road?"

"Maybe I will," Mike said.

He was about to take the beer over to their table when the door opened. The man who came in wore a security guard's uniform, and had a huge grin on his face.

"You look like you've won the lottery Frank," the barman said.

"Near enough," the security guard said. "I got an order from the high-head honcho to let this rich American bugger into the Palace tonight. I waited for *hours* for him. But when he did turn up, he gave me a hundred quid to give him the run of the place. Hell, for a hundred quid I'd throw the wife in as well."

Everyone in hearing range laughed, but Mike started for the door, motioning for Sam to follow. He only caught part of the guard's next sentence, but it was enough to get him moving even faster.

"I wasn't too sure about the guy he had wi' him though. He smelled worse than a wet fart in a phone box and…"

Mike and Sam were already out of the door, heading for the Palace.

33

Seton prized the board up with the tip of his knife. Patty saw him feel around in a hollow space behind it.

"What have you got?" she asked.

"Yes Alex," a cultured voice said behind her. "What *have* you got?"

Patty turned to look. A tall gray-haired man stood at the far end of the library. The pale man, Ross stood beside him.

Ross looked even worse than he had just that morning. His skin had taken on a green tinge, and Patty suspected that the sudden odor in the room, like a cow-pat on a hot day, was coming from him. He stood stock still, staring straight ahead. But the gun in his hand was pointed at Seton.

"Mr. Adams," Seton said. "I wondered when you'd turn up."

"I want those four pages," Adams said. "You know the lengths I'm prepared to go to get them."

Seton laughed. It echoed around the library, a sudden chorus of madmen. He held what looked like a block of wood in his hand.

"I'm afraid we've both been misled," he told Adams. He showed Patty the wood.

She had to angle it in the streetlight coming through the window.

It was a woodcut, finely detailed.

"*Volate*" it said in gothic lettering at the top, and showed a volcano in full eruption, sending out a lava flow that engulfed a huge fortification on its flanks.

"I've seen this before," she said. "It's one of the Concordances, isn't it?"

Adams spoke before Seton could reply.

"Throw it over. Carefully."

Seton slid the woodcut across the floor. It stopped at Adams feet.

As the older man bent to lift it, Seton's hand whipped out and sent the flashlight across the room. He missed Ross's head by less than an inch, but the man never moved, and the light tumbled away into darkness down the stairs.

"Would you like to try that again?" Adams said, smiling.

"If you insist," Seton replied and something silver flew across the room. Ross didn't even flinch as the penknife cut into his cheek just below his left eye, and the gun didn't waver as the knife fell away to clatter on the ground. It left a gray mark on Ross's face. There was no blood.

"Still the showman I see, Alex," Adams said. "Please don't try anything else. Ross is a bit unstable at the moment, and I'd hate for the gun to go off, accidentally or otherwise."

He lifted the woodcut, examined it, turned it over, and back again.

"OK," he said. "It's very pretty. What does it mean?"

"It's a clue," Seton said. "Probably to where the four pages you're after can be found."

"And what's the clue?"

Seton laughed again.

"You've got me on that one. Who knows what was in old Samson's mind when he left it there?"

Adams just said one word.

"Ross."

The man moved the gun so that it was pointing at Patty.

"Again, Alex. What's the clue?"

"It's all melodrama and cliché with you Adams, isn't it? You should try honey instead of vinegar sometimes."

"I tried that, remember?" Adams said. "Ross. Shoot the woman."

"No!" Seton shouted.

Adams smiled.

"You were saying about vinegar?"

Seton sighed.

"The woodcut, like its double in the *Concordances*, is symbolic. It signifies the volatile nature of the compound at this stage in the process, in that the oxide produced becomes gaseous on exposure to air. And spiritually, it symbolizes the fact that the person must become capable of letting go of worldly things and…"

"Enough," Adams shouted. "Enough of the *spirituality* bullshit. You said it was a clue. Where does it point to?"

Again Seton sighed.

"Old Samson was a literal sort of fellow by all accounts," Seton said. "So at a guess, I'd say we're looking for a volcano, a volcano with a fortification on it."

"And?" Adams said. Patty saw that the older man was getting impatient, but Seton did not seem too concerned.

"And the only one of those I know is less than forty miles away. Samson is pointing us to Edinburgh Castle," he said.

"Why?"

Seton shrugged.

"I need to examine the woodcut more closely," he said. "But at the moment, I've no idea."

"Ross, shoot the woman," Adams said again.

"No!" Seton shouted, and threw his body between Patty and the gun.

Adams laughed.

"Just testing."

"Bastard," Seton said.

"You're not the first to suggest it," Adams said. "And no doubt you won't be the last."

Seton still kept between Patty and the gun.

"So," Adams continued. "The missing papers are in Edinburgh Castle?"

"Maybe," Seton said. "And maybe there'll just be another clue."

"And what are we looking for?"

"As I said, I'll know when I have a closer look at the woodcut," Seton replied. "But it's still a long shot that there'll be anything there, after all this time."

"Let's hope for your sake that's not the case," Adams replied. "Get up. We're going on a trip."

Seton stood carefully, and took Patty's hand to help her up.

"Where to?" Seton asked.

This time it was Adam's turn to laugh.

"To the Castle of course. It might cost me a bit, but I'm sure I can find someone to let us inside."

"Our stuff," Patty said. "It's in the hotel."

"I'm afraid we'll have to leave it there," Adams replied.

"The book, the *Concordances*. We might need it," Seton added.

Again Adams laughed.

"Way ahead of you. I have that already. Staff in provincial hotels are always susceptible to bribery."

He patted at the inside pocket of his jacket where Patty noticed a prominent bulge.

"Ross. Show them to the car," he said.

Ross motioned with the pistol.

Seton took Patty's hand and they walked ahead of Ross as they went back down the wide staircase and out into the street.

34

Mike and Sam waited until the other four exited the Palace before emerging from the shadows at the foot of the staircase.

"Did you get all of that?" Mike asked.

"Yes," Sam said. "I take it we're going after them?"

"Damn right," Mike said, heading for the door. "If that bastard Ross didn't have a gun I'd have taken him already. Come on."

He took Sam's hand and headed for the door.

Sam pulled him back.

"Then what?" she said. "As you said. The bastard's got a gun Mike, and we're way out of our jurisdiction."

Mike smiled grimly.

"I'm not sure I care anymore. I just want to find out what this has all been about, and maybe, just maybe, get a chance to take down the bad guys."

He looked Sam in the eye.

"Or are you saying you want to give up?"

She smiled and gripped his hand tighter.

"Nope. I want to kick their asses. I just wanted to make sure *you* still did."

Mike pulled her closer and kissed her, quickly.

"That's my girl. Now come on. We've seen a Palace. Let's go see a Castle."

Sam picked up the discarded flashlight that had landed at their feet.

"We might need this later."

Mike checked outside, peering round the edge of the door. Adams and Ross were getting into the front of a black SUV. He assumed that Seton and the woman were already in the back. He waited for ten seconds and looked again. The SUV was pulling away down the street.

He almost pulled Sam behind him as they ran for the car. By the time they got going and headed out of town the SUV was almost out of sight, headed up a hill.

Mike put on a burst of speed and closed up to a hundred yards behind, then slowed, maintaining the distance. The traffic was a lot lighter than earlier, only the occasional car passing in the other direction. Even after they got onto the motorway leading south, the traffic was light and patchy.

"Seriously Mike," Sam said after a while. "Do we even have a very *small* plan?"

Mike laughed.

"I've been too busy having fun to think about it. We could have a car chase?" he said, and pushed hard on the accelerator, just for a second.

Sam laughed along with him.

"I don't think they go in for that over here."

She looked thoughtful.

"Back there," she said. "In the Palace. It certainly sounds like Seton and Doyle are innocent in all of this?"

Mike nodded.

"That's what I thought. There's something about this that has Adams all riled up though, and I can't for the life of me figure out what all this creeping around in historical buildings has to do with anything."

"So what are we going to do about it?"

"Follow them to the Castle," Mike said.

"And creep around in a historical building?"

Mike laughed again, and was still laughing as they crossed the road-bridge and headed into Edinburgh.

35

Adams drove, while Ross sat in the front passenger seat staring straight ahead.

The smell in the car was almost overpowering.

"Your boy is getting a bit ripe," Seton said.

"Open a window if it bothers you," Adams replied. Ross didn't even twitch. Patty could see the gray tear on his cheek where the penknife had entered. A flap of skin hung loosely from the wound, but there was no sign of redness, no blood.

Seton passed Patty a cigarette.

"For the smell," he said.

Patty lit up gratefully.

"What's the matter with him?" she whispered.

Adams barked a loud laugh.

"He doesn't travel well," he said.

"I told you it wouldn't work," Seton said softly.

"After your escape, Ross was adamant he wanted to try," Adams said. "I couldn't really refuse him."

"Escape?" Patty said, confused.

"It's a long story," Seton said.

"How much have you told her?" Adams said to Seton.

Seton kept quiet.

"You haven't told her?" Adams said, astonished. "How the hell did you get her to follow you then?"

Seton still said nothing.

"He's been lying to you all along," Adams said, this time addressing Patty.

She shook her head.

"You're the liar here."

"Tell her then," Adams said to Seton. "Why don't you tell her the truth?"

Seton still said nothing, but his eyes had taken on a cold hard stare that Patty hadn't seen there before.

"Ross. Shoot Seton."

Before Patty could move Ross turned and in one motion raised the pistol and shot Seton in the chest. Seton gasped, exhaled once, and slumped against Patty's shoulder. His cigarette fell from his hand to the floor of the car.

"Alex?" Patty said. "Alex!"

Seton's slumped further against her.

Adams laughed.

"Don't worry about him," he said. "Worry about yourself. You're here on false pretenses."

Patty couldn't see for sudden tears. Adams noticed in the rear-view mirror.

"Don't cry for him," Adams said. "He's not worth it."

Adams went on talking. Patty was only half listening, aware she was once more in shock, but unsure as to what to do about it.

"I first heard about Seton some ten years ago," Adams said. "And at first I assumed it was just another fairy story. Then I heard about *The Concordances*. I spent a very large amount of money tracking that manuscript down. And in the process, I came to Seton's attention. He started to poke into my affairs, and in return, I poked into his.

"When I discovered exactly what he was, I knew I had to have him. So we invited him to the lab. There we did some tests, and asked him a few gentle questions. Imagine my surprise when we found it wasn't a fairy story after all."

"I've no idea what you're talking about," Patty said dully. "Alex would never lie to me."

"That's my girl," Seton said beside her. He sat up and coughed. There was blood at his lips. He coughed again and spat into his hand. He showed his palm to Patty. There was a bullet sitting there.

"A bit melodramatic," Adams said. "But it proves my point."

"Which is?"

"Ms. Doyle, the man you're sitting beside is Alexander Seton, an alchemist. As far we can ascertain, he is over four hundred years old, and he may well be immortal."

Seton winked at her.

"*It's a kind of magic*," he said in a French accent.

Despite herself she had to laugh.

"You're no Lambert, that's for sure."

Seton lit another cigarette. For a man who'd been shot he looked remarkably well. His front was a mess of blood, but when he sat up straight his eyes once more held a twinkle.

"Sorry dear," he said and took Patty's hand. "I didn't tell you. I didn't think it was that important."

Adams barked again.

"Not that important? There's nothing more important."

Seton looked deep into Patty's eyes.

"Yes, there is."

He raised Patty's hand to his lips and kissed the back of it.

"This man here," he said, looking at Adams. "Thinks that the trick to living is to survive for as long as possible. To prove it, he injected Ross with some of my blood. As you can see, it hasn't quite had the desired effect."

"That's why we need the four missing pages," Adams replied. "I will have your secret Seton."

"And as I told you, it won't do you any good. And I won't let you experiment on any more people."

"I don't think you're in any position to argue," Adams said smoothly. "After all, Ms. Doyle here might not take a bullet quite so easily."

"She's the only reason you're still alive," Seton replied

Adams smiled.

"More melodrama. Here," he said, and passed the woodcut back to Patty. "Find out where we are to go. That's all that's keeping you alive."

Patty stretched to put on the overhead light. Seton stopped her, and kissed her on the cheek.

"No need," he said to Adams. "I know exactly where to go. Just get us to the Castle, and I'll do the rest."

He stroked Patty's hand.

"I'm sorry," he said again.

She looked in his eyes, and saw pain.

She stroked his cheek.

"I'm just glad you didn't get dead."

"Me too," Seton said, and smiled. He coughed again, and once more there were flecks of blood on his lips. He brushed Patty's hand away gently.

"Don't worry," he said. "I've had worse."

Adams spoke before Patty could.

"So all this subterfuge was for her benefit? You've known where the papers were all along?"

Seton shook his head.

"No. After the *experiment* I found I had an urge to travel. I left the papers with old Samson. Before I knew it a century had passed, and Samson, and the papers, were long gone. I always assumed he'd done as I asked and sewn them up in the *Concordances*. I was surprised when they weren't there."

"And I suppose I should thank Mr. McGuire from Linlithgow for uncovering them for us?" Adams said.

"Aye. Tam has a knack for sniffing out secrets," Seton replied.

"Had a knack, I'm afraid," Adams said. "Mr. Ross paid him a visit. It got messy."

Seton looked like he might launch himself across the car. Patty held onto him and pushed him back in his seat.

"Do as the lady says and be a good boy," Adams said. "We'll be at the Castle soon, then we can finish this, one way or another."

Adams went back to driving. After a while he took out his cell phone, dialed, and started talking.

"Douglas. I need a favor."

Seton once more stroked the back of Patty's hand.

"This could get messy," he said quietly.

She pointed at the blood down his front.

"It did already. Don't spend time worrying about me. Just do what you have to do."

He nodded.

"It's because of you I'll do it. Just keep an eye on Ross. I doubt he's quite as stable as Adams thinks he is."

Patty looked at the silent gray-faced man.

"So what exactly *is* wrong with him?"

"At a guess, I'd say massive overload of his immune system. His metabolism has been speeded up far beyond what a human body was built to take. Now he's breaking down, from the inside out. By the looks of things there's not much left."

Ross turned in his seat and stared blankly at Seton.

He brought up the pistol and pointed it at Seton's head.

His mouth opened, and he tried to talk. All that came out was a croak at first, and when he finally managed to say something it was a harsh rasp. His tongue looked like a white stone in a dry cave.

"Enough left to deal with you," he said. "More than enough."

36

Mike held back at the top of the Royal Mile as the black SUV drove on to the empty esplanade in front of Edinburgh Castle.

They watched as Adams walked up to the guard's post and talked to the Officer of the Watch. He handed the officer his cellular phone, the officer talked to someone, and the barrier was raised to let the SUV through into the castle proper.

"Well, that's us screwed," Sam said.

Mike banged on the wheel in frustration. It felt so good he did it again.

"I didn't realize this place was a damned fortress."

"It's the Home Headquarters of the Royal Regiment of Scotland and 52 Infantry Brigade," Sam said.

"How the hell do you know that?"

She pointed.

Directly outside her car window was a large poster depicting the Castle's history.

"It says their duties are largely ceremonial, if that helps?" Sam said and smiled.

"That rifle the sentry is carrying looks a bit more than ceremonial."

Mike banged the wheel again. He was looking at his hands as an orange light came and went across their back. He looked up to see a police car passing along the High Street outside the main gate of the Castle.

"McCall," he said.

"What about him?" Sam asked.

"He'll get something done. Stay here. I think I saw a phone booth just over there."

He'd remembered right. And the machine took payment by credit card. He got through to Partick CID at the first attempt, and was put on hold as they tried to find Detective McCall. He survived twelve bars of *The Girl from Ipa Nema* before the big man came on the line. There was no preamble.

"Where the hell are you," McCall shouted.

"Edinburgh," Mike replied, trying to stay calm. "Where are you?"

"As if you didn't know. I'm in McGuire's house, looking at your mess."

"Not mine big man," Mike said.

"We'll see about that. I want you and your partner at Partick CID as quick as you can get there. If my Chief is hungry for somebody's balls, I'll make sure they're not mine."

Mike nearly laughed then thought better of it.

"We've found him," he said instead. "The killer I mean."

There was a silence at the other end of the line.

"You'd better no' be jerking my chain Yank," McCall said.

"He's here. In Edinburgh," Mike said. "He's in the Castle."

"What? Embra Castle? You are jerking my chain."

"No. He's got Adams with him, the drug company man we told you about."

Mike could almost hear the clockwork as the big man's brain chugged into gear.

"Where are you at the moment?" McCall asked.

"On the esplanade outside the Castle. They went in two minutes ago."

"I'm on the way," McCall said.

"Bring backup," Mike replied. "He's got a gun."

"Just keep him there," McCall said.

"How?"

"Do something violent and messy," McCall said. "You know, some of that *John Wayne cowboy shit* I was talking about before? You Yanks are good at that."

37

Seton took the lead after they got out of the SUV. He led them to the highest point of the castle. A small, squat building stood on the skyline.

"This is the oldest building on the rock," Seton said. "In fact, the oldest building in Edinburgh. It's a chapel, so show a little respect Mr. Adams."

He led them inside.

The room was little more than a square box, stone below, wood above. The high arched ceiling looked like an upturned boat. Where the wood and stone were hidden, the walls were hung in heavy red velvet drapes.

Two tall candles lit the far end, and it took several seconds for Patty's eyes to adapt. The candles stood on tall metal poles on either side of a cubic stone altar. The candlelight cast long shadows over the chapel floor. The only furniture consisted of two long wooden pews, one on either side of the room.

Ross stood by the door with his pistol in his hand while Patty followed Adams and Seton to the far end.

"This is the Chapel of St. Margaret," Seton said. "On his death bed in 1329, the Bruce, who had ordered it pulled down fifteen years before, issued orders for the chapel's repair, with some forty pounds Scots being put aside for the purpose.

"Get on with it Alex," Adams said. "And spare us the history lesson."

"If it wasn't for history, none of us would be here," Seton said. "Besides, this is the point. The man entrusted with the building work on the Chapel was a Seton. He too was a follower of the Great Path. And when he went to the great architect, he was buried, here."

Seton walked over beside the altar. Several long stone slabs lay on the floor all inscribed with names and dates. He knelt beside one, and traced a word with his finger.

Volate.

"We need to get this slab up," Seton said.

Adams smiled.

"I'm not stopping you."

Seton took the tall candle off the metal pole nearest him and used the pole to try to lever the slab.

"It will never work you know," he said to Adams. "Not for you."

"So you keep telling me. Just don't give me that *spiritual dimension* B.S. again, please. Biology and chemistry, that's what it boils down to. The scientific method will get to the bottom of your secret."

Seton smiled.

"And it's been having so much success with that so far, hasn't it."

He motioned towards where Ross stood, still and silent at the door.

"There are always some small failures on the path to progress," Adams said.

"And there's exactly why it won't work for you," Seton said quietly. "You're too much of a heartless shit."

"What, and heartless shits can never be immortal?"

"Wrong question," Seton said. "Why would they want to be?"

"Power and influence," Adams said.

"But you've got them already, surely?"

"A man can always use more of both."

"And less," Seton said softly.

Adams laughed.

"It's wasted on you, I can see that," he said. "But I intend to put it to good use. When people see what it does for me, they'll be queuing up in their millions to get hold of it."

"Then what?"

"Then I get richer," Adams said.

"Then what?"

"I don't understand."

"No," Seton said sadly. "You don't."

There was a sudden grating of stone on stone and the slab he'd been working at slipped to one side revealing a hollow beneath it. Seton reached down and came back with a skin bag.

"We should destroy this," he said. He was talking to Adams, but he looked straight at Patty.

"Mr. Seton," Adams said. "It's late and I'm getting bored listening to you running off at the mouth. Just open it up and let's see what we've got."

Seton stood. He had the oilskin in one hand and the metal candlestick in the other. Ross stepped forward and pointed the pistol at him.

"Best put the pole down," Adams said. "It looks like it makes our friend twitchy."

Seton laid the pole next to him, leaning it on the altar but still within arm's reach. Patty and Adams leaned over the altar as Seton opened the skin bag, He took out what looked like a chicken's egg, and rolled it over in his hand. When Patty looked closer she saw it was a smooth piece of white stone.

"What the hell does that mean?" Adams said, almost shouting.

"What came first?" Seton said, looking at Patty and smiling. "Old Samson is telling us to go to the beginning, and the end. The place where the experiment started, and where I became what I am."

He tossed the egg in his palm, and kept looking straight at Patty.

"And?" Adams said.

Seton stayed silent.

"Come on Seton," Adams insisted. "Or shall I have Ross shoot the woman?"

Seton still looked straight at Patty.

"A smart person should be able to figure it out," he said. "With a map and those loose papers Samson put in the *Concordances*. Give me the first page and I'll show you."

Adams took the loose papers from his jacket pocket.

"Just remember who has the gun," he said as he handed them to Seton.

Seton kept the stone egg in his right hand and opened the papers with his left.

"Look," he said. "It's right here."

He read from the page.

"*Extractio Animae Solis: or a Triall upon Sol, for the Extraction of Philosophical earth. The Author has putt doon the consequences of his Experiments therein, from the beginning to the end, by way of Journal; in the sure and sertin hope of the resurrection and the life, in this year of oor lord sixteen hunner an forty. Putt doon here in the keep by the wee port by the shore.*"

He said the last sentence again, all the while looking at Patty.

Putt doon here in the keep by the wee port by the shore.

"Now all you need is a map," he said, and winked.

Things happened fast after that.

Seton tossed the stone in the air one more time. As soon as it landed in his palm he drew back his arm and, like a baseball pitcher, threw the egg. It hit Ross on the head with a dull crack.

"Run," Seton shouted.

As Patty turned towards the door she saw Seton lift the candlestick and aim a blow at Adam's head. The older man belied his age and stepped aside so that Seton, carried by the momentum, fell slightly off-balance.

"Run!" he shouted again.

She didn't wait to be told again.

Ross was on his knees at the door, clutching his head. As she ran past him he put out an arm, but she was able to jump over it, and a second later was outside into the night, running down a cobbled path away from the chapel.

The loud crack of a shot made her look over her shoulder. Ross stood in the chapel doorway, but he had not fired at her. He was aiming back into the chapel and as she watched he fired again, twice.

Alex.

There were new tears in her eyes as she ran down into the darkness.

Mike saw the flash from the shots first, and heard the sound a moment later. By that time he was out of the car and running. He got halfway across the esplanade before he even realized he was moving on cop instincts.

The guard at the gate saw him coming and raised his rifle across his chest.

"Stop there sir," he said.

Sam caught up with Mike and they walked quickly towards the guard.

"I said stop," the guard said. Mike noticed that he was fresh-faced, wide eyed, and, at this moment, more than a bit scared.

Shit. He's only a kid.

Mike flashed his badge and tried to bluster his way through, but the kid wasn't that scared. Mike was looking down the barrel of the rifle when the guard next spoke.

"This is loaded," he said. "And I've just about had enough of this shit."

Mike laughed.

"OK son. But there's trouble up there in the Castle, and we just want to help."

Another shot rang out. Then they heard footsteps on the cobbles, running, getting closer.

The guard tried to keep an eye on Mike and look over his shoulder at the same time. The rifle barrel wavered alarmingly and Mike stepped inside it. He threw a right hook that caught the guard on the side of the head and sent him falling away as Mike grabbed the rifle.

He got it pointed in the right direction just as Patty Doyle ran down the incline behind the guard-rail.

She saw Mike standing there with the gun, and stopped in her tracks. A shadow moved behind her, and Mike raised the rifle.

"Ms. Doyle," he said. "Come this way. It's OK. We're here to help."

Another shot rang out. The flash came from the shadow behind Doyle. Mike sent an answering shot that way, and heard a grunt of pain, just before the tall figure of Ross launched itself forward down the slope.

Patty Doyle was already at Mike's side. Mike aimed the rifle again, and was about to fire when the guard got to his feet and grabbed at the butt. Sam also got involved, trying to hold the guard off. The ensuing comedy of errors gave Ross all the time he needed to reach them.

The guard managed to wrest the rifle from Mike, and caught Mike a glancing blow on the side of the head with the barrel as he brought it up and pointed it straight at Ross's belly.

"I don't know what the hell is going on," he said. "But just stay right there mister."

Ross ignored him and kept walking. He had the pistol hanging in his hand by his side.

"Just shoot him," Doyle said.

"Stop!" the guard shouted.

Ross started to bring up the pistol.

The guard shot him, from only ten feet away. Mike saw the cloth of Ross's jacket billow as the blast went through him, but there was no blood, and the man kept coming.

The young guard dropped the rifle and backed away.

Ross aimed the pistol at Doyle, who had also turned to run, but Mike knew with a sickening feeling in his gut that it was too late.

He waited for the shot to come.

But it never happened. A slight figure fell on Ross from the battlement above and took him to the ground. Seton's face, smeared in blood, showed ivory white in the light, but his eyes blazed as he looked straight at Doyle.

"What bit of *run* don't you understand?" he said, laughing as he wrestled on the ground with Ross.

Then Seton had no time for talk as Ross tried to stand, still trying to come forward towards Doyle. Seton manhandled the bigger man and together, in a manic grotesque waltz, they staggered across the esplanade.

Seton managed to get Ross backed up against the battlements.

Mike caught a movement at the corner of his eye. The young guard had regained some composure, and was bending to lift the rifle. Mike put his foot on the barrel.

"No son, I don't trust you to get the right target."

It became a moot point seconds later. Seton bellowed in rage, and lifted the bigger man off his feet. At the same instant Ross threw himself backwards, grabbing at the Scot.

Both of them went over the battlements, and fell, silently, into the night.

"Alex!" Doyle shouted, and started to run in that direction. Sam grabbed her and held her back.

"Arrest those people," someone shouted. Mike looked up the incline. Adams was walking towards them, accompanied by four armed soldiers.

"Time to go," Mike said. He grabbed Doyle's other arm and between them they dragged her to their car.

A shot pinged off the cobbles at Mike's feet as he got the doors opened, and another hit the rear bumper as they got inside.

Mike got the car in gear and put his foot down, having to swerve hard to avoid another car that was heading onto the esplanade. He just caught a glimpse of McCall's enraged glare before they left the Castle grounds and headed at speed down the cobbles of the old High Street.

39

They clattered and bounced down the cobbles, with Patty being thrown around like a doll in a washing machine. Finally the man slowed down.

Patty sat back in her seat and looked at the two people who'd manhandled her away.

"So who *do* you work for?" she asked. "It's obviously not Adams' mob, and you're not the Scottish police. So who are you?"

The woman turned in her sear and showed her badge.

"Sergeant Sam Mendoza," she said, and motioned towards the man. "And this is Lieutenant Mike Turner. NYPD. We've been trying to catch up with you for a while."

"So you know what's going on?"

The man, Turner, laughed.

"Oh yes. We're *really* on top of this case. But at least we've got you now. That's something. And when we get you back to the States, you can explain yourself there."

"We can't go back," Patty said calmly. "Not yet. We've got a chance to finish this. I owe it to Alex to finish this."

"Lady, you don't get a say in the matter," Turner said, but Mendoza put a hand on his shoulder.

"Let's hear her out Mike. We came for Ross, didn't we? And if she can give us a chance at getting Adams as well, don't we want to take it?"

Turner sighed.

"I know when I'm beat. So, what about it Ms. Doyle. Fill us in."

Patty shook her head.

"Maybe later. But right now, we need to hurry. I need a map."

The cops looked at each other, but said nothing.

"We've come too far not to follow through," Mendoza said.

Mike nodded, and looked at Patty in the rear view mirror above the steering wheel.

"A map it is then ma'am. But I'm a stranger here myself, so it could take a while."

They followed the road down the Royal Mile away from the Castle. Patty checked out the back window, but there was no sign of pursuit.

"Adams will be held up, at least a bit," Mike said. "McCall will want to know what's going on. And he won't take No for an answer."

"McCall?" Patty asked, then held up a hand. "No, don't bother. It'll just confuse matters. You're cops, you tell me, where's the best place to buy a map in the middle of the night?"

It was the female cop, Mendoza who answered.

"A gas station?"

Patty nodded.

"Let's get out of this tourist area and find one."

Mike gave her a mock salute.

"Yes ma'am."

"I don't suppose either of you has a cigarette?" she said. Neither of them replied, and Patty sat back in the seat again.

She couldn't get the image out of her mind: Alex and Ross, locked together, going over the battlements. She had no idea how far the fall was, but she'd seen pictures of the Castle and knew that the chances were it was a long way down. She felt like she should be crying, but no tears would come. Instead all she felt was a steely resolve to get the job done.

And quickly at that.
Adams won't be far behind.

They found a gas station only a few minutes later. While Turner filled up the car, Patty went inside. The maps were by the door. It took less than ten seconds to find what she was looking for.

Putt doon here in the keep by the wee port by the shore.

She traced the shoreline to the east of Edinburgh, and the name almost leaped out at her.

Mendoza came and looked over her shoulder.

"Here," Patty said. "We need to go here, right away."

She pointed at the name, *Port Seton*, and on a promontory on the north side of the town, their goal.

Auld Sandy's Keep.

40

Mike drove through the quiet city streets, expecting at any moment to see the flashing lights of a pursuing police car behind them. He was becoming increasingly more aware of just how long it had been since he'd slept and he found it hard to concentrate on the driving.

Sam navigated, as best as she could, but already they'd taken a couple of wrong turns on a journey that Mike still wasn't convinced was necessary.

The woman in the back had bought cigarettes in the gas station and the smell of them started to sting in his throat and nostrils. He rolled the window down on his side and let fresher air wash over his face. It smelled of city, but also of something else that took him a second to register. It smelled of the sea.

"Tell me again," he said to Patty. "Why are we going to this… what did you call it?"

Sam replied.

"Auld Sandy's Keep. A keep is like a small castle. That's right isn't it?"

Patty nodded.

"And Sandy is a shortened form of Alexander."

"I get all that," Mike said. "But *why* are we going there?"

"It's where the experiment took place," Patty said.

"The one that turns people into immortals?" Mike said sarcastically.

The woman didn't rise to the bait.

"Adams believes that to be the case. If you believe nothing else, believe that he will be there, at some point. Our job is to get there first."

"I still don't like it," Mike grumbled.

"What's not to like?" Sam said. "We're on the run from a foreign police force, trying to stop a rich industrialist from misusing the secret to eternal life."

"Well, when you put it like that," Mike said, and started laughing. Soon the two women had joined in. They were still at it as they pulled up at a set of traffic lights.

A small, very drunk, man hung onto the pole beneath the light. He looked up blearily at the sound of the laughter. He waved them through as if he was supervising the crossing. That set Mike off even louder.

"Hey mister, can I have some o' what you're on?" the man shouted as the lights changed and they drove off.

The Keep proved surprisingly simple to find. They drove into Port Seton, and there it was, a black shadow against the night on a spit pointing out on the estuary. Mike drove on to a slip road and parked in a small parking bay there.

"Looks like we got here first," he said as they left the car. He lifted the flashlight from where they'd stowed it under the car seat. It flickered the first time he turned it on, but once he'd banged it hard on the palm of his hand the light stayed on strong and steady.

"After you," he said to Patty.

41

Patty had no idea what she was looking for.

The Keep was a ruin, little more than three walls of crumbling stone that might fall in at any minute. They'd already walked around the inside and outside, shining the flashlight in all available corners, and had seen nothing that might tell them why they'd been sent here.

She yelped as she stubbed her toe and looked down. The ground underfoot was strewn with loose rubble and lumps of stone that had already fallen from the walls.

Putt doon here in the keep by the wee port by the shore.

She shifted some of the rubble with her foot. There seemed to be smooth stone underneath.

"Here. Flash that over here."

She kicked more rubble aside.

"There's a floor here."

"So?" Mike said.

"*Put doon,*" she said. "That's what Seton said. What we're looking for is *under* the keep."

The three of them cleared as much rubble as they could and stood back.

They had uncovered a smooth floor of large stone slabs, some of which had rough indentations that might once have been inscriptions, but were now mostly worn by time and the elements.

"Now what?" Sam asked.

Patty bent for a closer look at the stones. Most of then had obviously been inscribed with text, but there was one large one that showed a rough figure of a man, his right hand pointing at a crude circle with rays coming from it, his left pointing to the ground.

As above, so below, Patty whispered.

"It's this one."

It took all three of them nearly ten minutes to manhandle the stone slab out of the ground and slide it to one side. Beneath it was a cramped passageway and a set of stone steps leading downwards into darkness.

"After you," Mike said again, and handed Patty the flashlight.

The first three steps were wet and slippery, but they were soon descending in a dry, almost musty corridor. Patty counted the steps, and laughed as they reached a flat area at the bottom.

"Thirty eight," she said. She saw the others look at each other in puzzlement, and that only made her laugh harder. The noise echoed.

She shone the flashlight around. They were in a large room with old dry straw on the floor, and a small fireplace in the far corner. The bulk of the room was filled by a long table, on top of which phials and retorts sat in a dusty pile. There were burnt and fused patches on the floor that spoke of spilled fluids and experiments gone wrong. Tall candles sat in sconces attached to the walls, and Patty started to light them with her cigarette lighter as she walked around the room.

Dust covered everything in thick grime that felt oily to the touch.

"What are we looking for again?" Mike asked.

"Four pieces of paper," Patty replied. "The key to the code in the *Concordances*."

She walked over to a huge oil painting that dominated one side of the room. It showed a figure that looked remarkably like Seton standing under an archway. There was an inscription written on the arch in Latin. Patty read it aloud.

"*He who can, without fraud, gain or deceit, tinge the basest metal with the argent colors, hath the gates of Nature herself opened to him. And from there he can inquire into further and higher secrets, and with the grace of God, obtain them.*"

"Help me move this," she said.

"Why?"

She pointed at the archway.

"The answer is behind the gates of nature."

Mike Turner shrugged.

"You heard the lady."

With the others' help Patty got the painting off the wall. Behind it was an alcove. There was a single shelf, and on it a small stone bottle sat on top of some loose sheaves of paper. She lifted the bottle and shook it. Something moved inside. It felt like a harsh powder rather than a liquid and made a sound like a shaken salt-cellar.

Patty left it to one side and picked up the papers. She read the top sheet.

> *Ye pictures, plain and insignificant in appearance,*
> *Concealeth a great and important thing.*
> *Yea, they containeth a secret of the kind*
> *That is the greatest treasure in the world.*
> *For what on this earth is deemed more excellent*
> *Than to be a Lord who ever reeketh with gold,*
> *And hath also a healthy body,*
> *Fresh and hale all his life long,*
> *Until the predestined time*
> *That cannot be overstepped by any creature.*
> *All this, as I have stated, clearly*
> *Is contained within these figures.*

After that there seemed to be a breakdown of the twelve Concordances, with detailed chemical instructions for each section. She read on a bit further.

> *Ye must expect to have it exceeding Black, within 40 days after you have put your Composition into the Glass over the Fire; if it be not Black, proceed no further, for it is unrecoverable: it must be as Black as the Ravens Head, and must continue a long time, and not utterly to lose it during five months.*
>
> *If it be Orange color, or half Red, within some small time after you have begun your Work, without doubt your Fire is too hot; for these are tokens that you have burnt the Radical humor and vivacity of the Stone.*
>
> *Know ye not, that you may have Black or anything mixed or compounded together with moisture: But you must have Black which must come and proceed of Perfect Metalline Bodies, by a real Putrefaction, and to continue a long time.*
>
> *As for the colours of Blew and Yellow, they signifie that the Solution and Putrefaction is not yet perfectly finished, and that the colors of our Mercury are not yet well mingled with the rest.*
>
> *The Black aforesaid is an evident sign, that in the beginning the Matter and Composition doth begin to purge it self, and to dissolve into small Powder, less than the Motes in the Sun; or a glutinous Water, which feeling the heat, will ascend and descend in the Glass: at length it will thicken and congeal, and become like Pitch, exceeding Black; in the end it will become a Body, and Earth, which some call Terra foetida; for then by reason of the perfect Putrefaction, it will have a scent or stink like unto Graves*

newly opened, wherein the Bodies are not thorowly consumed. Hermes doth call it Terra foliis, but the proper name is Leton, which must be blanched and made white.

Patty laughed.

"*This* is what it's all about? It's just as much gibberish as the *Concordances* themselves.

"Not to someone versed in Medieval Chemistry," a voice said. She knew who it was before she turned.

Adams stood at the foot of the stairs, a pistol trained on the three of them. A series of dull thuds came from behind him. A bloodied figure fell into the room and groaned.

Alex!

Seton spat out a wad of blood at Adams' feet and looked over at Patty.

"Hi honey, I'm home," he said, smiling although his face was a mask of blood and bruises.

Patty moved to run to him, but Mike held her back as Adams raised the pistol.

More dull thuds sounded on the steps, and Ross stepped down into the room. He looked even worse that before, his skin looking like wet paper. A flap of scalp had torn off and it hung loose over his left ear exposing gray bone beneath.

Seton tried to get up onto his knees. But Ross put a foot on his back and forced his face to the floor.

"I brought these two just in case I got here first," Adams said. "But it looks like you have what I came for. Give me the papers."

He raised the gun and pointed it straight at Patty.

"You don't need them," Seton said from the floor. "What you need is in the bottle. That's all that's left of it."

"OK," Adams said, motioning with the pistol. "Give me the papers, and the bottle."

Patty looked at Seton.

He nodded.

"Give him the bottle," he said.

She took him at his word. She tossed the bottle toward Adams. Even as it was in the air she took the cigarette lighter out and lit the bottom of the sheaf of papers.

Adams screamed, but had to move to catch the bottle in the air, and the gun veered away from pointing at her. She dropped to the ground, still clutching the papers. They hadn't quite taken. The bottom corner smoldered but the flame went out. She spun the wheel of the lighter again.

"Ross!" Adams shouted as he grasped for the bottle. The tall man leaped across the room, heading for Patty.

He didn't make it. Mike Turner stood in his way.

42

Over Ross's shoulder Mike saw Adams catch the bottle, but at the same time giving Seton a chance to go for the pistol. Then his view of them was obscured as Ross tried to go through him.

Ross grabbed Mike's arm and pulled Mike towards him. As he tried to regain balance, he tripped, falling face-first to the floor where the rough stone scraped across his face.

He was roughly turned over and looked up into Ross's bland stare. He heard a harsh click, loud in the confines of the room, and caught a glimmer of silver as a flick knife was brought up in front of his face.

"Not so smart without your big gun, are you?" Ross said.

He didn't give Mike time to respond. Mike felt quick lancing pain then the hot rush of blood against his neck as Ross drew the knife through his left earlobe. He saw the smile on Ross's face as he did it and he knew then that reasoning wasn't going to work.

Ross brought the knife up again and it headed for Mike's cheek. He laughed, an evil, cold thing, and drew back the knife to strike.

Mike got his left arm in front of it. The blade sliced easily through his jacket before bringing a burst of red heat as it found skin, then muscle. It scraped as it hit bone.

Mike squirmed, trying to get some leverage, and tried to fight back the pain as he pushed.

Ross suddenly fell away, and Sam loomed over Mike. She had a heavy iron wall sconce in her hand which had pieces of Ross's scalp hanging from it.

Mike reached for her to get helped up, but Ross wasn't finished yet. He got off the floor and backhanded Sam away. Sam fell in a heap to the floor, the sconce clattering down on the stone slabs.

And the rage took Mike.

Should have done something Mikey.

The red mist came down as he lifted the sconce and launched himself at the pale figure standing over Sam. He smashed the sconce on Ross's head. The skull caved in on one side, cracking with a sound like a hard-boiled egg dropped on a stone floor. Ross went to one knee, and brought the knife around, slicing across Mike's shin.

Mike felt no pain. He brought the sconce up and down, again, and again. Ross fell beneath it and lay still, but Mike kept pounding, until Sam put a hand on his shoulder.

43

The papers finally took and Patty had to drop them as they went up in a yellow flame, then just as quickly fell into ash, drifting to the floor.

She saw Turner head for Ross with the metal sconce in his hand. On the far side of the room, Seton and Adams grappled for control of the pistol, the barrel of which wavered alarming. A shot pinged against the wall by her ear.

"Anne!" Seton shouted. And that distraction gave Adams an opening. He wrested the pistol free and raked the barrel across Seton's nose, bringing a gout of blood. Seton fell away.

Adams fired two shots into the ceiling.

"Enough of this shit," he shouted.

The room suddenly fell quiet.

Seton rolled away from Adams and, half-crawling, half-stumbling, made his way over to Patty's side. She grabbed him tight to her.

"I'm OK," she said.

He laughed, coughing blood.

"It's not you I'm worried about."

Patty saw Mike Turner kick at the body of Ross at his feet. It didn't move.

"Is he dead?" Adams asked.

"I hope so," Mike replied. "But I've thought so before."

Adams motioned Mike and Sam over to join Patty and Seton.

"Well, I've got most of what I came for," he said, holding up the small bottle. "The papers?"

Patty sifted the ash at her feet.

"Gone," she said. "Now you'll never know the secret."

Adams jiggled the small bottle.

"I have several thousand research chemists working for me, all with state-of-the-art facilities. I think we can safely say there won't be a secret for long."

"But you'll try it yourself first, won't you?" Seton said softly.

"Of course. Wouldn't you?" he said, looking at Patty.

"Nothing I can say will change your mind?" Seton said. "I've told you. It won't work for you."

"And I've told you, I don't believe your mystical B.S. I'll trust the chemistry... and your record of how to use it," he said, and patted at his pocket.

He kept the gun trained on them.

"But I have a problem with what to do with you four. Give me one good reason why I shouldn't just shoot you."

It was Mike Turner who spoke first.

"Jock McCall," he said. "You met him. He wouldn't give up."

"The big fellow?" Adams said. "No. I suppose you're right. I guess I'll just say goodbye then, and leave you to your own devices. Don't bother trying to follow me. And don't bother trying to tell your story. You know no one will believe it anyway. Maybe we'll meet again."

He was looking at Seton.

"If you use what's in that bottle, you'll have less than a month. Trust me," Seton said.

"We'll see."

He turned, and headed away up the steps.

"Maybe in a century or so."

His laughter echoed away with him up the stairs.

Patty started to follow, but Seton held her back.

"No, it's over."

"But he has the elixir."

Seton laughed through bloody lips.

"Yes. But as I said, it won't do him any good."

Sam Mendoza started to patch Mike up as Seton led Patty to the large picture they'd taken from the wall and pointed at the inscription.

"*He who can, without fraud, gain or deceit, tinge the basest metal with the argent colors, hath the gates of Nature herself opened to him. And from there he can inquire into further and higher secrets, and with the grace of God, obtain them.*"

"*Without fraud, gain, or deceit.* I'd say that rules Adams out on all counts, wouldn't you."

He kicked at the ashes on the floor.

"No. The real secret went with those papers. We've done what we came for."

He stood up straight and stretched his back. Turning to Patty once more, he took her arm and smiled.

"Now darling, it's time for breakfast. Kippers or porridge?"

44

It took a month before Mike and Sam could get a warrant for Adam's arrest. In that time they had to explain all of Ross's actions, to both the Scots police and their own Captain, find a story that would be believable and stick to it, tie Adams in to it all, and keep Seton and Patty out of it as much as possible.

The amazing thing to Mike was that he managed it. And all without the help, or need, of any booze. He had Sam to thank for that. She held him together, even through the pain after getting his damaged arm stitched up.

And at night, when he woke, sweating, his head full of rage as he pounded, again and again on a dead man's head, it was Sam who was with him to soothe and comfort.

Now she was with him again as they went back to Adams Pharmaceuticals with the warrant.

"Ten to one he won't be there," Sam said as they pulled into the same parking space as the last time.

Mike shook his head.

"He'll want to be close to his technical people, in case of problems."

"You still think he'll be trying the experiment?"

"Seton was convinced," Mike said as they got out of the car. "And I can imagine the old man to be arrogant enough to try. Can't you?"

Sam nodded.

"And what if it works?"

"Then he'll have even more years in jail ahead of him," Mike said grimly as they walked into the reception area.

They were shown to one of the ward areas almost immediately.

"He said you would come," the young doctor said as he led them along the neon lit corridor. "He wants you to see."

The doctor stopped outside a door with a small window at eye level.

"We have him isolated. He's been almost catatonic for days now, but we're under strict orders not to enter. Not until the thirty days have past."

"And when's that?" Sam asked.

"The doctor looked at his watch and smiled.

"In about ten minutes. I'll be glad when this nonsense is over and I can get back to some real medicine.

Mike and Sam stepped forward and looked into the room. It was an eight-foot cube containing a mattress. The only source of light was a small bulb in the ceiling, and the six-inch hole in the floor was only a way out for fluids. Adams lay on the mattress naked as the day he was born. He stared straight at them, unseeing.

"Open this door," Mike said to the doctor.

"I can't," the young man said. "I'm under orders."

Mike waved the warrant in the doctor's face.

"Open this door now, or I'll take you in for obstructing justice."

The doctor looked like he might argue further, but something in Mike's glare must have shown him how useless that might be.

"I'll lose my job for this," he said as he took out a key and opened the door.

"I'd start looking anyway," Mike said as he walked into the room. "Your boss is going away for a long time."

He strode over to Adams and took the man's arm.

Adams blinked, and stretched, as if coming out of a deep sleep.

He raised his hand on his face and immediately burst into tears.

"It's working," he said. He showed Mike his hands. His wrinkles were gone, smoothed out into new flesh, new skin. The hairs on the back of his hand were thick and strong.

He used a finger to prod into his mouth and pulled back his lips to show two new rows of teeth, just beginning to poke through the gums.

"It's *working*!"

Mike pulled Adams to his feet.

"Get him some clothes, he's coming with us," Mike said to the doctor who stared, mouth open at Adams.

"It's working," Adams whispered.

"Yes. You said that already," Mike said.

Adams started to convulse, jerking like a puppet on too few strings. The doctor pushed Mike aside and laid the man back down on the mattress.

"I need a crash team, stat!" he shouted.

Adams started to foam at the mouth and thrash from side to side.

The doctor shooed Mike and Sam out of the room as a crash cart arrived.

They watched the medics work on the old man, getting more desperate at first, then more resigned as time wore on.

The young doctor called the time of death half an hour later.

In a mud hut on a parched plain in Ethiopia, in the middle of the severest drought in a century, a baby was born.

She opened her eyes, looked around.

And screamed.

About the Author

William Meikle is a Scottish writer with twelve novels published in the genre press and over 200 short story credits in thirteen countries.

He is the author of the ongoing Midnight Eye series among others, and his work appears in a number of professional anthologies. His ebook THE INVASION has been as high as #2 in the Kindle SF and Kindle Horror charts.

He lives in a remote corner of Newfoundland with icebergs, whales and bald eagles for company. In the winters he gets warm vicariously through the lives of others in cyberspace, so check him out at www.williammeikle.com/